Sc

M000020736

The Final Move

Thanks
for
reading!.

Victoria
Denault

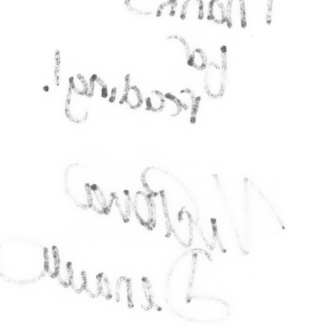

The Final Move

VICTORIA DENAULT

FOREVER
YOURS

New York   Boston

Forever Yours
Hachette Book Group
1290 Avenue of the Americas
New York, NY 10104
hachettebookgroup.com
twitter.com/foreverromance

First published as an ebook and as a print on demand edition: December 2015

Forever Yours is an imprint of Grand Central Publishing.
The Forever Yours name and logo are trademarks of Hachette Book Group, Inc.

The publisher is not responsible for websites (or their content) that are not owned by the publisher.

The Hachette Speakers Bureau provides a wide range of authors for speaking events. To find out more, go to www.hachettespeakersbureau.com or call (866) 376-6591.

ISBN 978-1-4555-3564-4 (ebook edition)
ISBN 978-1-4555-6405-7 (print on demand edition)

For Crystal Richard

Acknowledgments

Thank you to my agent, Kimberly Brower. I wouldn't be on this path without you. You're amazing and your advice on when to delete kissing scenes is spot-on. Nothing makes me giddier than happy faces from my editor in the margin of a manuscript, so thank you, Dana Hamilton, for giving me lots on this one. You've been so brilliant to work with on the whole series and I was so excited that you loved Callie as much as I did. Thank you, Leah, Marissa, and every part of the Hachette / Forever Yours team that touched this book—and the series—through editing, PR, and more. You've been invaluable to me.

I'm grateful to my mom, Luce, my mother-in-law, Celine, and all my relatives who read my books and support them even if the content isn't meant for your "demographic." And thank you, Dad, for not reading it and blindly supporting me anyway. To Jack, thank you for being my rock. Thanks to all the fellow authors, like Lex Martin, S. M. Freedman, Ray Mouton, Peter Milligan, and DeAnna C. Zankich, who welcomed me to the club with advice and support.

And to you—yes, you—the person who is reading this book and read the other Hometown Players books before it: thank you for letting the characters from my head into yours. I can't tell you how much I appreciate it.

The Final Move

Prologue

Devin

Five years ago

I walk toward the barn eager to steal a little solitude for a few minutes. The day has been a whirlwind. I'm happy—and I'm happy that everyone who loves me is happy for me and here to show it. Everyone wants to talk to me, shake my hand, hug me or—in the case of all the local girls—flirt with me. I guess signing a seven-million-dollar contract and winning the Stanley Cup in the same year will do that. I'm grateful for the attention—from all of them—but it's exhausting. Especially the girls, which I know sounds crazy. I swear to God every girl in Silver Bay showed up to this barbecue—even ones who never gave me the time of day in high school. Seven of them have already given me their phone numbers and four more have subtly offered to "show me a good time" while I'm home this summer. I really wasn't interested in that, which Jordan loved to point out made me insane.

I was only twenty-one and most normal guys my age weren't looking for serious relationships yet. But I wasn't a normal guy. I was a guy who had worked with insane focus to reach all my goals since I was a toddler—and I always reached them. I wanted to be in the NHL, and I was drafted in the first round. I wanted to win a Stanley Cup, and I won one. I wanted a big contract, and this week I signed one with the Brooklyn Barons. I got what I wanted—and now I wanted a serious relationship. Something with hope of a future—like a family of my own. It was weird, maybe, but I loved my large, tight-knit family, and being away from all of them for nine months of the year, I realized how badly I wanted one of my own. The way I saw it was my parents married in their early twenties and they were still madly in love. I could have that too if I worked hard enough at finding the right person to have it with.

As I reach the barn door I realize it's half open. As I slide inside, I hear a giggle. I know it's Callie. After years of her family mixing with mine for holidays and meals and everything else, I know her laugh as well as I know my mom's or Jordan's.

It's still bright outside but in the barn the light is so low it seems like dusk. Still, I find her form quickly—she's up against the wall in the far corner of the barn near the apple-red vintage tractor my dad uses during farming season. I take a few more steps and realize she isn't up against the wall, she's up against Owen Kaminski, one of my buddies from my junior hockey team. He's a big guy, almost as tall as me but much heavier, and he's all over her like a fat kid on the last piece of cake.

I clear my throat loudly. He jumps and turns. When he sees me, he looks instantly guilty. I give him a stern look and then give

Callie a disappointed one. As Owen starts to walk away, she rolls her eyes.

"See you back at the party," I say to Owen firmly.

"See ya there." He nods and disappears, closing the door behind him.

Callie doesn't move from her position leaning against the far wall. Annoyed, she has her arms crossed over her chest.

"Are you drunk?" I can't help but wonder aloud.

"I tried to sneak a beer—twice," Callie explains unhappily. "Both times Wyatt caught me and took them away. He said if it happens again, he's going to lock me in Cole's room until the party is over."

I laugh and walk toward her. "Thank God for you Caplan girls. You make it a lot easier for us boys."

"How do you figure?"

"Well, with you sneaking alcohol—and boys," I tell her and raise my eyebrows judgmentally, "and Jessie running away, my dad is probably more grateful than ever he has boys."

"Jessie didn't run away," Callie replies in a sad but stern voice. "We know exactly where she is. She's just...never coming back. Thanks to Jordan."

I don't say anything to that because there is nothing to say. I was in Brooklyn when most of the drama unfolded between my younger brother and her older sister and I still don't have all the details. No one seems to want to talk about it. Jordan is miserable this summer—his first summer back from playing hockey in Quebec—and Jessie isn't coming back to Silver Bay for the summer. Rumor has it she'll never come back here again.

I get back to the subject at hand. "Kaminski, Callie? Really?"

She shrugs and smiles a little self-consciously. It's a rare moment to catch Callie Caplan insecure about something and it makes her more pretty than she normally is—which is very.

"He's had a crush on me for years," she tells me and shrugs again, letting her arms fall to her sides. "And he has no hope of being a professional hockey player now. Just a regular boob like the rest of us."

"Is that a requirement for you?" I question as she pushes off the wall and walks closer to the tractor. "That they're hockey failures? What are you, some kind of consolation prize?"

"Ha. Ha," she says sarcastically before she climbs the giant piece of machinery. She doesn't sit but leans forward, hands on the steering wheel as she stands in front of the seat. "I just wouldn't want to deal with the drama of dating a pro hockey player. All the away games, and cheating, and puck bunnies, and egos."

I laugh and decide to climb up on the tractor with her. It's weird to have to look up at her. "It's not nearly as salacious as you think."

She gives me a disbelieving stare and swipes my half-empty beer bottle from my hand, taking a swig. "Okay," I admit. "It can be like that…but it doesn't have to be like that. I'm not like that."

I slip past her and drop down into the driver's seat. She turns to face me and sits on the engine casing. She's essentially straddling the engine, her bare legs dangling on either side. Her sundress is bunched up around the top of her thighs. She looks like a naughty girl from a country music video. It's beyond hot.

"You've never banged a puck bunny? Not once in the two years you've been pro?" Callie asks me skeptically.

"Every girl I've slept with, I've gone on actual dates with. No random hookups," I explain with a shrug. *"I want something real. Something that leads to something more than sex."*

"Oh my God, you're such a chick."

I smile lightly at that. *"And you're such a dude."*

She puts her hands on the metal engine casing in front of her and leans forward on them, her brown eyes staring right into mine. *"You're a catch, Devin Garrison. It's such a shame you're going to deny the world that."*

"What makes me a catch, my big paycheck?" I say, feeling sorry for myself.

Callie gives me a look like I'm an idiot. *"I'm not going to lie—that's a bonus to some girls because most twenty-one-year-old guys can't afford a used car, let alone much else. But screw the money. You're good-looking. You come from a loving family. You're built like a fucking Greek god and you're a sweetheart when you aren't so focused on overachieving...or cock-blocking my hookups."*

I laugh out loud at that. It echoes off the barn walls. She's grinning widely. *"What were you going to do, Callie? Bang him right here on the tractor?"*

"No, but there's nothing wrong with a little harmless groping on the tractor, is there?"

I smile despite myself and shake my head.

"Not all girls have to be about romance and soul mates and all that crap," she contends, pulling her legs together to dangle off the front of the engine casing.

"How old are you again?"

"Eighteen."

"*How many guys have you been with already?*"

Her big brown eyes flare in shock at that question and then she looks at the floor of the tractor, embarrassed. I instantly feel like shit. "Contrary to popular belief, I've only had actual sex with one guy. Sure, I like to make out a lot, and maybe fool around, but there are tons of ways to get a guy off without actual sex."

There is something very wrong, yet very accurate, about that statement. A hundred things run through my head—blow jobs and hand jobs being at the top of the list. And as I think about Callie doing those things, I feel my shorts getting tight. I have always thought she was hot as hell.

"I'm sorry, Callie," I say and I mean it. "It's not that I think you're easy or anything. I just…you're wild. And I guess I just don't want you to get hurt or anything."

She looks at me now with a confused expression, and I lean forward and grab her hand as if to prove how sincere I am. "You worry about me?"

"Yeah. Of course," I reply and tug on her hand. She slips off the engine casing and stands in front of me once again. It's weird to have her looming above me, so I stand up too.

"See, the cool part about being wild, as you call it," Callie says, tilting her head to look up at me, "is that I never get all emotional over some stupid guy, so I don't get hurt."

"How do you not get emotional? How do you not fall for someone?" I can't help but ask because every girl I've hooked up with I've dated. I don't just screw for the sake of screwing. It's never been something I've tried.

"Just never go for the ones you know you could really like," she explains with a small smile.

"*So you hook up with people you hate?*"

She laughs and squeezes my hand, which I just realize is still holding hers. I also realize it feels good. "No, you don't hate them, dumbass. You're just in lust with them instead of in like with them."

I don't know if I get it. It seems ridiculous. My face must reflect my confusion because she continues to try to explain it. "Devin, have you ever seen a girl and just thought, man, she's fucking hot?"

I nod. "Yeah."

"Who?"

I think about it. There's obviously been more than one hot girl I've admired in my life, so I'm trying to narrow it down. And then I decide to do something really dumb and also very honest. "You."

She blinks and her mouth drops open the slightest bit. She turns her hand around in mine so now we're full-on holding hands. "So have there been times when you just thought, man, I would love to bang Callie?"

Holy fuckballs, she did not just say that!

"Callie…"

"No, seriously," *she insists without any embarrassment visible on her pretty face.* "Hypothetically. Have I ever come over in, like, a short dress, or a tight pair of jeans, and you've just wanted to give it to me, hard?"

I swallow but there's barely any saliva in my mouth suddenly. I use my free hand—the one she isn't holding—to take back the remainder of my beer and finish it off in one gulp.

"Yeah. Of course." *There. I finally answered. She smiles.*

"So if you were like me, Devin, you just go for it. You just do it," she explains like she's giving me the recipe for a peanut butter sandwich or something equally mind-numbingly simple.

"Just…have sex with you?" I never blush—ever—but I'm blushing now.

She giggles. "Well, I'd start with something simple, like a kiss."

It takes me about thirty seconds to absorb what she said and then realize that I should act on her words. Or rather, enact them. I bend my head and kiss her. I've thought about doing it on and off for years. Callie is gorgeous and sexy and wild—everything I am not. Not the type of person I ever thought would be attracted to me, but the kind I'd always kind of secretly wanted to attract. Still, I knew we had nothing in common and that she didn't want anything I wanted in life, so pursuing something seemed futile.

But now that I'm kissing her…I can't believe how fucking hot it is. Within seconds of our lips connecting, the kiss intensifies. She slides her tongue out to tease my bottom lip. I open my mouth and her tongue finds mine and I grab the back of her head, tangling my long fingers in her silky hair.

"Fuck," she gasps when we finally pull apart.

"Yeah," I breathe back and kiss her again.

This time she moves her hands down my chest to the front of my shorts and I know she can feel my dick hardening. Instead of giving in to embarrassment, I put a hand on her ass and push her into me. I don't know what the fuck I'm doing, but I don't want to stop doing it.

"Who's the wild one now?" she whispers against my ear before she kisses the sensitive spot right under it.

"*Just following your lead,*" I remind her, biting her earlobe gently.

She shudders and pushes me down into the seat of the tractor. Before I can do anything, she's straddling me and kissing me blind again. My hard-on is at full mast now and aching.

Callie holds my face in her hands and grinds herself against my crotch. My hands grip her thighs as I fight the urge to come in my pants. Her sundress is bunched up around the top of her thighs; my fingers slide under it and I feel the elastic edge of her panties.

Her tongue dances with mine. I feel disoriented. I don't know how we got here. What the fuck am I doing? A few minutes ago—or was it seconds ago?—I was thinking about wanting a wife and a family and Callie was ready to jump Owen. And now we're making out and dry-humping each other on my dad's farming equipment.

I may be disoriented and confused, but I am also horny and needy. Callie Caplan may not be wife material, because she always says she'd rather die than be someone's wife, but she was fantasy material and I had fantasized about her, a lot. So I don't stop her as she undoes the button and zipper on my shorts and slides her hand inside.

"*Holy fuck, Devin, you're big,*" she murmurs in shock, and I fight a smile.

I kiss her hard again and slip my tongue back into her mouth. My hands slide up her taut little body and cup her breasts through the top of her dress. I'm never this forward. Never. But then again I've also never slept with a girl I wasn't dating, either. This is a whole different world on every level. She pulls my cock *right out of my underwear, shocking me. Her hand wraps around the base and she rubs me—long, firm, perfect strokes.*

I wish I were the type of NHL player she talked about earlier. Then I would have had way more experience with girls' hands on my dick and I wouldn't be so close to blowing a load right now. Fuck.

"Is this what you do, Callie?" I ask, softly kissing a trail down her neck. "You like to jerk a guy off?"

"Yes," she replies breathily as I fondle her breasts. "You like getting jerked off, Devin?"

"Yeah..."

"You like sex more, though, don't you?" She breathes against my ear as her hand continues to pump me. "You like to fuck?"

"Yeah," I all but grunt at her. Holy fuck, this is as close as I've come to dirty talk in my entire life and it's making me hot and crazy.

"If you had a condom, Devin, I would let you fuck me," she promises as her hand trails up my dick and her thumb glides over the tip.

"Back pocket."

She freezes. Her hand stops moving. Her lips stop kissing. Her mouth stops speaking. I open my eyes and she's looking at me. It's hard to focus and gauge her reaction because she's so close.

"I have a condom in my back pocket," I repeat quietly. I always carry one—ever since high school. Because as much as I want a serious relationship and a family, I don't want one accidentally.

I pull back and can finally focus on her face. I think I may see panic or even fear in it. I can't be sure, because I've never seen those emotions before on Callie. Before I can figure it out, or de-

cide what to do next, she's in control again. She pulls herself off me. Now I'm just sitting there, the cool air swirling around my exposed dick, and she's staring down at me with her big chocolate brown eyes.

"Take it out," she tells me softly.

"It's okay if you don't…there's a bunch of people just outside and…"

"Take it out," she repeats firmly as her hands drift under the hem of her tiny sundress.

A second later I watch a pair of tiny white panties with red and pink hearts drop to her ankles. She steps out of them. I hurry to pull the condom from my back pocket. As soon as it's out, she tells me to put it on, so I do. And then she's standing with one leg on either side of my lap and she bends over and kisses me hard and wet. Our tongues meet and it's a full-on battle for dominance. My hands drift up her thighs and over her bare ass. Boldly, I move my fingers to the inside of her thigh and let three of them brush her slit, one after the other. Her breath audibly catches and then she kisses me even harder and starts to drop lower. I use one hand to hold my cock out, in the right place for her descent. She buries her face in my shoulder as I feel my tip enter her.

"Don't move," I command and grip her hip tightly.

She freezes, and with my other hand firmly on my base, I slowly drag the head of my dick across her opening once and then twice.

"I need your wetness," I tell her softly and kiss her cheek. "It'll be easier."

I glide across her once more and she shudders and then pushes *down again. It's so warm but so tight. I swear to God she's almost too small. It almost hurts, but not quite. I know she feels it too because she sucks in her breath and doesn't exhale.*

"If it hurts, you can stop," I promise her but I really want to keep going. "It's okay. Just stop."

"No," she pants in my ear, her hands gripping the back of my neck as she leans back a bit and continues her descent.

I push up the hem of her dress. I want to see her take me in. I still can't believe we're doing this. But we are, and a few seconds later I'm completely inside her. Our eyes meet as she sits perfectly still. My dick is throbbing inside her wet, hot walls.

"I can't believe you fit," she confesses shyly. "I didn't think you would."

"Are you okay?" I ask tentatively.

She nods and, as if to prove her point, pulls herself up a tiny bit and then back down. The friction is the most intense feeling I have ever felt in my life. She does it again, moving higher so more of me is exposed, and then slides back down more quickly.

"I like this," she sighs and does it again.

I kiss her shoulder and then bite down on it lightly as her next movement is faster and harder than the last. And then I hear Jordan's voice.

"I'll check the barn, Dad!"

The sunshine slices across the room as the heavy barn door is flung open. Callie flies off my lap. I'm too stunned to react right away but Jordan isn't.

"Oh crap!" he bellows and turns away from us, shielding his eyes with his forearm.

I shove my condom-covered cock back into my shorts and half jump, half trip off the tractor, zipping myself up as soon as I land on the ground. Callie is just standing there with her hands over her face. Thankfully, her dress conceals her lack of panties from Jordan. He obviously knows what's going on and probably saw my dick hanging out of my pants, but she wasn't exposed, and for that I'm thankful.

"Dad was wondering where you went," Jordan mumbles, still hiding his face. "And I don't want to tell him now. Can you just go out there? Please."

I glance back at Callie and she nods emphatically and makes a shooing motion with her hands. I grab Jordan's arm and drag him out of the barn, sliding the door closed behind us to give Callie privacy.

"Dude!" Jordan says with wide, horrified eyes. "You're sleeping with Callie?!"

"No."

"I saw your dick, Devin."

"Lucky you," I snark, because I don't know what else to do.

I start walking back toward the house and the party. Jordan grabs my arm and stops me. "So what the hell?"

"Look, we've been drinking. We were just messing around. Not a big deal."

"It's…she's like family. It's a big *deal!" Jordan argues and I give him a hard, pointed stare.*

"Unlike you, Jordan, I'm not going to cause a Caplan sister to leave town with a broken heart," I snap at him harshly and turn away, but not before seeing the hurt pass through his eyes. I ignore the guilt that drops like a stone into my gut and leave him standing in the middle of the lawn. My dad calls me over to pose

for a picture with my cousin, his wife and their newborn. It's going to be an awkward picture because my smile is strained. All I can think about is getting the condom out of my underwear.

I excuse myself, head into the bathroom and clean up. When I get back outside a few minutes later, guilt gets the better of me and I look around for Jordan so I can apologize. But instead of finding him, once again someone is waving me over. Kayleigh Ratford, whom I've known since elementary school, is smiling broadly at me. She introduces me to her sister Ashleigh, whom I don't ever remember meeting before, even though Silver Bay is so small I must have.

We walk over to the picnic table filled with food, and I watch them fill their plates and I suggest things for them to try, like my mom's bacon and blue cheese potato salad and my dad's ribs. I chat with them as they eat but can't stop glancing around trying to spot Callie.

Prologue

Callie

*W*here did you go?" Rose asks me when I walk into the living room, where she and Luc and some of Devin's cousins are playing video games. I open my mouth and then close it. I can't tell my little sister—in front of Luc and all these people—that I was just in the barn fornicating with the reason for today's shindig.

"I was wandering around." I simply shrug and sit down beside Rose on the wide ottoman.

I pretend to be completely absorbed in Luc's character in the video game as it shoots its way through the levels against some pudgy, sunburned Garrison cousin I haven't officially met yet. My eyes are glued to the TV screen but all I'm really seeing are the images in my mind of what just happened in the barn. Devin's lips on mine, his hands on me, his huge dick—inside me.

"Are you feeling okay?" Rosie asks, suddenly pulling me from those glorious visions. She raises a hand to my forehead. "You look flushed, like you have a fever."

I realize I've been blushing. I smile self-consciously and swat her hand away lightly. "I'm fine. I'm going to get food."

"Bring me back some!" Rose calls out, because she's clearly not willing to leave Luc's side. I have a feeling she's starting to develop a little crush on him. I'm totally going to have to talk her out of that later. I can't believe watching Jessie fall apart wasn't reason enough to deter her feelings for one of these idiot hockey players.

Outside, the first thing I notice is Devin, standing by the big oak tree, with Kayleigh and Ashleigh Ratford hanging all over him. He notices me watching them and his face contorts with guilt for a second.

Oh no, I think as dread fills me. I don't want him to feel like that! I look away and walk swiftly to the food table. As I fill two plates—one for me and one for Rosie—I feel him come up behind me.

"Are you okay?"

"Yeah. I'm great," I say firmly. "And look at you with the Ratford babes all over you. Way to go!"

"They weren't all over me," he argues quietly.

"Dude, they both want you. I can tell," I tell him confidently and give him a smile before turning back to the food.

"Callie…listen…I…"

I interrupt him before he can continue. "Devin. It was fun. I'm glad we messed around, but that's all it was—messing around. I don't want anything from you."

I glance at him. He's standing there blinking his big hazel eyes at me. He's clearly confused but I can also see relief there.

"I'm not Jessie. I'm not going to get all heartbroken or anything," I reconfirm and pat his chest with my free hand. "I don't

want what she wants—to have a Garrison fall in love with me. I don't want anyone to fall in love with me. I just want to get Rosie through school and get the fuck out of this town. That's it."

"I just don't…I don't do things like that with anyone," he explains, telling me what I already know. "I just want you to know I didn't…I don't regret it but I…"

"Enough," I say, raising a hand to get him to stop talking. "It was fun and fucking hot. Let's just leave it at that. I don't want what you want, Devin, but there are a ton of other girls who do, and two of them are standing over there. Go show them what a great dick you have."

He blushes at that. It makes me feel victorious. I love making boys blush. It means you've taken away their control.

"You're something special, Callie." He bends down and kisses my cheek lightly. It makes me feel warm. Just before he walks away I grab his hand and give it a quick squeeze.

"If you ever stop wanting one of those silly, suffocating relationship deals, call me and we'll finish what we started."

He laughs and nods. "Deal."

Chapter 1

Devin

The porch light is on as I walk up the front stairs. I can see a faint glow behind the pale curtains in the living room. Conner is still sobbing in my arms. I sigh heavily. "It's okay, slugger. It's okay. You're home."

"Mama," he bellows and my heart breaks. Before I can knock, Ashleigh has the door open and she's reaching for her only child.

"Mommy!" Conner wails and wraps his tiny, chubby arms tightly around her neck.

We stare at each other. For a second—but only a second—I see sympathy in her eyes. Ashleigh hugs him to her chest and runs her hand over his hair. "It's okay, baby."

"I didn't know what else to do," I confess, feeling helpless and angry all at once.

"It's going to take time, Devin," Ashleigh replies as she places Conner on the ground. He wraps his arms around her leg, not wanting to let go of his mother, but at least his sobs are slowly halting.

"Maybe," I reply and catch her eye. "But maybe it's a sign we shouldn't be doing this. We shouldn't be putting our son through this."

"Devin, please," she says in her frustrated voice—the only one I've heard come out of her mouth for months. She presses her lips together in a tight line and bends down, rubbing our son's back gently. "Conner, honey, can you go into the den and play with your Legos?"

He sniffs but nods and untangles himself from her legs and shuffles off. He glances back at me and gives me a wave and a feeble smile. My heart starts to crumble once again and I run a hand through my hair in aggravation.

"He just isn't adjusting," I say firmly and lean on the door-frame, because she hasn't invited me in—*to my own fucking house.* "If you let me stay in the fucking guest room, like before, he would at least be able to sleep at night."

"He sleeps fine here," she counters, but I know that's not completely true. She's had to call me several times at night to talk to him over speakerphone and calm him down. He wants his daddy to tuck him in when he's with her and he wants his mommy to tuck him in when he's with me. "And you moving back in defeats the purpose of giving each other some space to figure this out."

"Space isn't going to figure this out," I shoot back harshly. "Counseling and effort and compromise is what's going to fix this."

"Callie called." Ashleigh changes the subject abruptly, tucking her long hair behind her ears. "She took a job on a show that's going to film here."

"What?" I'm stunned.

"She's moving here. New Jersey area, I think. And she wants to see us," Ashleigh continues.

"When? For how long?" I'm even more aggravated than before. This is not what I need right now.

"I don't know. She didn't say in the message and I haven't called her back," Ashleigh replies, crossing her arms over her chest. "I'm not going to lie anymore, Devin."

I want to punch the shit out of something—not her, of course, but a wall or a door or something. I haven't told my parents or even my brothers that Ashleigh asked me to move out for a bit. I didn't *want* to tell them either. They would make a big deal out of it. Or, more accurately, they would make me face the reality that it was, in fact, a big fucking deal.

"I'll handle it," I say swiftly.

"Devin…"

"I should go before Conner comes back," I say flatly, holding back the anger and pain that's building inside me. "I have an early practice tomorrow, and if he sees me leave, he'll flip out again."

Ashleigh does nothing but nod her head gently. I turn and head back down the stairs. I call Callie on my cell as I walk back toward the three-bedroom brownstone I started renting a few weeks ago when Ashleigh told me she needed space for a while. Callie's voicemail picks up and I curse, but I curb my frustration when I hear the beep.

"Hey, Callie! Ashleigh mentioned you called. You're coming to Brooklyn?" I swallow and work hard to keep my voice cheerful. It sounds forced, even to me. "Why don't you call me back on my cell and we'll make plans to hang out. Make sure you call my cell, okay? Thanks!"

I disconnect and sigh. How did my life end up here?

I wander the streets aimlessly. Brooklyn is quiet on this fall night with only a few people walking by me. A block before my rental home, I turn left and head for one of the busier commercial streets toward a place I've been going a lot lately—a pub. I can't go back to that townhouse. I hate it there as much as Conner does. Maybe more. If I could get away with throwing a fit and crying my eyes out—if I thought that would make Ashleigh stop this bullshit—I would.

Does she really not love me anymore?

She *has* to still love me; otherwise, she would just ask for a divorce. She never would have come back here with me this season. She would have stayed in Silver Bay…right? But even if she loves me, does it even matter at this point?

Do I still love her?

I love the child she gave me and I love the vision we both once had for our life together. I wanted that vision to be a reality. I always wanted that. But can I say, without a doubt, that I still love her? No. But I *want* to love her again and I want to make it work, because divorce is failure, and I'm not ready for failure. That's all I can say right now.

I walk in and take a seat at the glossy, dark wood bar. Vinnie, the bartender, gives me a friendly smile. It's sad that I know his name. It's sadder that he pours me a Sam Adams lager without me even having to ask. I smile gratefully and take a sip.

I still blame myself a lot for ending up here. I knew Ashleigh's first year in Brooklyn had been rough. She hated how big the city was and wasn't comfortable being left for road trips. She missed her family and friends like crazy. I'd spent thousands of dollars flying her loved ones out to spend time with her, but it wasn't enough. She wanted me to be there more and there was just no way I could make that happen.

She'd worked through it. I'd made a point of calling her a few times a day from road trips and emailed and texted her constantly. It was the best I could do. She didn't like a lot of the other hockey wives either, so the fact that, when I was home, there were a lot of team events they wanted us to attend didn't help matters. She complained constantly that we didn't have enough alone time.

After our first year in Brooklyn, I was honestly panicked at how strained our relationship had become. She told me flat out she didn't think she could return to Brooklyn next season. Desperate, I had taken her away to Europe—just the two of us. The trip did bring us closer. We went back to the way we were when I asked her to marry me—in love and happy and devoted to each other. She got pregnant with Conner on that trip. That was the happiest we'd ever been. Maybe the happiest we would ever be. God, I fucking hope not. I don't want my marriage to end. I really don't. I am not ready to fail.

"Captain!"

I recognize the voice before I even turn around. Tommy Donahue is standing at the other end of the bar, waiting on Vinnie to pour him a pitcher of beer. He smiles at me happily.

The kid is always happy. He just recently turned twenty-one, but with his freckles and dark red hair he looks more like a teenager from a cheesy sixties sitcom—if they'd made one about a kid with a killer wrist shot.

"Hey, Boy Band," I say casually, but somehow I feel embarrassed about being caught drinking alone.

He rolls his eyes at the horrible nickname the team gave him—insinuating he looks more like a goofy boy band member than an elite athlete. The moniker stuck like glue since he came up from the minors last year.

"Are you waiting for your wife?" he asks, and I realize I'm great at keeping secrets. The team doesn't have a clue what's going on—well, except for our goalie, Mitchell Lupo, whom I told outright because I crashed at his house when Ashleigh first asked me to leave.

"Nope. Just some alone time," I reply with a forced smile. "You take it easy. We have practice early tomorrow."

"Yeah, of course." He nods and pays Vinnie, then hesitates. "You want to join? We're at the back watching the Winterhawks game on the big screen."

I think about it. Watching my brother Jordan's team play and hanging out with some teammates is definitely better than sitting alone stewing in my frustrations. I nod, hop off the stool and follow him back to the seating area with the TVs on the wall.

At the table are three other guys I play with: Todd Anderson, Zach Klaussner and Riley Adams. There are also three girls—all of them wearing too much makeup and not enough clothing. The boys all call out jovial greetings to me as I sit down at the end of the table next to Tommy and turn my eyes to the big screen against the far wall.

The Winterhawks are playing the San Francisco Thunder. The guys talk through the game. Tommy critiques the plays the coaches are calling. Zach makes snarky comments about the players, calling every single one of them a pussy. Riley explains the game to the girls—using layman's terms and the salt and pepper shakers as makeshift players for visual cues. Halfway through the second, I watch Jordan deliver a solid hip check, sending a Thunder forward to the ice on his ass. Our table cheers and whistles its appreciation.

"I taught him that," I joke cockily and they laugh. It feels good to have an authentic smile on my face. I order another round for everyone and add shots of tequila to the mix.

When I get up to take a leak between second and third period, one of the girls from our table is walking back from the restrooms. She smiles at me and licks her lips. "So you're the captain of the team? That means you're the best, right?"

I chuckle and shrug. "It means I'm one of them, I guess."

"You look like you're the best," she says coquettishly and rests her hand on my shoulder. "At a lot of things."

She drifts past me, continuing down the narrow hall and back to the table, her tight ass swinging under her short skirt. I feel my dick twitch in my pants. It's not that I think she's all that pretty, or that I'm actually attracted to her. It's that I haven't had sex in a long time. Way too long. Well before Ashleigh asked me to move out.

Back at the table I order another round and Tommy gives me a cautious stare, though he's still smiling. "Garrison, you told me to take it easy, remember? I can't take it easy if you keep buying rounds."

I shrug. "You can handle it, Boy Band."

In the dying seconds of the third, Jordan is battling for the puck in the corner. He gets it and makes a sloppy pass, which is intercepted by the Thunder's biggest star, Theo French. French gets a shot off, which sails by the Winterhawks' goalie but, luckily, hits the goalpost and stays out of the net.

"I didn't teach him that," I remark and the guys laugh again.

"You know him?" the eager blonde from the restroom incident asks me, leaning over to touch my arm.

"One of my brothers," I reply and finish my beer.

"And he's a professional hockey player too?"

"Yep." I always find it amusing when a girl is so starstruck she wants to fuck a player of a game she knows nothing about. How does that happen?

This woman, whose name I don't know, turns to me and lets her eyes sweep the whole length of my body without even trying to hide it.

"I'm from a hockey family too," Riley says, obviously desperate to get her attention. "My dad played."

She nods, her eyes never leaving me. "Are all your brothers dirty blond and beautiful, like you?"

I chuckle at that. "They're all involved with someone—like I am."

"Oh." She doesn't even attempt to hide her disappointment.

About an hour later I decide I should go. The game is long over and I'm pretty drunk. I decide to call an Uber so I can get home quickly. When I'm drunk, I can usually sleep through the night—something that hasn't happened a lot since I moved out. So I don't want the cool fall air or the long walk ruining this buzz. I use the app on my cell and lean against the brick building as I wait.

I smell her even before she reaches out and touches my hips. Her perfume is overpowering and sickeningly sweet. My eyes open and I find her standing inches from me, grinning.

"You look sad," she announces and gives me a pouty bottom lip.

"I am," I tell her honestly, because what can it hurt? I will never see her again and I don't care what she thinks.

"I can make you happy," she says softly and steps into me, so our bodies are pressed against each other from chest to hips.

"I'm involved," I remind her.

"Not with the right person if you're so sad." She pushes up onto her tiptoes and now her face, her lips are much closer to me. Much too close. Or not close enough…depending…

"I'm married."

"I don't care," she whispers and leans in. Her lips make contact with mine and I feel a lightning bolt of guilt shoot through me, followed by panic. I firmly but gently put my hands on her waist and push her backward. She takes a step and then another, and I slip away from the wall and take several steps into the center of the sidewalk, away from her.

"I'm married," I repeat a little harshly. "And I don't cheat."

She makes a face like I'm overreacting. Like I'm the crazy person here. "Okay. Whatever."

With that, she stalks back into the bar, and thankfully, I see the Uber pull up to the curb. I jog over to it and jump in the back. I tell the guy my address, close my eyes and pinch the bridge of my nose. I just turned down sex. Free, easy sex with a girl who wants me because I'm fighting to save a marriage I'm not sure I even want. Life fucking sucks.

Chapter 2

Callie

The afternoon sun is bright and I actually get a little itchy as I drive slowly down the narrow tree-lined street with the picturesque brownstones lined up like a wall on one side and the scenic park on the other. It's not quite full-on suburban hell, since Park Slope is still in the middle of a bustling urban jungle, but it's the New York version of that existence, and I swear I'm allergic to it.

As the street curves left, I see the numbers I'm looking for carved into the thick stone above one of the doors. I parallel park between a silver Mercedes and Ashleigh's Range Rover and tell my little 2009 Volkswagen Bug convertible not to feel inferior, before getting out and stretching. I had opted to drive here from California, which had been grueling. And New York isn't a city that makes driving easy or even necessary, but I like the sense of security and freedom my car gives me. I can just jump in it and drive away, from anything and everything, if the need arises.

I glance at Devin and Ashleigh's home. It is the typical Brooklyn house, well, for the wealthy, anyway. Three narrow stories, all stone, with a bay window to the left of the stairs leading up to the double oak doors, which have leaded glass and wrought iron inserts. It looks exactly the same as the ten beside it, and when I step onto the sidewalk and glance down the block, it almost makes me feel like I have double vision—I just keep seeing the same thing, over and over.

As I walk to the door, I try to picture Devin and Ashleigh's existence. I bet he comes home from practice and plays with Conner in the big park across the street while Ashleigh scurries around the kitchen making pot roast and cookies.

I stand on the wide front stoop with the oversize black lacquer planters filled with colorful flowers, and ring the doorbell. It's a long few minutes with no response, but I know that's Ashleigh's Range Rover because it still has Maine plates. She *must* be home. I turn and scan the park across the street to see if maybe she's there with Conner. Finally, seconds before I'm about to give up, the door flies open and Ashleigh is standing there in a bathrobe looking irritated. When she realizes it's me, her face morphs to shock and…guilt? Why would she look guilty?

"Callie!"

"Yeah," I confirm like an idiot and step across the threshold to hug her.

She hugs me back, halfheartedly at first, but then her shock wears off and she hugs me more tightly.

"Devin was supposed to call you," she stammers, releasing me and adjusting her robe, tying it tighter.

"He did," I say and smile, hoping it makes her smile and removes the awkward look from her face. It's making me uncomfortable. "I didn't talk to him. He just left a message. Is he on a road trip?"

"No. He's…" Ashleigh falters and then shakes her head. "You should call his cell."

"Why?" I ask. She glances up the staircase toward the second level. "Ashleigh…what's going on?"

"Callie, you know I love you but…this is something you should talk to Devin about," Ashleigh tells me quietly. "Call him."

"I could just hang out with you and Conner until he comes home," I suggest.

"Conner is with Devin. And I'm busy. Can you just call Devin?"

"Ashleigh…" My mouth stays open but I stop speaking as I hear her name.

A male voice I don't recognize is calling it from somewhere behind Ashleigh, inside the house. I glance over her shoulder and see a guy—stocky, brown eyes, brown hair, five o'clock shadow—standing in the archway to the kitchen. He's wearing an untucked dress shirt with a tie loosened around his neck. I take a step toward him.

"Who the hell are you?" I demand. He looks nervous suddenly. Ashleigh swivels to face her male guest.

"You need to go," she tells him flatly. He simply nods and starts toward us and out the front door.

"Call me if you need to talk some more, Ash," he says firmly as he passes me on the stoop.

Stunned, I watch him get into the Mercedes parked near mine and drive away. I turn to Ashleigh, not even attempting to hide the shock and suspicion covering my face. "Who the fuck was that and where is your husband?"

"Devin is at his place across the park," Ashleigh spits back hotly.

I blink. My heart stops beating momentarily and all the blood in my body seems to plummet into my Converse-covered feet. "What the fuck are you talking about?"

"Devin and I are separated," she says in a hard voice.

"You are fucking kidding me."

"Callie, can you just please go?" Ashleigh asks in a strained voice. "Just go and call Devin."

"And say what?" I ask her, and suddenly I'm not shocked anymore—I'm furious. "Hey, Dev, was just at your house but there's another guy there. What's up?"

"I would appreciate it…" She shakes her head and there are tears in her eyes. "I would appreciate it if you didn't jump to conclusions here and run and tell Devin things you don't know."

"I'm not a Sherlock Holmes, Ashleigh, but you're in nothing but a bathrobe and there was a man here with you," I reply fumingly. "And last time I checked, separated didn't mean divorced. Separated doesn't mean you fuck random Mercedes owners!"

"It's complicated, Callie," Ashleigh insists. "If you want to hurt Devin, then go ahead and tell him what you *think* you know. But if you care about me—or him—at all, you'll keep quiet until I can discuss things logically with my husband."

"You have a man who loves you and wants to take care of you and helped you create a beautiful son and a perfect life," I explain to her in a low, even tone. "There can be nothing logical about a conversation explaining why you're throwing it away."

I turn and storm down the steps and to my car. I glance back once and see her on the stoop looking distraught. I get four blocks away and pull over, parking at the curb as I dig my cell out of my purse. I can't believe what just happened. What the fuck is Ashleigh doing? Poor Devin. Holy hell. Does anyone know what the fuck is going on with him? Did he tell Jordan or Cole or his mom or Luc? Anyone?

I dial his cell and he answers on the second ring.

"Hey, Cal," he says in a tone I realize is forced lightheartedness. "I'm glad you called me back. When do you arrive?"

"I'm already here," I say quietly. "And I know."

There's a brief pause. I hear him sigh.

"You went to the house?" he asks.

"Yes. Now where are you? We need to talk."

"I'm at the park across the street from my rental. Conner loves it here," he says in a defeated voice and gives me the address.

"See you soon." I hang up the phone, punch the address into my GPS, and follow the directions.

Chapter 3

Devin

Ten minutes later, as I wait to catch Conner at the bottom of the corkscrew slide on the jungle gym, I see a car pull to the curb and Callie get out. As she puts money in the meter, I catch Conner and study her. She looks exactly like she did this past summer: tall, lean, curvy with that long brown hair and her full, pouty mouth. Callie's beautiful and wild; everything about her has always exuded those two qualities. She has always annoyed, amused and terrified the crap out of me, usually in the same instant. My brain darts back to that time in the barn a million years ago and I chew my bottom lip. Fuck, that was something. I knew right then and there, without a doubt, she was more than I could ever handle. But, as she slipped down around my cock, I also toyed with the idea of dying trying.

Now she walks swiftly and with purpose—it's almost more of a march. I feel a humiliated flush hit my cheeks. She knows Ashleigh left me. She knows I've been rejected. She knows I failed. I don't know what to expect as she approaches. I put Conner down and he runs for the swings a few feet away. When Callie reaches me, she immediately throws her arms around me and traps me in a bear hug.

She's so warm and soft and I'm overwhelmed by how badly I've been missing human contact. It occurs to me that the only touching I've had in my life since Ashleigh and I started having issues was body checks on the ice. Suddenly, I can't take a deep breath.

I drop my head to her shoulder and bury my face in the crook of her neck. Her hand smooths my hair and lovingly holds the back of my neck. It's the same gesture my mom used to do to me when I was Conner's age. Oh God, it feels so good.

"Devin, you don't deserve this," she says in a throaty whisper.

"It is what it is," I tell her with as much confidence as I can muster, which is hardly any. "I'm trying to get it back on track. For Con's sake, if nothing else."

She hugs me harder.

"Daddy!" Conner calls as he toddles back toward us. "I want swing, please!"

We pull apart and Callie turns to my son. She smiles brightly.

"Hey, Con!" she calls out excitedly and jogs over to him with her arms out.

"Callie!" he shouts with a grin, and I'm happy he remembers her. They did spend a lot of time together at my youngest brother Cole's wedding last summer. She scoops him up in her arms and swings him around, causing him to burst into a fit of giggles. I smile as I watch Callie drop him into a junior swing and start to give him small pushes. He kicks his feet as he grins. God, I love my kid.

"What happened?" she asks me softly as she pushes and Conner starts humming to himself. "I know you guys were having issues this summer but I didn't know they were this big."

I nod. "Neither did I. I thought…I mean, I knew she was angry I wanted another kid but…I didn't think that was a deal breaker."

"She doesn't want more kids?" Callie looks stunned, which makes me feel better about the fact that the news stunned me too.

"She says it's too hard raising Conner by herself and she can't imagine having another one as long as I'm in the NHL," I say, repeating Ashleigh's rationale almost word for word.

"She's not raising him alone," Callie argues quietly. "You're the most dedicated dad I have ever seen—besides Wyatt. And you're not going to be out of the NHL for at least another ten years, for crying out loud. She knew this going in."

"I know. I told her that too." I nod in agreement. "But she says she didn't know how bad it would be, how lonely it would be, until it happened."

Callie just shakes her head and sighs. Her chocolate brown eyes find mine and they're filled with concern. "Are you sure it's just about that?" she asks softly.

My brow furrows. "Yeah. I mean what else would it be?"

She doesn't say anything for a minute and then changes the subject. "Does anybody else know?"

I shake my head. "I almost told Luc…but changed my mind."

"Your parents? Jordan and Jessie? Cole and Leah?"

I shake my head. She gives Conner a fairly big push and he squeals in delight. She turns to me, letting him swing solo for a few.

"You need to tell your family," she insists. "They love you, Devin. They'll help you."

"I don't need help," I counter and give her a small, tight smile. "I just need her to make an effort. And she will, eventually."

She doesn't say anything. In fact, I see her bite her lip like she's fighting to keep her mouth shut. She turns back to Conner and stops his swing, tickling his sides for a minute before she lifts him out of the seat.

"Is he staying with you tonight?" she asks.

"He's supposed to, but he doesn't like his room in my temporary place," I explain. "I usually have to bring him home around nine o'clock, wailing. And then he cries when I leave him there. He wants me to stay with him and mommy."

Callie looks heartbroken. She glances down at Conner. "Hey, big guy, how about we go get some ice cream?"

"Really?" he asks hopefully.

"Yeah! Let's go!" Callie says as she links an arm through mine and holds Conner's hand and starts walking toward the street. "Is there ice cream around here?"

"It's New York. There's everything around here," I tell her with a cheeky wink.

As we walk the block and a half to a gelato place I've taken

Conner to a few times, we talk about her little sister Rose and our good friend Luc and how well things seem to be going with them since Rose moved to Vegas to live with him. She tells me about the show she's here to work on. It's a teen drama about a poor family with four daughters who are all in love with the same rich boy. Typical teen angst—the type of show Ashleigh would love.

"Where are you staying?" I ask her.

"A motel in Jersey," she replies sheepishly. "At least until I find a place."

"Stay with me," I blurt out suddenly. I didn't plan on offering but it makes perfect sense. I am renting a furnished three-bedroom townhouse that is too big for just me and sometimes Conner. And she knows my only secret now. It would be nice to have someone around. Someone who is such a good friend.

"Really?"

"Yeah. I have the space and…I could use the company," I confess. I hate how much of a fucking loser it makes me feel like to say it aloud.

She smiles and nods. "Okay. As long as I get to spend time with this gorgeous nugget." She wipes the chocolate mess from Conner's face with a napkin.

When we get back to the house, I give her a tour. It's a nice enough place. A big living room with high ceilings and massive windows that looks out onto Prospect Park. A nice kitchen with funky blue granite countertops and cherry cabinets. A small office with built-in bookcases, which are empty because, other than my clothes and my laptop, everything stayed at Ashleigh's. Upstairs my master bedroom spans the whole front of the house. It has huge windows, a walk-in closet and a giant bathroom complete with Jacuzzi tub and separate marble and glass shower you could comfortably fit five people in at the same time.

The other two bedrooms are fair sizes and share a nice bathroom between them. She makes a face as she walks from one bedroom through the bathroom and into the other. I'm panicked suddenly that she's changing her mind about staying here. I know it's stark—just a queen bed on a metal frame and a dresser—but surely it has to be more appealing than a motel in Jersey.

"Which room is Conner's?" she asks me.

"This one. See the teddy bear on the bed? That's Sid. He's Conner's favorite. He brings him every time he comes over," I explain.

Callie smiles at that but then her face gets serious. "Sid isn't enough, Dev. This room is stark and bare. It's unwelcoming."

"Well, it's not permanent," I say defensively.

"He doesn't get that," she replies and starts pointing around the room. "There should be toys over there and a poster of something he likes above the bed, and some color. Something fun and happy. He has to stay here. He should feel comfortable."

"You think that will make him want to sleep here?"

She nods emphatically and pats my shoulder reassuringly. "Don't worry. I'll take care of it," she tells me and turns to Conner, who is sitting on the hardwood floor. He looks up at her. She walks over and squats down in front of him. "I'm going to go get my stuff and check out of my motel and then I'll come back and we can have a campout! Does that sound like fun?"

"A campout?" he asks in his inquisitive three-year-old voice.

She smiles brightly "Yep. We'll make a fort in the living room and eat s'mores and have a sleepover."

"With Mommy and Daddy?" he asks hopefully.

"Daddy will be there but Mommy can't be," she says simply, like it's no big deal at all. "But you'll have me and Sid. Is that okay?"

He thinks about it for all of three seconds and grins. "Okay!"

Callie stands up and smiles at me. "I'll be back in a couple hours."

She starts for the stairs. I don't know for sure that this sleepover idea is going to work but Conner honestly seems okay with it.

"There's an extra set of keys on the table in the hall. And Callie?" She glances up at me, her long, dark hair dangling behind her. "Thank you."

She smiles. "Don't thank me."

She disappears out the door. I pick up Conner and carry him down to the living room. I feel better. Not much better, but a little bit better. And I'll take anything right now.

Chapter 4

Callie

My first day on my new show was coming to an end. It had lasted fourteen hours. I was used to the long hours from previous wardrobe jobs but the jet lag and the chill of New York fall—which feels freezing to me thanks to my years in Los Angeles—and the crick in my neck from sleeping on Devin's living room floor under a bedsheet, broom and cushion tent with Conner made the day harder than normal.

Luckily, on my way in this morning Rose had called me back. I'd left her two messages last night. Luc's team was on an eastern road trip and she and some of the other wives and girlfriends—WAGs, as they were nicknamed in hockey—had tagged along to bond with each other and go to the games. Last night they'd been in Boston. Tomorrow they would be in Philly. I told her about Devin and Ashleigh. It was a horrible conversation to have with her, and listening to her relay it all to Luc made it even worse, but it had to be done.

"Are you absolutely positive?" Rose had asked me after I

heard Luc in the background repeating "No way. No fucking way. She's mistaken. Ashleigh would never."

"Well, I didn't actually see her banging him, but when I accused her of it, she didn't deny it or even try to look innocent or shocked," I replied, exasperated. "What does Luc want me to do, go back and get cell phone pictures of his dick actually inside her?"

"Callie!" Rose complained. She's never been as crass as I am. "I don't know...I just...I think he can't believe she would do this to Devin. I know I can't."

"He deserves to know," I said firmly.

"Callie." Luc was suddenly the voice on the other end of my cell; clearly he had taken the phone from Rose. "It's just a lot to take in. I'll...I'll deal with it. I'll help Devin...but give me a minute to figure out what to do, okay?"

"Sure. Yeah," I told him.

"And you're staying with him?" he reconfirmed.

"Yep. Until he kicks me out...which may be the second he finds out I told you," I replied.

"It'll be fine. You did the right thing," Luc told me, and it made me feel slightly better.

I got a text from Rose around noon and she said Luc was handling it. I didn't ask details because I didn't want to know. It was a family matter and I trusted Luc to be able to handle it. Luc had lived with the Garrisons as a teenager so he was basically family. And I knew it would be easier for Devin if Luc helped him than his brothers Jordan and Cole. Devin, Jordan and Cole have some weird competitive vibe between them that Devin and Luc don't.

I wave good-bye to the producer and the set designer. The sun is in the process of setting and the sky is a gorgeous golden color. I haven't seen much of the East Coast yet but I do have to say it's full of pretty colors. There's vibrant fall foliage, bright blue skies, golden sunrises and kaleidoscope sunsets. It's different, but equally beautiful, scenery-wise, as L.A. Now if only it weren't so chilly.

All I want to do is head back to Devin's, crawl into my bed in the guest room and sleep. I have to be back on set by eight tomorrow morning and that's almost less than twelve hours away, but I need to fix something first.

I follow my GPS to the closest toy store. I also manage to make it to the paint store minutes before it closes for the night. I make one last stop at a sports store, knowing Devin will kick my ass for buying the poster I purchase, but it's worth it.

Devin has a game tonight. Conner is back with Ashleigh. My credit card is in the hole for more than a hundred and fifty dollars, but if it makes that precious, blond angel smile, it's worth it.

I lug the bags into the house and head straight to Conner's room. As I begin to take my purchases out of the bags, I think about Ashleigh again.

She knew getting into a marriage with Devin how important kids were to him. Devin loves his family. He wanted one of his own for probably as long as I've known him. And I know he made that clear to Ashleigh from day one. She herself had talked about wanting a little girl next, almost immediately after Conner was born. And when he met her, she was about to graduate from her education program and wanted to work with kids. She always looked at Devin like he hung the fucking moon. What the hell changed?

I start to open the small can of red paint and unwrap the paint roller I bought. Then I move Conner's dresser away from the wall and throw down some newspaper I grabbed from a newsstand by the toy store.

It's almost 11:30 p.m. when I finally finish decorating Conner's room. My brow furrows a little bit. Devin should be home from his game by now. I think about calling him but decide against it. I assume he and his teammates have decided to either celebrate their win or commiserate their loss. Either way, the guy deserves to blow off a little steam. Exhausted, and fighting a headache, I head into the guest room and collapse onto my bed.

Chapter 5

Devin

We won, and for the first time all season, I actually had a lot to do with it. It was a 3–1 victory over the Comets and I had a goal and two assists. I was the first star of the game for the first time this season. Being that we were a month in, I felt like it was a much overdue accomplishment.

Everyone knows I am competitive, but no one knows just how much. Every game I play, I strive—and flat out work—to be the best player on our team. I don't think that is much of a secret, but what was a secret is that I also have another goal every game—to get more points than the best player on the opposite team.

Levi Casco is the Comets' golden child. My inner secret mission tonight was to get more points than him—and I had. When we play the Winterhawks, I try to get more points than Jordan—because my brother can never, ever beat me. It ruins my night if he does, which, sadly, happens a lot more often than I would like since he joined the NHL.

The reporters came in and I gave a few decent sound bites, talking about strategies and giving credit where credit was due. Alex Larue, who had been traded to our team from the Winterhawks last summer, was a rock star out there tonight. And Mitchell Lupo—or Loops, as we called him—had been on fire, keeping all but one of the thirty-three shots out of the net.

After the reporters left and I showered, I started thinking about what had been my personal turning point. For the last few weeks—since I moved into my own brownstone—I had been floundering on the ice. My shots were missing the net, I was turning over pucks, and I was taking stupid penalties. Not all the time, not a full-on meltdown, but enough that the coaches were concerned, and I was too. But today—everything was almost back to normal. I was back to making smart, controlled passes, my shots hit the net and I didn't take a single penalty.

I figure it had to do with Callie. Well, her impact on Conner. He was so happy last night and it was the first night he actually stayed the whole night with me. And subsequently, it was the first night I got a decent amount of sleep. Night after night I lay in that memory foam, pillow-topped, king-size bed in a beautiful master suite and couldn't get more than a couple of hours of sleep in a row. Last night I'd slept on the couch, with a bedsheet tented above me as a roof and my kid and Callie sprawled out on the floor below me, and I slept like the dead for seven hours straight. It wasn't a normal night, by any means, but it was the most normal I had felt in a long time.

Was it because my kid had finally settled down? Was it

because I wasn't alone in a big room with nothing but my thoughts? Was it because someone finally knew my big, shameful secret? Was it because sharing that secret hadn't resulted in pitiful stares or words of scorn or judgment—either internally by my own traitorous brain or externally by Callie? Or was it that Callie Caplan, as usual, has this weird way of unnerving me and making me feel stable at the very same time? She had been doing that to me since we were kids. It's probably all of that to varying degrees. Whatever the cause, I'm just extremely grateful for the end result.

As I'm buttoning up my shirt and tucking it into my suit pants, our assistant coach, Phil Tucker, walks in.

"Hey, Garrison," he says in an upbeat voice. "Luc Richard is here to see you."

I spin around quickly with a completely shocked and confused look on my face.

"He said to tell you he would meet you in the parking lot. He's got a pretty little thing with him too."

"Rose," I murmur and hurry to finish dressing.

Luc and Rose obviously know Callie is here so maybe they came to see her. I know his team is playing in Philly tomorrow, and had probably flown in last night, so he was in the area. But why is Rose with him? Although it isn't unusual for him to meet up with me when his team is out this way, he usually calls first.

I drape my suit jacket over my arm and nod good-bye to the guys left in the locker room. As I head down the hall toward the player exit that leads to the reserved parking lot, another potential reason for their visit has me stutter-step. Callie told them about Ashleigh and me. As soon as the thought pops into my head, I know it's the truth. Damn her.

When I get to the parking lot and see Luc and Rose, my worst fear is confirmed. I can tell before anyone even says anything. Rose's eyes are wide and sad. Luc's are narrowed with concern. I stop abruptly a few feet away. Rose comes rushing over to me and hugs me, but I don't hug her back.

"Your sister has a big mouth."

"Don't be mad at her, Dev," Rose begs me, her cheek against my chest as she clings to me. "She can't keep secrets and she's worried about you!"

"Callie did the right thing, Dev," Luc says as he steps forward and pulls his girlfriend off me, obviously knowing this kind of sympathetic outpouring is exactly what I don't want. "You should have told us—and your parents, and Jordan, and Cole."

"It's not your business," I reply coldly.

"You *are* our business, dumbass," Luc counters firmly. "We could have helped you."

I shake my head. "There's no help needed. It's fine. We're working it out."

They both give me skeptical looks.

"Are you going to counseling?" Rose asks meekly.

"We couldn't fit it in this week, or last week, but we'll go soon."

"Are you fucking around?" Luc asks, and Rose looks just as shocked as I do that he would think he has to ask that.

"Luc, fuck you."

"It's not unheard of, Devin. We all know there are girls in

every city who throw themselves at professional athletes. If your wife isn't…"

"Luc!" I snap. "I am *not* cheating on my wife."

"Is she cheating on you?"

"What?!" I seriously want to punch him. "No!"

"Are you sure?" he asks quietly, his tone deadly serious.

I stare at him, anger spreading like hot lava through my body, and then I turn to Rose, who has been suspiciously silent. When I catch her big, dark eyes, she looks away instantly.

"What?" I ask harshly.

Rose continues to look at the pavement. Luc takes a step toward me, his hands buried deep in his pockets and his shoulders slumped forward. "Devin…Callie thinks she saw something when she dropped in on Ash the other day."

"She doesn't think," Rose finally speaks. "She *knows* she saw something."

"Saw what? Where?" I demand, getting frustrated and, if I'm honest, slightly frightened by where this conversation may be going. "Could you two just spit it out, for fuck's sake? I want to get home and get some rest."

"When Cal went to your house yesterday, there was a guy there with Ashleigh," Luc blurts out.

"Who?"

"She didn't ask," Rose explains in a strained voice. "Ashleigh told him to leave right away."

"Maybe it was a plumber," I say and my mouth is incredibly dry. "The sink in Conner's bathroom has been dripping."

"Callie accused Ashleigh of sleeping with him," Luc announces in a pained voice. "And she didn't deny it."

"And she was in a bathrobe," Rose whispers.

I stand motionless. I don't know what to do or say. I don't know what to feel. This can't be right. Callie has to be wrong. Every possible emotion is ripping through me: embarrassment, fear, rage, betrayal and humiliation.

I start toward the street.

"Devin! Where are you going?"

"Where the fuck do you think?" I holler back and storm to the subway station a block away.

Her car is at the curb when I storm up the street. I don't bother ringing the bell or knocking—first of all, it would wake Conner, and second of all, it's my fucking house. I use the key I still have and open the door.

The front entry is dark. I clench my keys tightly in my hand and head for the back of the house. The kitchen is straight ahead and the family room is attached to it. I can see light coming from that direction. I enter the kitchen and hear her before I see her. She's laughing quietly. It's a throaty, sexy, soft sound and it makes my blood run cold—because the only person I've ever heard her make that sound for before is me.

Our big chocolate-brown leather couch is positioned facing the fireplace with its back to the kitchen, where I'm standing. I see her feet hanging off the side of the couch. She's wearing her favorite monkey slipper socks.

"I really needed that laugh," she says with a smile in her voice. "But I should go…Of course I miss you but…"

I drop my keys loudly on the granite countertop of our kitchen island. She jumps and her head pops up over the back of the couch, her cell phone falling from her ear.

"Who are you talking to?" I ask, my voice so low and menacing, I know why she looks terrified. She picks up the phone again as she stands up.

"I have to call you later. Devin is here. Talk to you later, Kayleigh." She ends the call and actually has the nerve to place her hands on her hips and try to look indignant. "What the hell?! You can't just barge in here in the middle of the night!"

"It's my fucking house. I can do whatever I want," I growl back. I grip the granite countertop in order to stop the rage from making my hands tremble.

Ashleigh walks into the kitchen and stands on the other side of the island, her back against the sink.

"Who was that?"

"Kayleigh."

I swallow hard. "So if I look in your call log and hit redial, Kayleigh will answer the fucking phone?"

"Devin, are you drunk?" she accuses. I can't help but notice she's clutching the phone tightly. "What the hell is wrong with you?"

"Are you fucking someone else?"

Her eyes narrow angrily. "Get out."

"No."

"Devin. Get. Out." She's furious—and still clutching her phone.

I take a step toward her and extend my hand. "Give me your phone."

"Get out. Now!" She raises her voice as high as she can without waking Conner.

"When I see your sister's phone number in your fucking call

log, I will leave," I promise and we stare at each other for a long silent second.

Her long, narrow fingers are still wrapped tightly around her fucking iPhone. I slam my hand down on the island. The crystal bowl Jessie sent us for our wedding, which Ashleigh keeps filled with apples, jiggles from the force. Ashleigh jumps and lets out a fearful squeak.

"Give me your motherfucking phone."

"Stop!" she all but screams, tears swimming in her eyes. "You're scaring me. You'll scare Conner if he wakes up. Devin, please!"

"Do you bring him here with my son?" I snarl, leaning toward her over the island. "Do you fuck him in my bed with my son down the hall?"

"I would never do that to Conner!" she blurts out and then her hand flies to her mouth. I feel like someone just stuck a serrated knife through my heart. It's a weird pain, though. It's not heartbreak so much as betrayal slicing through me. I was forcing myself to make things work and she was fucking someone else. Tears roll down her pale cheeks. "I didn't mean for it to happen."

"You didn't mean for *what* to happen? Destroy our fucking marriage? Rip our family apart?" I want to throw things. I want to ram my fist through the wall. I want to throw myself into traffic. "Who is he?"

She shudders and sobs. "It doesn't matter."

I grab my keys off the counter and storm around the island to stand in front of her. She actually cowers, like she really thinks I would physically hurt her. Like she thinks *I'm* the monster here. I roughly grab her phone and wrench it from her hand. I spin and hurl it as fast and hard as I can. It sails across the kitchen, into the family room, and slams into the wall beside the flat screen. The force knocks one of our framed family photos off the wall and it lands on the floor on top of the destroyed iPhone, glass shattering.

"You're a fucking whore," I growl and stalk out of the house.

She chases after me yelling something, but my head is screaming and I hear nothing. Luc's rental car is pulling up as I'm marching down the street. I don't even stop. I just continue straight ahead down the idyllic street that just became my living nightmare.

Chapter 6

Callie

I was so exhausted I slept like the dead. When my alarm goes off at six a.m., I head straight into the shower and go through my morning routine like a zombie. Twenty minutes later, my hair is damp and hanging loose around my shoulders and I'm dressed in a comfortable pair of old jeans and a baby doll blouse I got at a vintage shop in East L.A. It's got small orange and yellow flowers all over and kind of looks like wallpaper an eighty-year-old would pick, but I dig it.

I grab my Uggs, and after glancing in Conner's room to admire my work from last night, I bounce down the stairs. The first thing that strikes me as odd is the smell of coffee.

Devin shouldn't be awake right now, let alone drinking or making coffee. I make my way from the stairs, through the small front hall and into the kitchen. Luc and Rosie are sitting quietly at the kitchen table with mugs in their hands.

"What the fuck," I say, shocked.

Rose stands and I walk into her outstretched arms, hugging her tight.

"We told Devin," Luc tells me.

"And it didn't go well?" I squeak, feeling guilty because they wouldn't have anything to tell him if I hadn't told them.

"Well, he stormed over to Ashleigh's and confronted her and then took off," Luc says, running a hand through his disheveled, shaggy hair. "So, yeah, it went fantastic."

"We've been driving around looking for him all night," Rose tells me with an exhausted but worried expression. "And we called all the guys he's close to on the team. No one has seen or heard from him. We even went to see Mitch Lupo at, like, three a.m. Devin had given him a spare key to this place, which he gave us."

"Fuck." I curse and cover my face with my hands. "This is all my fault."

"It's Ashleigh's fault," Luc tells me flatly. "It's not yours."

"Did she…did she tell him she was cheating?" I ask as Rose walks over and pours me a cup of coffee.

"Pretty much." Luc shakes his head in disgust. "She tried to rationalize it to us after he stormed out."

"'He is there for me when Devin can't be. He doesn't travel half the year without me. He loves me,'" Rose mimics Ashleigh in a wickedly whiny, high-pitched voice.

"*He* loves her? Her husband fucking loves her! Screw this other guy!" I snap furiously.

"His name is Andrew and he's their accountant. Oh, Rosie told her that and a hell of a lot more," Luc says in a proud voice as he flashes my sister a little smile. "She ripped Ashleigh a new asshole. Told her she was a selfish bitch, that Devin was the best thing that would ever happen to her and Conner is proof of that. That she was ruining Con's life, not just Devin's."

"He had to make me go wait in the car while he finished talking to her," Rose admits and she doesn't look the least bit shameful about it. "I made her hysterical."

"Oh, *you* make her hysterical." I roll my eyes. "How the fuck does she think she made Devin feel, destroying his trust and their wedding vows?"

Before anyone can say anything else, the front door slams—hard. We all jump. My heart starts to beat frantically. Luc is the first to make it into the front hall. I follow behind and Rose is right on my tail.

Devin looks like shit. His dirty-blond hair is askew, his suit is wrinkled and his eyes are puffy and red. I realize he may have been crying and it breaks my fucking heart. He doesn't make eye contact with any of us.

"What are you still doing here, Luc? Go back to your team," he says gruffly and starts for the stairs.

"Devin…"

"Go, Luc!" he yells so fiercely it makes me jump.

Devin stomps up the stairs. Luc moves to follow him but I grab his arm. "I'll handle it. You guys should just go."

"Are you sure?" Rose looks concerned but I nod and give her a brave smile. She hugs me and then I hug Luc and watch as they head out the door.

I climb the stairs two at a time and hurry down the hall. His bedroom door is open and I step tentatively into the room. He's standing with his back to me. His suit jacket is lying in a heap at the end of the bed and he's stepped out of his shoes.

"Devin, I'm sorry."

"For what?" he barks. His shirt falls from his shoulders and he drops it on the ground.

"I'm sorry about Ashleigh," I manage to tell him, despite my wildly hammering heart. He's so angry I can feel it in the air around me and it's freaking me out.

"You're not sorry you betrayed my trust and told Luc?" he growls and turns, bare-chested, his dark eyes narrowing angrily on me.

"No. I'm not sorry for that," I tell him calmly. "I didn't know what else to do."

"You could have minded your own fucking business!" he screams so loud and hard the veins in his neck pop out and his face goes instantly red. "You could have fucking respected me when I said I didn't want anyone to know!"

"Your family loves you and you need that around you right now," I reply quietly and clasp my hands together to keep them from trembling.

"My wife fucks other guys? You think Luc is going to make me feel better about that?" He's still yelling, eyes bright with anger. "You know nothing about what I need. Fuck off!"

I stare up at him, trying to remain calm, and as his gaze sweeps my face, the fire and darkness in his eyes soften and he heaves out a breath. "Callie, I'm sorry; I just—"

"Don't be. I did betray you. But I felt I had to," I tell him and fight like hell to keep the quiver of fear out of my voice. "I'll go."

I turn and leave him in his room by himself. I head straight to my room and send up a prayer of gratitude that I didn't un-pack very much. I shove everything haphazardly back into my suitcases, zip them up, grab the handle on the biggest one and start down the hall toward the stairs.

I'm moving as quickly and quietly as possible. I've never seen Devin—or anyone—so filled with rage in my entire life and I just want to get the hell away from it. As I pass Conner's open door, Devin steps out into my path.

I literally jump and let out a squeak, then slam a hand over my open mouth. He looks truly shocked by my overreaction, like he has no idea why in the world I would be on edge. His half-naked body is still rigid and his eyes are still red and puffy, but they don't look as angry.

"What are you doing?"

"Leaving."

"For good?"

"You asked me to go."

He stares at me and then turns his head to glance into his son's room. He's obviously taking in the toys and accessories I bought last night. "You did all this?"

I can't tell from his facial expression if it makes him want to strangle me or hug me. I nod proudly, because no matter what he thinks, doing this was the right thing for Conner.

"He needs to feel like this is his room. He needs to want to be here," I explain.

Devin glances back into the room, his eyes sliding over the red stripes across the wall behind the dresser. "Don't go."

I don't say anything. Devin takes a deep breath, holds it a minute and then exhales loudly. "Conner needs you here."

"Okay," I say simply and wheel my suitcase back into the guest room. When I come back into the hall, he's leaning against the railing by the stairs.

He looks up at me, his face completely devoid of emotion, which is definitely better than the rage that was all over it before. But it's also scary in a different way. "It's my night with Conner tonight. I don't want to see her. Can you pick him up for me later?"

"Of course," I agree and nod. If he doesn't want to see her, he shouldn't have to. I don't want to see her either, but I'll do it for Devin. "I have to go to work. I'm late."

"Okay."

"Devin…" I open my mouth to say something but I don't know what.

"See you later," he says and walks back into his room.

Chapter 7

Devin

I call the coach and tell him I'm sick and won't be at practice. He wants to send the team doctor over to check me out, but I refuse. Maybe he can tell from my voice that something is up because he doesn't argue like he usually does. Or maybe Loops told him what's going on. I don't know and I honestly don't care anymore.

I lie in bed but I don't really sleep. I'm exhausted, both emotionally and physically, after spending the night walking around aimlessly with nothing but my dark, angry thoughts. But despite the fatigue, my brain still won't shut off.

I go through every single moment of my marriage to Ashleigh. All of it—from the wedding day to Conner's birth, to the day she told me she needed space. How much of that was this other guy involved in? How many of those memories were tainted and I didn't even know it? If Conner didn't look exactly like me, I would ask for a DNA test. I contemplated doing it anyway just to hurt her.

She looked hurt last night. She looked devastated and that made me angry. I hadn't done a fucking thing to hurt her. I had done everything I could to keep her from getting hurt. She had cheated and she then had the nerve to look destroyed about it? I wonder when she became that kind of woman. Was she always like that and I was just too stupid to see it?

And when I can pry my mind off of Ashleigh for a millisecond, all I can think about is my family. I have to tell them about this now because I am not going to be trying to make things work. I am not going to stay married to this woman. I also feel sick at the idea that my parents will be disappointed and that I will look like I fucked up. My ego isn't willing to tell everyone the whole truth—that my wife decided I wasn't enough and fucked someone else. I am just not ready for the world and my family to know that. So eventually, I will muster up enough strength to tell them we are separated, but not the reason why. Not anytime soon, anyway.

And then my thoughts turn to that sexy, loudmouthed brunette who betrayed my trust in less than twenty-four hours. I know Callie meant well. I know she wanted to help me, but telling them—having Luc and Rose look at me with those sad, sympathetic stares—made me furious. That "Poor Devin, he isn't perfect after all" face they both gave me was worse than keeping any of the secrets I'd been keeping.

Half of me wanted to let Callie get the hell out of my house this morning. Half of me didn't care if I ever saw her again, but then I looked in Conner's room. She'd taken the time and the care to make it into something special. That's when I begrudgingly realized she needed to be here. In my current state, I am in no shape to take care of my child on my own. Having Callie around—with her loudness and happy-go-lucky attitude—will, hopefully, keep Conner from noticing his father is a fucking mess on the inside, my emotions surging back and forth between complete rage and utter relief. The relief comes from knowing that because Ashleigh did something completely unforgivable, I can stop the exhausting mental exercise of trying to find ways to redeem her and our unhappy life together. And then there is the added bonus that having Callie around means she can save me from having to face my poor excuse for a wife. I had no plan of ever seeing Ashleigh again.

I call our home phone number and when Ashleigh answers, sounding strained, I blurt out that Callie will be picking up Conner for me that afternoon and abruptly hang up. Then I turn my cell off. Luckily, I don't have a landline here so she can't get a hold of me that way.

If I could get away with it, I would never have an actual conversation with her ever again. I have nothing to say. And there is nothing she could say to make this better. By noon, when it is clear that my mind won't shut off on its own, I go downstairs in search of something to make it shut off. I find a bottle of Jack Daniel's on the bar cart in the dining room, open it and start to drink.

Chapter 8

Callie

After work I pick up Conner at Ashleigh's. She looks distraught and tries to talk to me about it, but I simply ignore her and walk away with Conner. When I get to Devin's, he's nowhere to be found. I take Conner upstairs and show him his newly decked-out room, figuring Devin might be there, but he's not. As Conner squeals with delight and starts exploring his new toys and admiring his posters and decorations, I dart down the hall to Devin's room. The door is cracked open, but it's dark inside.

I peek my head inside, and when my eyes adjust to the darkness, I can make out his form in the bed. I sneak in, intending to wake him up, and as I get closer I realize he's naked. He's facedown, his dirty-blond hair completely askew. The sheets on his California king bed are covering one leg and half an ass cheek but nothing else.

I don't even pretend not to admire his well-muscled back or his perfectly round, tight ass or the hard, thick muscles in his exposed thigh. I realize that even though we sort of had sex, I've never seen Devin naked. It's impressive. I lean in to wake him and am completely assaulted by the stench of liquor.

I sniff. Whiskey, if I'm not mistaken. Barf. I touch his bare shoulder and give it a shake. His skin is warm and sweaty. "Devin! Wake the hell up! Conner is here."

He grumbles into his pillow. I shake him harder.

"Get! Up!" I bark.

He moans and rolls over. The covers do not cover anything now. The girly girl in me—the one I like to keep locked up in a dark corner of my mind—wants my hand to fly up and cover my eyes. But luckily, too much of me is an anti–girly girl, badass horndog and I resist the urge. So I stand there and stare down at him as his eyes flutter open.

"Conner's here," I repeat in a low but firm voice. "And you smell like a distillery."

"Sorry…" His voice is thick and gravelly. He puts his hands to his eyes and rubs them.

"And you're totally naked right now."

His hands fly from his eyes and he looks down his body and grabs at the sheet, pulling it up over his legs to his waist as quickly as humanly possible. His eyes find mine again and he looks embarrassed.

"Well, don't just stand there staring!" he demands as his face goes red.

"I didn't. I took pictures with my cell phone," I quip, and turn and head back to Conner's room.

We're on the floor in Conner's room playing Legos when, half an hour later, Devin wanders in. He's showered, his hair still damp, and he's wearing a plain white T-shirt and a pair of Brooklyn Barons sweats with bare feet.

Conner's whole face lights up when he sees him, and Devin kneels and captures his son in a big hug. His caramel-colored eyes land on me and they're even more bloodshot than this morning. The liquor is to blame this time.

"Daddy, my room is special!" the little blond bundle of adorableness says to Devin.

"It is!" Devin agrees enthusiastically and he glances around it again. He sees it—above the bed—and he gives me an amused look with an eyebrow cocked.

"Really, Callie?" he questions. "In *my* house?"

I look up at the poster of Avery Westwood, captain of the Seattle Winterhawks and one of my conquests, and smile. "He loves Avery and besides, he can stare at you and his uncles anytime he wants."

Devin almost laughs at that. Almost, but it's still a victory.

Later that night I'm in the kitchen cleaning up the remnants of the spaghetti dinner I had whipped up, as Devin comes into the room after tucking Conner into bed.

"He's out like a light," Devin says with some relief. "Not one tear."

"Good." I smile softly.

He leans against the counter looking drained. "What did she say when you picked him up?"

"Do you really want to know?" I reply quietly as I load the dishwasher.

"Yeah. Why the hell not?" he smiles mirthlessly.

I take a deep breath and catch his eye. "Ashleigh says she is trying to stay away from him. She wants time to think."

He doesn't appear to react to that—at least not on the outside. He tips his head back, closes his eyes and lets out a long breath. I act on instinct, on the need to get his shoulders to stop trying to attach themselves to his ears and his thick, dirty-blond eyebrows to stop pinching together. I step closer, reach out and wrap my hands around each of his shoulders, where they curve into his neck, and I begin to knead.

He lets out the most fucking delicious little grunt, so deep and needy that I feel it between my legs. His head falls forward now, eyes still closed, and his neat blond hair becomes a tousled mess covering his forehead. Holy hell, he's still just naturally the hottest boy I've ever met. I keep massaging his shoulders for several minutes in silence, and as his shoulders finally begin to sag, I ask, "How do you feel?"

He pulls his head up and opens his eyes. They're a light hazel color tonight and the flecks of amber seem more noticeable than normal. He reaches up and cups my face for a brief second, leaving a trace of heat behind on my cheek.

"I'm done feeling," he tells me and starts out of the room. "'Night, Callie."

Chapter 9

Devin

As we start filing off the plane, I turn to Loops.

"Want to grab a beer?" I ask hopefully. "I need to unwind."

He looks hesitant but he nods. "Sure. Let me just call Tara and let her know."

I nod. The mention of his wife makes my heart ache. That used to be me—with a wife and a son waiting for me at home. I walk through the airport with him as he calls his wife. They talk for a few seconds about what's been going on while he's been away and then he asks if he can head out for beers.

I wait for the inevitable fallout I always got from Ashleigh if I didn't rush right home to be with her after a road trip. But Loops just laughs into the phone. "Okay, if you want me to, I'll do it. Give Henry a kiss for me and tell him I'll see him soon."

"All good?" I ask, trying not to look surprised or envious.

"Yeah. But she says I better come home tipsy so she can take advantage of me," he says with a chuckle.

Wow, I think. Tara is amazing.

We decide to head to a pub called McSorley's. Alex Larue and Tommy Donahue join us and as soon as we sit down, they all order beers. I order a Crown and Coke, finish it, and order another before they can finish their first pints.

My phone rings three times during the hour and a half we sit around chatting and drinking. One of the times is Callie. The other two are Ashleigh. I send all of them to voicemail.

"Anyone up for heading to the club down the street?" Tommy asks hopefully. "I'm supposed to meet some guys there. It's got talent on a Friday night!"

"Talent?" Loops asks, raising a bushy brown eyebrow in confusion.

"Yeah. Hot women," Tommy clarifies. "Talent means hot chicks."

"Ahh. Talent." Loops laughs, standing up and dropping some cash on the table. "I'm out. My wife wants to take advantage of me."

Alex whistles at that and Tommy chuckles. I give my best friend on the team a tight smile and swallow down the jealousy. It's not his fault I picked a cheater and he didn't. As we say good-bye to Loops outside the bar, he grabs my shoulder.

"You okay?" he asks finally. I know he's wanted to ask that since the start of the road trip. We haven't talked at all about Luc showing up at his house in the middle of the night or why I looked like, and played like, death warmed over the entire trip. Instead of telling him anything, I just shrug and walk away.

Tommy wasn't kidding. The club—a fair-sized dance club

with a huge dance floor and a mechanical bull in the corner—is hopping with gorgeous women who are just as hot as the wannabe puck bunnies from the last time I was out with Tommy, only they're way classier looking.

My eyes fall on a dirty blonde by the edge of the dance floor. She's wearing a short silver-gray dress. Her legs are long, toned and tanned. Her hair is natural blond, not bottled. She's talking with a shorter brunette that Tommy pointed out earlier.

I order another Crown and Coke and wonder, if I were single, would I have the balls to take her home tonight?

My phone vibrates in my pocket. I grab it and see HOME on the call display. I sigh, leave my drink on the bar next to Alex and head into the hallway that leads to the bathroom.

"What?" I snap into the phone.

"Devin? Where are you?" she asks and I know she had to raise her voice so she could be heard over the background noise she can hear through the phone.

"Out. Is Conner okay?"

"He's asleep. We need to talk."

I hang up and turn off my phone. I still have nothing to say to this woman and there's nothing she can say that will make me want to go back to the hell that was me trying to save our marriage. I head back toward the bar to pay my tab and say good-bye to Alex and Tommy. When I find them, they're talking with the girl I was admiring before and her friends.

I walk over and touch Tommy's shoulder. "I think I'm going to go."

"Really? Are you okay?"

"You should stay for a drink," the dirty blonde says out of

nowhere and I look over at her. "You look like you might need one."

I hesitate. She smiles and gets even prettier. "My treat," she adds.

"*My* treat," I insist and head to the bar. She follows me. Tommy and Alex stay with her friends.

"A Crown and Coke and a…" I turn to her so she can tell me the poison of her choice.

She's standing behind me, and when she leans in toward the bartender, her body presses up against mine.

"A gin and tonic, please—and two broken-down golf carts." She smiles and winks at me. "We'll call them broken-down Zambonis for you."

I laugh at that. She knows who I am. "Guess the guys told you what we do for a living."

She shakes her head. Her hair tumbles over her shoulders. "Your face is on billboards and I've gone to a game or two. My dad is a big sports nut. So why did you become a hockey player instead of a male model?"

Oh, this one's brought her A game. Before I can figure out how to respond, the bartender has put our drinks, and the shots she ordered, in front of us. She reaches in and takes the shot glasses and hands me one. We clink glasses and down them together. As we reach for our drinks, her big gray eyes that almost match her dress fall to my hand. My *left* hand.

"You're wearing a wedding ring?" she questions.

"I'm wearing a ring," I correct her and sip my drink. She sips her own drink wordlessly, her eyes sweeping over my body without even trying to hide it. "Does it matter?"

"Not to me," she responds easily and leans toward me. She smells of cinnamon and something musky. "But maybe to the person that gave it to you."

"She doesn't give a fuck," I tell her.

Her lips are precariously close to my ear. My dick starts to get hard. It's been that fucking long. Her lips brush my ear and the side of my cheek as she pulls back a little bit. "Then I only have one more question. Your place or mine?"

Chapter 10

Callie

The noise pulls me from my much-needed sleep. If there is anything that makes me a bear—a vicious, seething bitch of a bear—it's having my sleep disturbed. When we were teenagers and Grandma Lily first started leaving us all alone in Silver Bay over the winters, Rose and Jessie were terrified at night. The old farmhouse creaked and groaned and the land outside was so dark and eerie because we were so far out of town, but I was never scared. God help any burglar, rapist or serial killer that broke in and woke me up. On more than one occasion I had thrown things—pillows, alarm clocks, water glasses—at my sisters for waking me up.

So when the sound—it's like a dog stuck in a fox trap—becomes relentless and makes it impossible to fall back asleep, I start to get irate. What the hell is it? I throw the covers off and walk over to the window and glance outside. I don't see an animal out there. I cock my head and listen more closely, trying to determine not just what the sound is but where it's coming from.

It still doesn't sound human, but I've at least figured out it's coming from inside this house. My brain is still groggy from sleep and I have a panicked moment where I worry it's Conner. As I run down the hall and into his empty room, I remember he's at Ashleigh's tonight. As I step back into the hall, I realize the sound is coming from Devin's room.

I freeze. What the fuck do I do? It doesn't sound like a noise he would make. I still can't even tell if it's human. There's a slight bit of light spilling out from the door, which is cracked open maybe half an inch. I pad quietly toward it. I pause outside it and raise my hand to knock, but hesitate as the noise stops and I hear a voice.

"Harder. Yeah. Like that. Fuck, you're so big!"

My blood runs cold from shock and at the exact same time my face flushes from embarrassment. Then the noise starts again. I shuffle back to my room noiselessly, making sure to shut my bedroom door tightly. I lean against it and my nose crinkles up as I think about this discovery.

Devin is fucking someone. Someone who is not his wife. I think maybe on some level I should feel horror or disappointment toward him because he's violating his marriage vows, but at the same time—is there anything left to violate? Ashleigh pretty much destroyed everything already, didn't she? I can't begrudge him a revenge fuck because I would do it too—if I were stupid enough to get myself in a situation where someone could rip my heart out.

I go over to one of my suitcases and dig around in the dark

until I can find my iPod and earbuds. I crawl back under the covers, shove the buds in my ears and hit play.

As I close my eyes and try to fall back to sleep, my thoughts roam.

I haven't been laid in a while. Almost four full weeks, which isn't actually that long. I've gone longer before. Hell, I was celibate for almost eleven months once, so why am I suddenly so sexually frustrated?

Maybe it's from being around so many guys. The TV show crew is ninety percent male and the people I work with directly are all male. And there is this total babe named Matthew who is the assistant to one of the actors and he and I flirted a lot. And then living with Devin…well, Devin is a stunning male specimen.

My mind drifts sleepily back to the evening I walked in on him sleeping naked. I had been joking about taking cell phone pictures but even if I'd taken them, I wouldn't have to look at them. I had his naked image burned into my brain. He was gorgeous—all of him. His flaccid dick was bigger than most men's hard ones.

Now my brain floats back to that little adventure in the barn when I was eighteen. I was so young and way more innocent than I liked to let on. I had only had sex once and it was fast and clumsy. The guy had rolled on top of me and given me a few awkward thrusts and rolled off. It was literally over in two minutes. That's why I hadn't been in any rush to try it again. But when the teasing and flirting with Devin in the barn somehow turned serious…I suddenly *needed* to try it again.

I'd always had a crush on Devin—ever since Jessie had

dragged us to the Garrison house one winter afternoon to "skate with my friend Jordy and his brothers." I had just turned ten. Devin was thirteen. I'd heard of him—everyone had heard of him. He was this hockey star who was going to be drafted to the NHL. People were actually saying that about him even then. That was a big deal in Silver Bay. I didn't care about the hockey skills. I had liked his boyish yet cocky smile, his pretty caramel eyes and those unbelievable lips. Devin's lips were wide and plump and I have been obsessed with them since that day.

But because of how close we became with his family, I never ever gave any serious consideration to fooling around with him, or any of the Garrison brothers. Once, at a birthday party at Billy's house, we'd played Truth or Dare and I dared Cole to kiss me. He'd done it without even blinking. Cole had been a good kisser but I had pretended it was Devin the entire time. Still, I knew that silly dare of a kiss was as close as I could ever come to crossing lines with those brothers. Because if I did anything else, it could cause a rift that took Wyatt and Donna out of our lives, and I loved them and needed them more than anything. They were the parents I never had.

My lovesick sisters hadn't realized what would happen—or hadn't cared as much about the risks. Jessie let Jordan take her virginity and everything had blown right up. Since everything was already obliterated when Devin had that party for his new contract, I wasn't taking any risks when I gave in to my fantasy. Still, I was a little bit stunned he played along. I'd never gotten any indication at all that Devin thought I was remotely attractive.

The words moaned by the random chick down the hall run through my head again. *Fuck, you're so big!* She wasn't just being polite. When I first felt Devin's dick through his shorts in that barn, it had actually caused a ripple of fear. I almost didn't go through with it because I wasn't sure I'd be able to make it fit. But it had fit—and it had felt incredible. And the friction when he started to move…*that* was what a sexual experience was supposed to feel like.

Damn Jordan—or as I like to call him, Big Bird—for interrupting us. I think I hated Jordan almost as much for that as for breaking Jessie's heart. Almost-sex with Devin had spurred me on to try it again with someone else—a guy from my community college named Mike who had adorable freckles on his nose and a great body. Mike had definitely been better than the first guy, but not quite as exciting as Devin. In the years and years since, I'd had some really fantastic sex and mind-blowing orgasms, but I always wondered if an orgasm with Devin might be better. It didn't bother me, though, that I would never know. You can't miss what you never had, right?

Curiosity gets the better of me and I pull my earbuds out of my ears. I hear nothing at first but as I strain I can faintly hear some grunting. It's a male grunt. Devin's grunt, but not the sound he had made with me. And then I hear her again—the moaning has changed to high-pitched squeaking. The rhythm of the noise indicates it's probably in time with some very hard thrusts.

I shove my earbuds back in my ears. A yawn overtakes me. I'm tired.

I picture Devin behind her pumping in and out of

her…rubbing her clit with one of his long, strong fingers. I try to conjure up an image of her as I yawn again and curl onto my side. Is she blond? Brunette? Redhead? Is her hair long? Is she short or tall? Pale or tanned? As I start to slip back into sleep, my brain starts playing tricks on me. The redhead I'm picturing morphs into a blonde and then a brunette, and then as I slip into the dream world, it morphs into me.

Chapter 11

Devin

It's pain in my head that feels like a mallet slamming a snare drum that tears me from sleep. I roll from my stomach onto my back and my shoulder bumps something warm and soft. Memories of last night explode behind my eyes. The bar. The phone call with Ashleigh. The heartache. The booze. The dirty blonde. The dirty blonde, naked. My eyes fly open and the pounding intensifies.

I turn to the left and see her, tangled up in my sheets, curled on her side, her hair fanned out on my pillow, her bare back exposed. She's probably a very lovely sight, but bile rises in my throat anyway.

I turn away and catch the time on the alarm clock sitting on the night table: 5:24 a.m. I quietly get out of bed. Luckily, I hadn't put away a basket of fresh laundry from before the road trip. I pull out a pair of workout shorts and a Barons T-shirt and I walk back over to the bed. Leaning over, I give her a light shake.

She stirs, turning onto her back and stretching under the

sheet. When her eyes flutter open, she seems a little stunned to find me hovering above her and not in bed beside her.

"I'm sorry but you have to leave," I whisper loudly.

"What?" She sits up, thankfully pulling the sheet with her so she's not exposed. "What time is it?"

"Almost five thirty."

"In the morning?!"

I nod. "Sorry, but I have a guest staying with me and it's not a good idea if she meets you."

"Is it your wife?" she asks stupidly.

I try not to frown. "No. My brother's fiancée's sister. I'm sorry about this but you really have to go."

She sighs and her brow furrows, but she doesn't argue. I bend down and grab her bra and dress from the heap at the end of the bed and hand them to her. Without another word I head into the master bath to give her some privacy.

I lean over the sink, look in the mirror and fight a sudden wave of nausea. What the fuck—I didn't think I drank that much last night. I splash cold water on my face and try to take deep, cleansing breaths. A second later she's standing in the bathroom doorway. She looks calm and unbothered. I guess that's a good thing.

"I'll walk you out," I offer and she nods.

She's carrying her heels in her hand and when we reach the front hall, I open the door as she slips them on. She smiles and I try to smile back. I must look as incredibly awkward as I feel, but she leans in and hugs me anyway. I wrap an arm around her waist; my other hand stays on the door handle, gripping it so tightly that my knuckles are white.

"Last night was fun," I offer lamely.

She nods, her hair brushing my cheek, and then she pulls back and presses a piece of paper into my free hand. "Let me know if you want to do it again sometime."

"Will do," I reply.

Thankfully, she leaves. I lock the door behind her and slowly head back up the stairs. When I get back to my room, I close the door, drop the piece of paper on the dresser and strip off my clothes as I walk to the bathroom. I turn on all the jets in the shower—the ones in the wall and the rain head above—and make it as hot as possible without scalding myself before stepping inside.

What the fuck did I just do?

I wasn't into one-night stands even before I got married. That incredible but crazy moment in the barn with Callie was the closest I'd ever come to random, no-strings-attached sex. I know Jordan had done it—a lot. And Luc even made a relationship out of "just sex" with that model ex of his, but it just wasn't something I ever wanted. It still isn't, so why the fuck did I do it?

The fact that I don't feel completely horrible about it is what makes it worse. It actually felt kind of incredible. Damn, I missed fucking. I missed orgasms that didn't come from my hand. Ashleigh and I had sex once in the last seven months. But now I feel like it made me just like Ashleigh. All those horrible words I had called her over the last week apply to me too now. My stomach lurches and I place my hand flat on the marble wall as I hunch forward and puke onto the shower floor.

Chapter 12

Callie

I skitter to a halt on the dark granite floor in the kitchen. Devin turns slowly from his seat at the kitchen island and gives me a half smile. He's in jeans, no shirt and bare feet. I allow my eyes a moment to slide down his sculpted shoulders, rippled stomach and then linger on his dark blond happy trail. A ripple of desire skids down my spine and pools below my belly. Fuck, he's sexy as hell, even all fucked up like he clearly is now.

"It's seven in the morning. What are you doing up?" My eyes dart around the room looking for the source of the animal noises last night. Either she left or she's still asleep in his bed. He looks a little sick.

"What are you looking for?" he asks me tentatively.

I shrug and make my way around the breakfast bar to the counter by the window, next to the stove. I pull two bananas and some apples out of the fruit bowl I filled yesterday and then head to the fridge and dig out grapes and the big tub of fat-free vanilla Greek yogurt. Then I grab the cutting board and head back to the breakfast bar and sit down beside him.

"I didn't know we had fruit," he murmurs, sipping his glass of water.

"We didn't," I reply, and start coring and chopping the fruit. "So I bought some—and some other essentials."

"Oh."

"So you never answered me," I remind him casually. "Why are you up so early?"

He's silent so I give him a sideways glance. His hazel eyes find mine and immediately look away. I guess he wouldn't be Devin if he weren't wracked with guilt, I think to myself and almost smile sadly.

"I couldn't sleep," he mutters and swallows more water.

I nod and finish chopping the fruit, then hop off the chair and walk over to the cupboard to grab a bowl. I swing by the pantry and grab the low-fat granola mix I also bought.

"I thought you'd be exhausted after last night's workout," I say simply as I scoop some yogurt into the bowl.

"WHAT?" he sputters, and I don't have to look at him to know he looks horrified.

"Is she still upstairs sleeping it off or did you give her the boot?" I glance at him just long enough to give him a soft smile.

"She's gone." His voice is sheepish and slightly sad.

"Was she walking like she'd ridden a horse for four days?" I joke and wink at him as I pour some granola into the bowl on top of the yogurt. "Because your cock looks even bigger than it did when I was seventeen and it sounded like you were really giving it to her."

"Holy fuck, Callie! Seriously?!" The words rush from him in an embarrassed whisper. I stare at him. His face starts turning crimson and he covers it with his hands, leaning his elbows on the black granite counter in front of him.

"And you were eighteen, not seventeen," he reminds me through his hands.

"So are you as big a mess on the inside as you look on the outside?" I venture quietly as I mix the granola with the yogurt.

"Pretty much," he responds, hands still over his face. "I'm not any better than Ashleigh now."

"Yeah, that's a load of shit," I argue swiftly and slide the fruit from the cutting board into the bowl. "Ashleigh betrayed a trust and violated a marriage contract."

"So did I."

"It was already decimated," I correct him firmly and then I lighten my tone. "And besides, do you have feelings for the lucky lady from last night?"

His hands drop from his face. "No."

"Then you are not even close to the same as your ex-wife," I tell him resolutely. "You stuck your dick in a girl after your wife ruined your marriage. Big fucking deal. Ashleigh shared her heart with someone, not just an orgasm, while she was committed to you. Now eat."

"This is for me?" He looks down at the bowl I just made.

"Yes. I get meals on set," I explain and hop back off the chair. "I'll see you tonight?"

"Conner will be here," he says, still more glum than I would like.

"I'll make something yummy for dinner," I announce and move to leave.

He reaches out and grabs my hand. His grip is firm but gentle, and when our eyes connect, that ripple of desire turns into a tidal wave. I suddenly want to ask him if he was satisfied last night and if he wasn't, I volunteer as tribute.

He leans a little closer and suddenly I wonder if desire is contagious, because he's looking at me like I assume I'm looking at him. "Thanks."

"Of course." I smile. He lets go of my hand and I hurry out the door.

Chapter 13

Devin

Loops is watching me carefully as I get dressed back into my street clothes after practice. He's been staring at me through most of practice and I'm done waiting for him to spit it out.

"I'm in a slump," I say as I pull my shirt over my head. "Happens to everyone."

"Dev, come on," Loops says quietly, his eyes darting around to make sure the last few guys left in the locker room aren't listening. "It's more than that and I know you know it."

"It's not."

"You've had slumps before. This is an all-out free fall," Loops tells me. "And I'm not just talking about on the ice."

I turn and stare at him but say nothing. He looks concerned and it makes me angry.

"I've been trying to give you space after that whole thing with Luc showing up at my house in the middle of the night but…" He swallows and searches for the right words. "I think maybe you should talk about it."

"Nothing to talk about," I reply curtly and grab my baseball cap out of my locker. "I have to go. I have Conner tonight."

"Devin."

"Look, Loops." I turn and face him and try to contain my anger. "Talking to you isn't going to help. You're happily married with a perfect family and you couldn't possibly relate."

He opens his mouth to say something but nothing comes out.

"And the coach spent an hour riding my ass this morning, so trust me, I know I have to get my shit together," I tell him flatly. My cell starts buzzing in my pocket. I pull it out and see HOME on the call display. I hold it up. "Now excuse me while I deal with my cheating wife."

I storm out of the locker room and head down the hall.

"Is Conner okay?" I say into the phone without so much as a hello.

"Devin. It's your mother." I'm confused for a second but it's promptly replaced with panic. My mother is at my house, here in New York. The house I don't live in anymore. "Your father and I are here with Ashleigh and Conner."

"Okay" is all I say, because what else can I do?

"Okay?" she mimics, stupefied.

"Meet me at my place." I pause. "My other place. Ashleigh can tell you the address."

"Devin, I don't think—"

"I'm not going over there, Mom, so your option is stay with her or come to my house," I say firmly. "This isn't your problem to fix."

"See you shortly," she says with a hard snap to each word.

It's the same way she talked to me when I was a teenager and she didn't like my attitude.

Twenty minutes later, as I turn onto my street, I'm so nervous I want to puke. My dad and son are sitting on the stoop. I can hear Conner chattering away and I know he's playing a game of I Spy as they look out at the park across the street. My mother is pacing on the sidewalk below them, arms crossed and a heavy scowl creasing her normally serene, fair face. Her blue eyes lock on me as I walk toward them and the frown deepens.

She doesn't reach to hug me like she usually does. Instead she just stands and scowls. I scowl back. "What are you doing here?"

"You play Jordan tomorrow night. We always try to come to the games you two play together," she reminds me, something that's been happening since my middle brother joined me in the league. I should have been prepared for this. I completely forgot we were playing the Winterhawks.

I nod at my mother curtly. "Right. Did you ring the bell or try the door?"

"Why would I do that?"

I was hoping Callie would talk to them before I got here. If she's in the brownstone, she didn't see them out front. The one time I'm banking on her big mouth to ease this for me and it didn't happen. Fuck. My. Life.

"Come inside," I say quietly.

Conner grins at me as I climb the stairs toward him. He looks so excited he could burst. I can't help but smile back at him and scoop him out of my father's arms. This kid, I remind myself, was worth marrying the wrong girl for. I swing open the door to my rental, and my father lifts his graying eyebrow because it was unlocked and there is a pile of high-heeled shoes and boots by the door as we cross the threshold.

"Someone else living here?" he asks in a tone coated in shock and dripping with condemnation.

"Yeah," I say sharply. "But it's not what you think. Thanks for having faith in me, though, Dad."

"Devin," my mother chastises and I ignore her.

"Hey! I'm home!" I call out.

I hear footsteps and heavy breathing. Callie rounds the corner from the kitchen holding a bottle of water up to her lips. She's wearing a tight gray tank top and a pair of tiny running shorts. Her long, chestnut hair is pulled back in a high ponytail and there's a slick sheen to her smooth skin. Her back is to us and she's swaying her curvy little hips to whatever is pouring out of her earbuds and into her ears. I have an instant, uncontrollable urge to still those hips with my hands and glide my lips over the damp skin on her neck.

Before I can quell the urge and calmly tap her on the shoulder, she spins—part of her little dance—and her eyes widen in shock when she sees her audience. I literally see what her brain is processing all over her face—fear because my parents are here, shock because she knows they must know and relief because she's happy she's not hiding this for me anymore.

"Donna! Wyatt! Oh my God! Hi!" She runs toward them and skitters to a halt short of a hug. "I'm disgusting. I just had a run."

"I don't care in the least," my dad replies and pulls her into a hug. "How are you, sweetheart?"

I know my mom loves the girls equally, but I think my dad has always had the softest spot for Callie. She hugs him back and she's smiling from ear to ear. She's so beautiful when she lets all her defenses down like that.

"I'm great! I didn't know you were coming!" she says and her eyes scoot to me quizzically as Donna hugs her too, despite the sweat. "Did Luc talk to you?"

My dad glances over at me and frowns. "Luc knows about this?"

"Who else knows?" my mother wants to know.

"Callie told Luc and Rose when she found out," I inform them. "I don't know who they've told."

"They've told no one," Callie assures everyone. "I told them to keep quiet."

My mother sighs again. Conner interrupts and asks if he can watch his favorite Disney movie for the hundredth time. I take him into the living room and turn on his movie as he settles on the couch. I walk back into the kitchen and find my mother and Callie whispering at the island.

"Look, you can talk about it with me if you want, but you can't talk about me with everyone else, okay?" I say flatly to my mom.

My father shakes his head ruefully from his position at the kitchen table. "Kind of hard to talk about it with you when you don't tell us about it."

"Ashleigh…" I glance toward the living room and lower my voice. "Ashleigh doesn't want more kids. She hates my job. She wants a husband that is home by six every night and spends weekends barbequing and gardening or whatever. That can't be me. We all know that."

They're silent for a long minute. My mom looks so sad it's devastating. My dad just looks disappointed.

"How is he doing?" my dad asks, nodding his head toward the living room.

"He's doing better," I say and look at Callie. "It's helped to have Callie here. She fixed up his room and she helps me stay positive around him. She also makes sure we both eat properly."

My parents turn to look at Callie, who looks suddenly uncomfortable with the attention. My mom takes her hand and gives it a grateful squeeze. She just shrugs. "Speaking of eating, I've got a chicken in the oven that should be big enough for all of us. And I was thinking mashed potatoes and some salad?"

"Sounds great." My dad nods and smiles.

"I'll just jump into the shower real quick," she says, starting toward the hall.

"I'll start the potatoes, honey," my mom volunteers.

For a few tense moments I watch my mom gather the potatoes and putter around my kitchen. My dad is just staring at me. Finally I stand up. "Can you keep an eye on Con while I go upstairs for a second?"

My dad nods and I head into the hall and climb the stairs two at a time. I knock lightly on Callie's door. She opens it in nothing but a towel—a small towel that barely skims the top of her thighs.

"Hey," she says, her big brown eyes wide with innocence. "I didn't tell them. I swear."

"I know," I say and sigh.

She opens her door a little wider and I step in. "I have never seen my dad look so disappointed in my entire fucking life."

"Because you weren't there when I told them Jessie moved to Arizona without saying good-bye," she explains, her expression darkening at the memory. "As soon as the words left my mouth, your dad turned to where Jordan was sitting in your kitchen and gave him the exact same look. It was awesome back then. Now, not so much."

I suddenly feel exhausted—and incredibly frustrated. I run a hand through my hair and let my body sag against the wall behind me. She tilts her head a little and gives me a concerned look. "If Wyatt knew what she did to you, he'd stop looking so disappointed."

"Yeah, then he'd look at me with pity. I'll take the disappointment," I reply firmly.

"Do you need me to move out? I can grab a hotel," she suggests suddenly. "After dinner I'll pack up and they can stay here with you."

I shake my head. "No. They can stay in the same hotel as Jordy's team. It'll be fine. I'd rather you were here than them right now. I can't handle the stares."

She just nods and pulls her hair out of its ponytail. I try not to focus on the hem of the towel as it lifts ever so slightly, revealing even more of her long, lean legs.

"Will you come with them to the game tomorrow night?" I ask, trying not to sound as desperate as I am. "I want you to keep them company and keep them from obsessing about this."

"Of course." She gives me a little snarky grin. "Can I wear your jersey and scream your name and make a sign that says 'Garrison Can I Hold Your Stick?'"

I laugh at that. Genuinely laugh. It feels completely unnatural. "Is that a sex reference?"

"Yup! I saw some girl waving it in the stands at the last game of yours that I watched on TV," she explains. "You really should look up in the stands every now and then. It would be good for your ego."

"I'll keep that in mind." I smile softly and then decide to hug her.

I reach out and pull her into me. The fluffy blue towel is soft under my arms and as I bury my face in her neck, I inhale—she may have gone for a long, sweaty run but she somehow still smells good—something fruity and warm. She wraps her arms around my neck and holds on tightly.

We stay like that for a long moment. It feels so fucking good. When I feel a slight tingle in my pants, I realize it's starting to feel too good and pull back. She looks flushed but I assume it's still from her run.

"I meant what I said down there. You make this easier," I tell her.

She smiles. "It's because I'm awesome."

I laugh. "And modest."

I close the door and head back downstairs to face the sad and disappointed stares again.

Chapter 14

Callie

I get home with just enough time to change before Donna and Wyatt pick me up for the Barons game against the Winterhawks. Today went great at work and now, after working twelve straight days, I am off for two whole days. I have been looking forward to exploring New York City and catching up on sleep.

I drop my keys on the front table and dart up the stairs. Devin is already at the rink. I throw open the door to my room and pull off my shirt. I kick off my leggings and walk over to the closet. I had unpacked most of my stuff now. I grab my girls-cut Barons T-shirt, pull it on and match it with my favorite jeans and a pair of brown leather high-heeled boots. I decide to refresh my makeup and pull my hair from its ponytail, adding a little styling creme to it to give it a tousled look.

Who knows? Maybe I'll find a hockey fan who's as cute as a player. Although it's hard to top Devin and his teammates. Maybe I can find Jordy after the game and get him to introduce me to that French Canadian hottie from his team, Sebastian Deveau.

Donna and Wyatt are pulling into the driveway just as I hit the front hall and peek out the window. I head outside and into the backseat of the truck. They both smile at me.

"How is your new job going?" Wyatt asks me as he drives through the busy Brooklyn streets toward the hockey arena.

"Good! I really like the crew," I tell him honestly as I watch the scenery blur by. "My assistant is fantastic and even the cast are pretty cool kids. I was worried because sometimes actors can be head cases but they all seem to be great. They're not squawking about the wardrobe at all."

"It's so great that you got such a big network show," Donna says. I know she doesn't really know much about what I do but she's trying. I really appreciate that. "Wyatt showed me your name on the Internet on a list and you're one of the youngest to have such a high-up job."

"What?" I'm confused.

"I was goofing around on the Internet Movie Database," Wyatt explains a little sheepishly. "I searched your show, you know, thought it would be fun to see your name up there. And then I just started searching other shows for fun. Didn't matter which show I went to, none of the costume designers on any of the other shows were as young as you."

"What Wyatt is trying to say is he's as proud of you as he was of Jordy for leading the league in shorthanded goals," Donna says with a chuckle. "I am too, honey."

Wyatt's eyes shine with pride as they catch mine in the

rearview mirror. I smile back at him. God, I love these two. They are the perfect parents, even when they aren't technically someone's parents.

"How was your day with Conner?" I ask, changing the subject because I've never been that comfortable with attention like this.

Donna lights up again and gives me a detailed report of how great Conner is getting at skating and how after his skating lesson was over, they went to the Museum of Natural History, where Conner was obsessed with the butterfly exhibit.

We pull into the small lot reserved for players and VIPs and Wyatt puts the car in park. "We invited Ashleigh to join us tonight but she said it was best if she stayed home. She thought she would throw Devin's game off."

"Clearly, she hasn't been watching the games lately," I mutter as we all get out of the car. "She would know she's already done that."

Donna gives me a quizzical look. "Devin told me I can't talk about this but…do you know what happened? It seems like it has to be more than just Ashleigh being lonely."

"It is," I assure her and then I give Wyatt a stern look. "And it's not anything Devin could have controlled or avoided. He's a complete victim here and that's what is making this so hard on him. You know he's always been the type of guy who controls his own fate. He fails at nothing. He had no control over this situation and can't fix it and it's killing him."

They don't say anything but exchange worried glances as we head into the arena through the private entrance the players use, which takes us into the bowels of the arena. I know I'm being cryptic but even though I think Devin should sell Ashleigh out and tell them exactly what a monster she is, it's not my place to do it for him. I have no choice but to talk around the real rift in their marriage.

"You and I may have to stage a fight in the stands. Give the press something to talk about," a familiar voice echoes off the concrete walls.

I peer past Wyatt's shoulder and see her—in a Winterhawks T-shirt and low-rise jeans—walking toward us with Jordan. I let out an excited squeal and charge her. My older sister Jessie opens her arms and we both start screaming as we hug each other and jump up and down at the same time. Some staff and trainers walk by and smile, amused. Jordan stands beside us and shrugs an apology at them as he hugs his parents in a much calmer manner.

"I can't believe you're here!" I say to my older sister. "Why didn't you tell me you were coming?"

"I only decided last minute," she responds as she pulls back from the hug and catches my eye. "Besides, apparently we don't tell each other everything anymore."

She's pissed I didn't tell her about Devin. I roll my eyes to let her know she's being ridiculous. Jordan clears his throat. "Don't I get any love?"

I glance up at Jordan in his pinstriped gray suit and sigh. "Yeah, hi, Big Bird."

"Stop pretending you don't miss me terribly." He reaches down and hugs me, lifting me right off my feet. I groan in mock protest, but willingly hug him back.

"You better be making my sister happy," I warn him.

Jessie smiles and it's as bright and beautiful as it has been since the minute they stopped being idiots and got back together.

"Never been happier," she assures me and I can't help but smile. She turns to Wyatt and Donna and gives them both a quick hug. "We'll meet you guys at the seats. I need some alone time with my little sister."

She hooks her arm through mine and leads me down the hall, away from her future husband and his parents. She asks me about my job for the first four questions and, God bless her, she actually pays attention to the answers. And I can tell she's truly happy and excited for me. I can also tell she has other things she wants to talk about.

"Why didn't you tell me about Devin?" she asks finally.

"I couldn't," I reply honestly. "He didn't want Jordan to know."

"You could have still told me," Jessie argues and I give her a hard look.

"You and Jordy don't keep secrets from each other," I remind her. "I'm not about to start asking you to."

"So you've just been living there with him the entire time? And he and Ashleigh are what? Separated?"

"Yeah. I guess," I say softly as we follow the curve of the hallway in no particular direction. "He had already moved out when I got here and he was a mess. He needed a friend."

"He needed his family too," Jessie adds, slightly scornfully. "Jordan has been really worried about him. He sees how badly Dev's playing. And I could have talked to Ashleigh. She probably needed a friend too."

"She doesn't deserve a friend," I snap and Jessie looks at me with surprise.

"Callie, come on. I'm sure this isn't all her fault," Jessie tries to rationalize. "I mean when Jordy and I had issues it wasn't totally his fault. I liked to think it was, but it wasn't. I made it harder than it had to be too."

"She's lonely. She hates the road trips and the hockey wife lifestyle. He can't change that," I explain. "She's being selfish and ridiculous."

Jessie thinks about it for a minute as someone in a Winterhawks tracksuit walks by and waves at her. He's too old to be a player, probably a trainer.

"See, if you'd told me, I could have talked to her," Jessie says finally. "I still can. I know it's hard. I live it too. But it's not impossible and..."

"She cheated."

"WHAT?" She stops walking as her voice bounces off the cavernous cement hallway we're in.

I shush her loudly and she covers her mouth with her hand. "See! This is why I didn't want to tell you. This and because if Jordan knows, Devin will go completely off the deep end. He's pretty close as it is."

"She cheated?" Jessie repeats the words as if they are some foreign language she doesn't understand. "Had sex with someone else? Someone other than Devin?"

"That's the definition, yes." I nod solemnly. "But worse than that, she has feelings for someone else. She says she's in love with this guy Andrew and with Devin. And that she kicked Devin out so she could have time alone to think."

"She can have the rest of her life to think, now that she destroyed her marriage, that cheating bitch," Jessie seethes and I can't hide my shock—or awe.

"Jessica Caplan!" I say with a smile. "Since when are you the irate, protective sister?"

"Since it involves someone hurting Devin and that precious little ray of sunshine he created," Jessie responds and sighs. "Poor Conner and Devin. My God, of all the Garrison brothers to do this to, he's the one that it might honestly kill."

"Oh, yeah, because if you cheated on Jordy he would bounce back." I roll my eyes and give her a playful shove.

"Jordan would be devastated, but he wouldn't self-destruct," Jessie admits as we continue walking again. "Devin is so proud and so scared of failure—because he's never experienced it. No wonder he's falling apart."

"You don't know the half of it," I whisper and Jessie catches my eye. I open my mouth to tell her about the booze and the random hookup but someone calls her name from down the hall.

"Jessie! Where's your worse half? It's almost time to hit the ice."

We both turn and see a guy walking toward us in workout shorts and a black dry weave T-shirt with the Winterhawks logo on the chest. His brown hair is tucked under a Winterhawks hat but there's no mistaking his pale blue eyes. I grab Jessie's hand and squeeze it—hard.

She glances at me with stunned green eyes and then turns to him.

"Hey, Seb. Jordan's with his parents," she says and uses the hand I'm not clutching to point to me. "This is my sister Callie."

Seb's eyes lock with mine. His lips tug up in a soft smirk that makes me smile. I let go of Jessie and extend my hand to shake his. His grip is firm, which is a total turn-on. I can't deal with guys who shake a girl's hand limply because they're afraid to hurt them.

"Callie," he says my name. "You are Luc's girlfriend?"

"The French Disaster? God, no!" I blurt out, and Jessie laughs.

"That's Rosie, our youngest sister," Jessie explains.

"I'm one hundred percent single," I proclaim, and he chuckles at that.

"Good to know," he says before adding, "I hope to see you after the game."

He continues down the hall. I turn my head to watch him go. Jessie is watching me with a raised eyebrow. I grin at her. "I want that."

"Oh my God." Jessie giggles and tugs me toward a door that leads to a staircase. "I don't know if he can handle you."

"Can we find out? Please?"

We head up the stairs to the main level, where our seats are located. "Well, Jordan wants to go out after. I'm sure Sebastian will be there and you're obviously welcome to come with us."

I'm excited now. But as we hit the bustling concourse, reality sets in and I grab her hand again and pull her close. "Jessie, Donna and Wyatt don't know what Ashleigh did," I explain in a hushed voice. "Devin will tell them and Jordan when he's ready, and we shouldn't do it for him, okay?"

Jessie nods. "I won't tell them."

Chapter 15

Devin

We've only been at the bar twenty minutes and I'm already more stressed and angry than I was on the ice. It's fucking stupid. My team won. I should be just as happy as Larue and Loops, who are clinking their celebratory beers together. But I know, despite the win, Jordan outplayed me. And worse, I know he knows it. He's not saying it—yet. He's just laughing with his teammates about something. He brought his buddy Sebastian Deveau, his goalie Chooch and some rookie named Kennedy with him. They are nice enough guys but I am so not in the mood for a big group tonight.

I head to the bar and notice Seb is over by the pool tables playing a game with Callie. Well, they're holding pool cues, but the balls look untouched and he's leaning in pretty close to her as she says something to him. He smiles and she laughs, tipping her head back, her long, wavy brown hair tumbling over her shoulders in sexy waves.

My shoulders get tighter. I order a drink and turn to find

Jordan standing right behind me. He must have followed me from the table.

"Don't let your little French Canadian Casanova get any ideas about Callie," I warn Jordan sharply.

He glances over at Callie and Seb and snorts. "Please, I'm more worried about Seb than Callie. Callie will have him begging for mercy."

"Whatever." I shake my head, throw some money on the bar and grab my drink. Jordan isn't moving out of my way. I glare at him.

"Can we talk for a second?" Jordan asks quietly.

"If you're just going to brag about the fucking face-off wins, then no."

He rolls his eyes. "Actually, I wanted to know how you're doing. Why are you in your own place?"

"Because my wife is a horrible bitch," I snap and move to get around him.

He grabs my elbow lightly. "Dev…come on," he chastises me softly. "Don't talk like that. You love Ashleigh."

"I thought I did," I reply, and it stings somewhere deep in my chest where my heart used to be.

"Is this just because she's hesitating about more kids?" Jordan rolls his eyes again and I want to punch him. "She'll come around. Let Jessie talk to her tomorrow. She's got the whole hockey wife thing down already."

He looks so proud and so happy and so in love. And even though I know how immature it is, I fucking hate him for it.

"You win face-offs and you pick the perfect woman. Gee,

Jordy, is there anything you can't fucking do?" I hiss and storm off.

He follows me, of course. Jordan never backs down—not even when he should. I get to the table and before I can sit down, his hand clamps down on my shoulder. I spin to face him. Our body language must be completely confrontational because his buddies Chooch and Kennedy stop talking with Jessie and stare up at us.

"What the fuck is wrong with you?"

"Nothing." I glance over to the pool tables again. The balls remain untouched. Deveau is leaning forward, his hand on Callie's shoulder, whispering something in her ear. Whatever it is, she looks like she likes it.

"Is your teammate always such a manwhore?" I snipe and drop my drink on the table and head toward them.

"What the fuck?" I hear Jessie whisper loudly but I keep walking.

Chapter 16

Callie

Seb and I are totally hitting it off. He's quiet, and at first I thought he might be shy, but he's all about the body contact—touching my arm, my shoulder, my hip—and he talks easily in his totally hot French accent about the game, his team, living in Seattle and growing up in Quebec.

"You are younger than Jessie?" he asks and I nod. "You seem more mature."

"I am," I reply easily. "But she's more mature than she appears. Jordan brings out the lovesick kid in her. That's okay. She deserves it. We had a rough childhood."

"It's hard to be immature when you didn't get to do it as a kid when everyone else did," he murmurs and our eyes lock.

He gets it. I wonder why. It makes me want to do more than stick my tongue down his throat and that worries me. I try to get us back on track. I move to the pool table, where we racked the balls but never bothered to break them. I lean forward and pause before taking the shot so he can admire my butt.

"You have beautiful eyes," he tells me right after I break the balls on the table.

I smile softly. He was so not looking at my eyes.

"And your smile…makes it look like you might be thinking dirty things," he says and winks.

"What can I say? Between those biceps and that accent"—I lean against the table—"I can't seem to keep my mind out of the gutter."

He stands directly in front of me—inches from me. He leans in and I feel his lips brush my ear. "Maybe you and I can do something about those dirty thoughts."

"Callie."

Seb and I both turn our heads to find Devin standing at the end of the pool table glaring at us like an angry parent. Seb doesn't say anything; he just takes a big step back from me and walks around the table to the side farthest from Devin and starts to line up a shot.

"Yes, Dad?" I say snarkily. "Is it past curfew?"

He doesn't even smile at my joke. He puts a hand on the small of my back and moves me out of Seb's earshot.

"What?" I ask, trying not to sound quite as annoyed as I am.

I know that he's going through a lot and I want to be supportive. I *have* been supportive, so I deserve a ride on Sebastian Deveau as a reward.

"Just forgot to mention the ground rules when you moved in," he tells me, his eyebrows pinched together in an angry frown. "No random hookups in my house."

"You're joking, right?" I can't believe he would dare to do this. "You had a random hookup just last week!"

That comment seems to wind him for a second but he recovers instantly and turns condescending eyes on me. "You seriously want to sleep with him?"

"Yes, Devin. He's what a sane woman would call a hot piece of ass." I give him a look like he's a moron. He gives me one back like I'm insane.

"That's your type?" He looks disgusted.

"Yes. Good looking, well built and sexy as all hell with bedroom eyes is my type," I snap and put my hands on my hips. "And before you go slamming the type of guy I like to fuck, remember you are one of them."

I storm back to Seb without looking back.

Chapter 17

Devin

Before I can follow her, Jordan is in my face again.

"Would you fucking talk to me?" he demands, his voice soft and urgent. "I want to help you."

"I don't need your help, Jordan," I snap. "Just go back to Seattle and your perfect little world with the love of your life and all that crap."

"I'm the first one to admit my world is far from perfect," Jordan replies. "I have no problem admitting that it was a whole lot of luck that brought Jessie back in my life. But it's a whole lot of work that is going to keep her there forever. I would never give up on us. What are you afraid of—the work? Why are you giving up on Ashleigh?"

I take a step toward him. We're literally toe-to-toe now, breathing in each other's faces. My shoulders are so tense they ache and my fists are balled up at my sides, ready to strike. I have never punched Jordan, but right now it's all I want to do. Jessie appears next to him and touches Jordan's waist. It just makes me angrier to see her concern for him. Did Ashleigh ever have concern like that for me?

"It's my fault? You think I just walked away because she didn't want another kid or because marriage requires work? That's how fucking shallow I am?"

"What else am I supposed to think? You won't fucking tell me anything!"

"Umm, guys…can we leave and talk about this elsewhere?" Jessie begs softly.

I turn and look down at her harshly and back up at Jordan. "When you put that wedding band on her finger and she fucks another guy, then you can judge me. Until then, go fuck yourself, little brother."

I shove him—hard. He stumbles into the table behind him and a couple of glasses full of beer tumble over. Jessie yells for Callie and grabs Jordan harshly by the arm, holding him back from going after me, because I can tell by the rage in his eyes he wants to slug me now as badly as I want to slug him.

Callie is there suddenly—right in front of my face on her tiptoes so she can come close to making eye contact. She grabs my shoulders and starts pushing me backward.

"Outside. Now!" she barks in my face. I could easily stand still—I'm way stronger than she is, but I also know Callie will never give up. She'd knee me in the balls and drag me out by my hair if she had to, so I turn and storm for the exit.

Chapter 18

Callie

I'm so upset by what just happened in there that I'm literally shaking. I can feel my pulse hammering in my throat and I can't take a deep breath. I have never seen them go after each other like that. Never.

I have been witness to a lot of Garrison brother fights. They constantly tease each other and call each other names and push each other's buttons. There have been a few times when lines were crossed and someone told someone else to fuck off and meant it. Jordan was the king of hurling sticks at his brothers in anger on the backyard rink. He'd also once thrown a lamp at Cole in the living room when Cole was picking on him about something and didn't realize how sensitive Jordy was. And then there was the time that Devin totally schooled Cole on the rink and scored after sending Cole to his ass in a heap. Cole had promptly gotten up, skated over and punched Devin in the face. Cole was eleven and Devin was fifteen. That was the only time I'd heard of them getting violent with each other.

But tonight…if Jessie and I hadn't stepped in, the two of them would have probably fought until the death. And that totally terrified me. Jessie, Rose and I didn't have a lot of things growing up—like parents or a strong biological family—but we did have patience, love and respect for each other. I know my sisters would risk their lives for me and my happiness and I would do the same for them, without question. I know that Cole would do that for any one of his brothers, and Luc—the honorary Garrison brother—would do it for them too, but I always question whether Jordan and Devin would do it for each other. They are just so…intimidated by each other.

"You are out of control," I tell Devin, fighting to keep my tone hard and even so he doesn't know how rattled I am.

"Who the fuck does he think he is, accusing me of being the one to give up on my marriage?" he barks at me in his own defense.

"Well, maybe if you weren't too fucking proud to tell him what happened and let him see you're fucking human, then maybe he wouldn't make assumptions!"

Seb and Alex Larue come out into the parking lot. They see us—Devin leaning up against the side of the building and me pacing furiously in front of him—and they both stop dead in their tracks.

Seb is the first one to step forward, which is very brave and makes me like him, unfortunately. "Callie, are you okay?"

"She's fine," Devin answers angrily.

I give him a death stare and turn and walk over to Seb. When I get there, he reaches out and takes my hand in his gently. Damn him, why does he have to be so likable? I may not be able to just fuck him and walk away now, which means I won't let myself fuck him at all.

"I'm fine," I assure him with a small smile.

His light blue eyes narrow with concern and he takes his free hand and pushes my hair back from my face. "You're shaking, *ma belle.*"

"It's not a big deal," I argue and glance back at Devin, who is staring a hole into the pavement at his feet. His hands are still balled into fists by his sides. "I just need to make sure Devin is okay."

He looks confused now. "I thought you were Garrison-free."

I sigh. "I thought I was, too."

Jordan and Jessie emerge from the bar. I pull away from Seb and walk back over to stand in front of Devin, blocking his path to his brother. Jessie and I lock eyes. I can tell she told her fiancé the gory details I told her at the arena and I don't blame her in the least. I am done waiting for Devin to do the right thing.

Jordan takes a couple steps toward us but stops a few feet away. Jessie is beside him; her eyes never leave me. I guess I look as shaken up as I feel. Alex and Seb disappear down the street, probably realizing that this is a family matter. Jordan shoves his hands into his pockets.

"I don't want to fight with you, Dev," he says in a quiet voice. "I honestly don't give a fuck if you stay married to Ashleigh or not. I just want to see you out of this place you're in—this dark, shitty place."

Devin says nothing. He doesn't lift his gaze. If I didn't know better, I would think he was dead. Maybe he kind of is on the inside. That revelation makes my heart ache. I reach out and take his hand in mine, prying his fingers out of the fist they're balled up in and lacing them with mine. He doesn't pull away.

"If you need anything, if Conner needs anything, whatever…just call me, okay?" Jordan tells him. "I'm sorry."

Jordan turns and walks back toward the bar. Jessie watches him disappear back inside but doesn't follow. She walks over and stands in front of Devin and waits patiently until he finally lifts his head and looks at her.

"He loves you so much," Jessie tells him in an even, matter-of-fact voice. "I do too. Never forget that."

She reaches up and hugs him. He doesn't hug her back but I can see the anger melt from his face. Now he simply looks defeated.

"When you're ready to get out of your own way and let us in, we'll be here," she says as she kisses his cheek and walks off.

We both watch her go back into the bar. Once we're alone in the parking lot again, he pushes off the wall and starts to storm down the street. I run after him.

"I need to get the hell out of here," he says in a strained whisper.

"Fine," I reply and follow him toward the sidewalk.

He turns to me with dark, hollow eyes and all I want to do is kiss that sad, empty look off his face. It's such an overwhelming urge that I have to bite my bottom lip and push my hands into my jean pockets to keep them from grabbing his face. Vulnerability in a man has never been attractive to me before. But with Devin it's so raw and charged with testosterone that I can feel my panties getting wet. "You should go get Sebastian and bring him home if you want. Do what you need to do."

"If only it were that simple," I reply ruefully, but I don't know if he hears me. He's halfway down the street already.

I head back into the bar. The atmosphere is still tense. I walk over to Jordan, who is standing by the pool table finishing the game I started with Seb, and I hug him and kiss his cheek.

"Okay, now I know the world is coming to an end," he jokes, but it's strained.

"Thank you for not being a total infant out there and just letting him be one instead," I tell him as I let go of his broad shoulders. Jessie walks over and hugs me around the shoulders from behind.

"The boys are off to Milwaukee in the morning," she says about the Winterhawks. "My flight back to Seattle isn't until four in the afternoon. Let's do brunch."

"Deal. I'll pick you up at noon," I tell her and kiss her cheek. "I'm going to go home."

"Check on Devin?" Jordan asks hopefully. I nod. "Can you keep me posted on things? Text me updates for the next few weeks? You know he probably won't be talking to me for a while."

"Yeah. Totally. I promise."

Jessie hugs me and I give Jordan a playful shove, then I call a cab on my cell.

Chapter 19

Devin

I couldn't go home. I knew Callie would show up there sooner rather than later and I don't want to talk to her—or anyone—about what just happened. I really am not in the mood for talking. I am in the mood for taking my frustrations out in a different way. I walk around in the cold, with no destination in mind, until I find myself in front of my local go-to bar, the same bar where I ran into Donahue a while ago. Back then I was trying desperately to hold on to my marriage. Now I know better.

I head inside, order a scotch and nurse it as I scan the crowd. I'm there about an hour when I see her. The girl from the last time I was here. I never did get her name. I don't care if I get it now either. I watch her as she dances on the tiny dance floor with two other girls. She's wearing a pair of black leggings and a cherry-red top that her cleavage is spilling out of. She's teetering on a pair of four-inch red leather pumps. Those shoes are the only things I will let her keep on tonight, I decide.

As I walk toward her, a part of me fills with dread because part of me doesn't want to do this. Part of me wants to go home and let Callie hold my hand again. But wanting someone's hand to hold—someone to count on—is what had made me want to marry Ashleigh. So I let the irrational, angry and sexually frustrated part take over. The part of me that wants to live in a drunken world of base pleasure and emotionless sex. The part of me that would rather die than fall in love with someone again.

She looks up as she swings her hips provocatively and sees me coming. It takes her a second, but her heavily made-up eyes flare in recognition. She smiles and waves. I walk over to her and wrap an arm tightly around her waist and instantly match the rhythm of her hips. Our groins are pressed up against each other and I'm already hard. I was hard before I saw her. This isn't about her.

"Remember me?"

"How could I forget?" she asks.

"Want to come home with me?"

"I thought you were married," she whispers hesitantly.

"Do you want to come home with me?" I repeat and let my lips graze her neck, before moving up and nipping her earlobe lightly.

"Yes."

Chapter 20

Callie

I must have fallen asleep on the couch waiting for him to get home and the sounds of the TV must have muffled his arrival. But nothing could muffle the high-pitched squeal coming from his bedroom. I sit bolt upright on the couch and stare into the hallway. I can see part of the stairs and the front hall. Devin's shoes are there and there is a tacky fake Coach purse beside them.

He did it again.

I had been hoping that, even though he didn't give in to his family's attempts at getting him to open up, it had at least made some kind of deep impact. That Devin would start to do a little self-reflection and stop lashing out—with his words or his dick—but apparently I was wrong.

He hadn't left the bar tonight to absorb everything that had happened and get a grip. He left so he could find himself a warm body to bury his feelings and his cock inside, once again. And stupid me had come home—and left that sexy, French, walking orgasm inducer Seb—to be with him. I'm suddenly consumed by anger. I jump off the couch and climb the stairs two at a time.

When I get to his bedroom door, I don't even knock. I just fling it open so hard it hits the wall. Some completely skanked-up bottle blonde is on her back, lying sideways across Devin's California king. Her leggings are halfway down her thighs. Devin is leaning over her, shirtless and wearing only his boxer briefs.

Her eyes get huge at the sight of me. Devin jumps up and spins around to face me. He looks embarrassed and furious. "Callie!"

I ignore him and point at her. "You. Get out."

"What?!" she squeaks, horrified.

"Get out. Go home," I command and point to the open door. "You're not fucking him tonight. Or ever. Go home."

"Callie, what the fuck do you think you're doing?" he wants to know.

"Are you the wife?" the bottle blonde asks, terrified.

I glare at her and figure what the hell. "Yeah. I'm the wife. Now stop fucking my husband or I'll kill you. Deal?"

I say it with absolutely no emotion—like I am reciting lunch specials at a diner. It sounds ridiculous, but it does the trick. She scampers off the bed and starts pulling up her leggings and charging down the stairs at the same time. I hang my head over the railing and watch her grab her bag and disappear out the front door.

"What the fuck is your problem?" he slurs furiously. He's clearly had too much—way too much—to drink.

There is actually an open bottle of Crown Royal on the bedside table. I shake my head. Classy.

"I decided your rule is a good rule," I tell him as I try to look intimidating, my hands on my hips as I stand in front of him in my hot pink pajama shorts and white tank top. "No random hookups in this house."

"I told you you could bring Seb home," he yells. "And who I bring home is none of your fucking business!"

I shake my head and step into him. We're maybe a foot apart and I poke my finger into his chest. "Yeah, I'm pretty much done with letting you figure this shit out on your own. You're making a bigger mess of your life than it already is."

He pushes past me and storms into the master bath. I follow. I don't even give a fuck if he's going to take a piss, he is not getting out of this conversation.

"What the fuck are you doing?" he bellows and turns on me. His normally caramel-colored eyes are as dark as coal. I feel a little ripple of fear but I swallow it down. I know he would never physically hurt me.

"You're done with the revenge fucking phase of this mess, do you hear me, Devin Garrison?" I shout and push past him and open the shower door. "Now it's time to start acting like a grown-up and figuring your shit out."

"So she's allowed to fuck whoever she wants but I can't?" Devin demands.

I turn on the cold water in the shower and flip the lever so it's coming out the rain head. I hesitate and also turn on the warm water. Yes, I want to shock him, but I don't want to kill him.

"This isn't about what Ashleigh's doing. It's about what you're doing to yourself," I tell him, trying not to scream but, man, I want to. "These randoms are not helping anything. So next time you want to fuck something…"

I grab his arm and yank him. He's so drunk it's easy. He's not resisting so, although it takes all my strength, I can push him into the giant marble shower stall. He almost slips and, as his back hits the far wall and the lukewarm water pours down on top of him, he yelps.

"Take a cold shower." I finish my sentence, raising my voice for emphasis.

"You bitch," he hollers and then lunges for me.

I wasn't expecting that at all and I have no time to react. He yanks me into the shower stall with him. The water splashes down on me and my whole body goes completely rigid. My eyes snap shut to block out the water, and a furious, shocked scream escapes my lips. I can feel his hands wrapped around my biceps. He's holding me right up against him and he has no intention of letting go. I struggle but it's useless.

My eyes fly open and I smack at his bare chest. But when I see the look in his eyes, I stop fighting. Gone is the anger and rage. His eyes are caramel again and his brow is slightly raised. His mouth is gaping slightly, his tongue on the edge of his bottom lip as his gaze slides over my body.

I glance down. I'm soaking wet. My little shorts are stuck to my skin and sagging slightly, exposing my lower abdomen. My white tank top is clinging to my chest and stomach and is completely see-through. I can't help but notice the same effect has happened to his white boxer briefs. I can make out every angle of his hardening cock as easily as he can make out the curve of my breasts and the dark circle of my nipples.

His eyes finally land on my face. I open my mouth to speak but no words come. He tugs on my arms again; my body jolts forward and his lips crash down on mine.

My body reacts before my mind does. My mouth opens instantly, and as our tongues meet, my body softens in his arms and I push myself against him. He moves and one hand goes into my wet hair as the other one grabs my ass. I reach between us and cup his dick, giving it a firm squeeze. My breath leaves my lungs with a *whoosh*. Holy fuck, I realize I have wanted to touch it since I saw him naked that day I woke him up. The thought is completely overwhelming both in how much I mean it and in how surprised I am by it.

His hands move and he runs them over my wet tank top, cupping my breasts and rolling my nipples between his fingers through the soaked fabric, turning them hard in seconds. His lips move to my neck and he sucks—hard.

I yank his underwear down and push my crotch into his exposed erection. If it weren't for the pajama shorts, I would be fucking him right now. Standing in this shower, tepid warm water coating us…no condom in sight. Thank God for pajamas.

He reaches for the front of my bottoms, clearly not feeling the same appreciation for clothing that I am, but I shove his hands away and drop to my knees. Without even the slightest thought or word, I wrap my hand around the base of his cock and take him between my lips.

Chapter 21

Devin

Her mouth is hot. Blazing hot. I shudder and moan, the sounds loud and guttural. I've lost complete control. Callie owns me right now and I don't even care.

She slides almost all the way down my cock, her tongue pushing hard against the underside as she slides almost all the way off it before rolling her tongue around the tip like it's a lollypop. She repeats the process, and the third time her free hand cups my balls firmly and she takes me so deep into her mouth that my tip taps the back of her throat. She fights a gag but keeps going, picking up speed.

My mind goes blank. My hands wrap around her long, wet hair and my head falls back against the marble wall. This is fucking heaven.

"Callie…I'm close," I warn and try to pull her off. She lets go of my balls and slaps at my hand that's pulling on her hair, trying to stop her, and continues to lick and suck on me.

Her hand at the base of my cock starts to move with her lips, trailing behind them and creating a perfect blend of friction and pressure. She is literally milking my orgasm to the surface. A moan escapes at the same time I lose the ability to breathe as my balls tighten and I let go right into her perfect mouth.

I say her name over and over in jagged breaths and she pumps me dry, swallowing everything. My knees start to give out and I slide to the floor in front of her. My eyes flutter open and the water splashes off my chest and her shoulders, sprinkling both our faces.

She leans in and cups the sides of my face and kisses me hard and firm on the lips. I grab the wet material of her tank top with my hands and start to lift it, but she pulls away and stands up.

"Callie…" I croak out her name and reach for her, but she steps out of the shower, dripping a giant puddle onto my bathroom floor.

"That's all you get from me," she says firmly.

"You've given me more before," my drunken, orgasmrocked brain argues aloud.

"I didn't give it to this Devin," she retorts. "This Devin doesn't deserve me. Not all of me. Now get your shit together."

She shuts the glass door of the shower and disappears from sight.

Chapter 22

Devin

I'm sitting in the lobby with two Starbucks in my hand when they start filing off the elevators. A few of them notice me and obviously recognize me. They nod or wave. It would be weird to have a member of another NHL team sitting in the lobby of your team's hotel except when it's me and the team is Jordan's or Luc's. Seb Deveau, his Winterhawks hat low on his head, makes eye contact as he saunters off the elevator. His gaze is wary but unwavering. I fight down the anger that starts to bubble at the sight of him. My mind drifts to Callie on her knees, water pouring down on her as her lips slide over my cock. Seb didn't have her last night, so I shouldn't be upset with him.

Finally I see Jordan lumber into view. He's talking with their captain, Avery Westwood. Jordan's head is turned away from me. As I leave the chair I'm sitting in and start toward them, Avery catches my eye and says something to my brother. Jordan's head turns and he stops walking. Avery takes Jordan's bag and nods at me with a small smile as he walks by and continues out of the hotel to the team bus.

I nod at Avery as he goes and I try to forget that he slept with Callie last summer at Cole and Leah's joint bachelor-bachelorette party. I walk over to my brother and hand him the tall americano I bought for him. He takes it from me wordlessly. I sip my own latte. We walk toward the restaurant, away from the constant stream of players heading out the front doors.

"I shouldn't have attacked you last night," I finally say. "Verbally or physically."

He looks truly shocked that I would apologize, but he recovers quickly and nods. "Don't worry about it."

We both sip our drinks. "Tell Jessie I apologize."

He nods again. "Are you divorcing Ashleigh?"

"I think I have to, even though I think it will hurt Conner."

"Do you still love her?"

"No."

He nods. "Whatever you decide, I've got your back."

I catch his eye. "What would you do?"

He sips his coffee and swallows, his big blue eyes catching mine. "What would I do if it was Jessie?"

I nod and we stare at each other. I can see the turmoil in his face. He opens his mouth but then closes it swiftly and bites his bottom lip. My shoulders sag.

"Jessie would never do that to you." I say the words he's scared to for fear his faith in his fiancée and their relationship would anger me again like it did last night.

"She never would," he whispers almost guiltily. "But that

doesn't mean we're perfect. You know we're not, Devin."

"Yeah. I know." I nod slowly. "You found a girl that gets you and loves you no matter what. I shouldn't begrudge you that. It's good that you've got Jessie. I know she's not like Ashleigh. It's fine."

One of their trainers walks into the lobby, makes eye contact with Jordan and waves him over. "We're heading out, Garrison!"

We walk out the lobby doors into the cool morning air. The bus is waiting at the curb.

"It's not fine," Jordan argues delicately and stops to face me under the awning of the entrance to the hotel. "You deserve someone like Jessie, someone trustworthy and unconditionally in love with you."

I say nothing. He hugs me quickly. "Love you, bro."

"You too, Jordy." He's about to get on the bus when I call out his name again. "Hey!" He turns and looks at me. "My face-off percentage this season is seventy-two percent. Beat that, Mr. Perfect."

Jordan laughs and flips me the bird before disappearing onto the bus. It feels good that things with him are back to normal, but now I have to make things okay with Callie. That seems like a much harder thing to do.

What happened in the middle of our argument was completely unexpected. When she threw me in that shower, I wanted to rip her head off. I grabbed her and pulled her into the water to punish her—make her as wet and furious as I was. But my anger evaporated when I saw her body through her wet clothes. And when I felt her wet skin against mine. My need to lose myself in those random girls from the bars was nothing compared to the crushing need I suddenly had last night to lose myself in Callie. And she felt so much better—made me feel so much better—than the other girl had.

As I drive to practice, I try to think what caused that. Was it because she was familiar? I'd been with her before—sort of. She is a friend. Touching her and being with her offered just the slightest bit of emotional grounding, which I clearly had been lacking since Ashleigh left. Was it because I have always wanted to finish what we had started in that barn? Because I always have. There is no denying it. That almost-sex with Callie had been a total fantasy and Jordan walking in on us was like being abruptly woken up from a glorious dream. You always want to slip back into sleep and try to catch it again.

What was even more confusing than the feelings and the need that bubbled up so intensely from me last night was the matching response from her. When I kissed her, she didn't put up one ounce of a fight. In fact, she matched my lust move for move and kiss for kiss.

Where the hell was that coming from?! Was she just so full of sexual frustration over not being able to screw Seb that she was taking it out on the only available male body? Or was it that I was just such a raging, seething mess that she wanted to do whatever it took to calm me?

Callie had once said she made sure she didn't hook up with boys she could really like. I guess I was officially a boy she could never like. Not only had she clearly decided last night that she didn't like me and therefore could give me a blow job (a mind-blowing, perfect blow job) but she'd also made it clear that she thought too little of me to give me the rest of her body. That had been one hell of a reality check. I had sat there on the shower floor until my skin pruned reeling with the shame, embarrassment and shock of that realization.

As I pull into the parking lot of the arena, I come to one steadfast conclusion. Whatever the reason either of us did it, it doesn't matter. What matters is figuring out how to deal with what we did. And in the end, I am thankful it had happened—I somehow feel more like myself than I have in weeks.

Chapter 23

Callie

The next morning I hear him leave really early. I don't know where he could possibly be going because it's too early for a hockey practice but I'm incredibly grateful I don't have to face him just yet. He's leaving on a road trip to play Canadian teams late this afternoon. With any luck I can avoid him completely and not have to deal with this until he gets back six days from now.

I lie in bed and feel a blush creep over my face. I still can't believe what happened last night. Holy fuck. What the hell was I thinking? What the hell was *he* thinking?

I know the answer to that: he wasn't thinking. He hasn't been thinking for weeks. That means last night was my fault. I should have pulled away. I should have stopped. I should not have given him a goddamned blow job in the shower.

I was just so…frustrated. I was frustrated with the way he was acting and stressed from that fight he'd had with Jordan and having to lie to my sister for as long as I did, and I was sexually frustrated. He had banged a chick before and it hadn't helped his situation. And of course I was upset that the first chance I got to stop thinking about Devin fucking and start fucking myself, Devin screwed it up. Still, that didn't give me the right to kick the one-night stand out and become one myself.

Fuck.

The worst part is I know, without the slightest doubt, that if he had followed me out of the shower and into my room, I would have screwed his brains out. That speech I gave—I meant it more than anything, but whether Devin deserved to screw me or not, I wanted him to do it more than I had ever wanted anyone in my life. And when he didn't follow me, I imagined him there in my bed with me anyway and touched myself until I came.

I groan, pull myself from my bed, traipse to the shower and concentrate on getting ready to meet Jessie for brunch. Every time an image of last night flashes into my brain I struggle to catch my breath and I blush. I decide to walk to Jessie's hotel. It's forty-five minutes at a brisk pace, and the fall air is crisp and heavy, like it may rain or even snow, but I need the time to get my head straight. When I get to the Sheraton, where the team had been staying, we grab a cab and I take her to Jimmy's Café because Devin mentioned it had an amazing all-day breakfast menu. Even on a Thursday, in the middle of the day, it's pretty packed but we manage to grab a small table toward the back.

"How was he when you got home?" Jessie asks, skipping small talk completely.

"He wasn't there," I explain honestly and scan the menu in front of me.

"Where did he go? Is he okay? Did he come home at all?" Jessie goes from concern to panic in a millisecond.

"Don't you think I would have called you and Jordan if he just completely disappeared?" I ask as the waitress brings us two lattes, a vanilla for Jessie and a caramel for me. "He came home."

We order with the waitress. I get steak and eggs with a side of grits and an extra side of corn bread. Getting a guy off always leaves me with a big appetite. Jessie orders chicken and waffles with extra gravy. I smirk. Guess she worked up an appetite last night too.

"So did you talk about it?" Jessie asks and I move my gaze to stare at my latte.

"Not really," I murmur. "It was late. He was drunk."

"Drunk?" Jessie repeats, horrified. "So he went out and got hammered? Jesus, Callie, he's off the deep end."

"Yeah, he was." I nod and sigh, finally moving my gaze up to meet hers.

Her green eyes bore into me and I know she knows instantly that something is up. Jessie is psychic when it comes to my feelings. It's scary, annoying and comforting all at the same time. "Something happened. What happened?"

She reaches across the table and grabs my hand. I sigh again and feel a blush creep up my face. Damn. "He came home with another random girl he wanted to hook up with."

"Another?" Jessie almost gasps. "What do you mean another?"

I nod. "Yeah, it's happened once before. Only since he found out about Ashleigh and this Andrew dude. Not before. He didn't cheat on her; she cheated on him."

"They're technically still married," Jessie argues.

"And Jordan was technically dating Hannah when he took your virginity," I remind her and her lips press together in a thin, discontented line.

"Not exactly the same thing," Jessie argues softly. "We were kids and not legally attached."

"It's a piece of paper," I remind her. She knows I have never put much value in marriage. After all, our parents were married and it didn't stop our father from disappearing.

"So you don't think the random women are a big deal?" she counters.

I shake my head, take a deep breath and try to figure out how to express my thoughts. "They're not a big deal because he's still legally married. They're a big deal because they're out of character."

She nods. Her eyes squint slightly for a second like she's focusing on something but I assume she's just thinking really hard. I sip my latte and pause the conversation as the waitress brings our meals over.

"I didn't think anything of the first one," I tell my sister as I reach for the pepper. "I would do it too, you know? And besides, you should have seen him, Jessie. He looked sick about it afterward."

I pause to take a bite of my eggs. I'm famished. I take another big bite, chew and continue. Absentmindedly, I push my hair over my shoulder. "But when he kept doing it I realized it was becoming a problem. Like he was forcing himself to be this unemotional fuck machine."

Jessie wrinkles her nose at that and sighs. "You're right. That's not like him."

I take a bite of my steak. "So last night when he brought home this one instead of dealing with his feelings and what had happened with Jordy, I kicked her out."

"You did what?" Jessie almost drops her forkful of waffle.

"I walked into his room and pretended I was his wife and kicked her out," I explain and swallow some grits. "He was furious."

She's smiling at me, but then her eyes narrow again. She cocks her pretty head to the left and her auburn ponytail swings out, grazing her shoulder. "So if you went home last night and kicked out Devin's skank, does that mean you didn't hook up with Seb?"

I shake my head and sip my latte again. "No. Everything was too dramatic. And even though I only talked to him a little bit, he was way too deep and insightful and charming...I could have liked him. You know I don't do like."

She smiles at that but it goes from a humored grin to a knowing smirk. "So then if it wasn't Sebastian, who left the bite mark on your shoulder?"

"What?" I drop my fork with a loud clang.

She laughs and reaches out, her fingers grazing the top of my shoulder, which is sticking out of the oversize neck of my powder-pink sweatshirt. As soon as she touches it, a flash of Devin's lips on my skin, sucking it between his teeth, clouds my brain and makes me dizzy. I blush. I hate my traitorous face right now. Her green eyes grow to twice their size.

"Callie. Who…?" Then she blinks and I can almost see the lightbulb turn on. "Oh, Callie."

"I didn't sleep with him!" I blurt out much too loudly. A couple at the table next to us turns and stares for a second.

Jessie waits until they go back to their own brunch and continues in a whisper. "Callie, you and Devin? Again? Now?"

"I didn't plan it or anything," I explain quickly. "I was so pissed at him and he was yelling at me and I told him next time he wants to do something stupid like fuck a stranger he should take a cold shower. Then I shoved him in the shower and he grabbed me and pulled me in with him, and the next thing I know we were kissing."

She absorbs this information silently, her eyes glued to her coffee cup for a long minute. When she looks up at me, she looks concerned, but not disappointed.

"You didn't sleep with him?" She wants to make sure and I can, without guilt, respond with a firm no. She sighs. "It was still a stupid mistake."

"I know. I know." I groan a little. "I have to talk to him about it."

"You do," she agrees and takes another bite of waffles. She wants to say more. She *really* does, I can tell. I know her better than she knows herself. But she's clearly just as confused as I am. Sure, Devin and I had that moment way back when, but neither of us even talked about it with anyone because it wasn't a big deal. There were no unrequited feelings. I mean, I still thought he was attractive and everything, but I didn't spend a second pining away for him after the barn. So this little make-out session was shocking. She would probably pass right out if I told her about the blow job—not to mention how much I loved it.

So I keep that part to myself and change the subject to her wedding—which she is supposed to be planning for next summer—and try to ignore the panic I feel about having to face Devin.

Chapter 24

Devin

I'm carrying my suitcase down the steps when I look up and see her walking slowly down the street toward the house. She slows almost to a halt as she sees me on the sidewalk and I wonder for a brief second if she might turn and walk the other way. With Callie, it's a distinct possibility.

Luckily, she decides to just keep walking toward our home. I lean against the concrete pillar at the end of our stairs and watch her as she slows to a stop in front of me. She has a tote bag full of groceries over her shoulder.

"Hi," she says and then smiles sheepishly. It makes me grin like a goof. "Off on the road trip?"

"Yeah…" I say and jiggle my house keys in my hand. "So, I went to see Jordan before he left today."

"Oh?" She looks surprised, but happy.

"Yeah. We're good," I tell her and she nods. We stare at each other for a long minute. I push off the pillar and glance into the grocery bag she's holding up against her chest. "Dinner?"

"Yeah."

There's another slightly awkward pause and we just stare at each other again. Finally, she smirks her typical sexy little Callie smirk.

"So yeah, last night was pretty much the hottest thing that has ever happened to me," I confess softly. "And also the most out-of-control and out-of-character thing I have ever done."

"Yeah," she agrees quietly and turns her eyes to the street, focusing on nothing. "Believe it or not, it took me by surprise too."

"I don't regret it," I tell her honestly. "I probably wouldn't have fixed things with Jordan as quickly if it didn't happen. I think I have a different perspective now. Or at least I'm trying to."

She starts to giggle self-consciously. "All that from a blow job? Damn, I'm good!"

I burst out laughing at that. Her giggles turn to full-fledged laughter too. "I should tell the U.S. military about you. You could probably stop terrorism."

She's blushing and tears of laughter are swimming in her beautiful brown eyes. I put my hand to the back of her head and kiss her forehead gently. I make sure to let her go quickly and step away so the gesture is friendly, nothing more.

"Have a good trip. I expect a goal a game, Garrison. Nothing less," she commands.

"I'll do my best," I promise her as my airport car pulls up behind her. "If you need anything while I'm gone or you're bored or whatever, call me or text me."

It's weird. I have never told her that before. And I know

I don't have to tell her now. If the house burned down or something happened to Conner or whatever, she would get in touch with me. I guess now I'm reminding her it's okay if she wants to talk to me without a disaster attached to it.

As fucked up as last night was, she pulled me back from the edge of complete self-destruction. I don't know how far I am from that edge, but it's farther than I was before last night. I don't want to slip back.

She nods and winks. "And remember, when in doubt—cold shower."

I laugh and slip into the backseat as the driver loads my bag into the trunk. I watch her climb the steps to the front door and admire the swing of her narrow hips and the perfect round shape of her ass. Then I give my head a shake as the driver heads toward JFK.

Chapter 25

Callie

The next night I sit alone in the living room with a glass of Pinot and a big bowl of my favorite pepper Parmesan pasta and watch the Barons–Ice Dogs game. My eyes follow the puck on the TV as Devin skates with it down the ice, making a picture-perfect pass to Donahue, who takes a screaming shot that hits the post. My phone vibrates on the coffee table with a text from Jessie. She wants to know how things are with Devin and me. As I text her back and tell her we're all good and just friends (again), nothing to worry about, the captain of the Hamilton Ice Dogs scores so they're now leading 2–1. There are only seconds left in the second period. A goal like that is a real morale killer. I swear under my breath as the camera shows a close-up of Devin skating to the bench with a hard scowl on his face.

In the third period the Barons come out full of intensity and get an early goal to tie it up. Devin has an assist on the goal, which makes me clap and bounce on the couch. By the end of the third it's still tied. Halfway through the five-minute overtime, Devin intercepts a Hamilton pass and makes a break for it. He's so fast and determined I know, even before his stick pulls back and slaps the puck, that it will sail easily through the goalie's legs and hit the back of the net—which is exactly what it does. I squeal and jump off the couch.

Later that night as I brush my teeth, my mind is on Devin. If I'm honest with myself, I've been thinking of him more than I should be since he left on this road trip. I'm worried about him but I'm also still a little flustered about that whole shower thing. We seemed to leave things on good, friendly ground again, like I told Jessie, but until we go about our normal daily routine—with both of us under the same roof again—I won't know for certain that things are okay.

I crawl into bed and send him a text message. *You didn't score in Montreal but the OT game winner in Hamilton makes up for that. However if you don't score in regulation in Ottawa, don't come home. ;-)*

Before I can even put the phone back down, he's responded. *Typical Callie Control Freak, telling me how to play. FYI—I'll score twice next time.*

I laugh.

Two days later, after the Barons win in Ottawa, the theme to the horror movie *Halloween* slices through the darkness of my room at three in the morning and I fly from my bed, suddenly wide awake. Fuck. It's November. I keep forgetting to change that damn ring tone. I snatch my cell from the nightstand and see Devin's number lighting up my screen.

"Holy fuck, you just gave me a heart attack," I say breathlessly as I fall back onto my rumpled bed.

"Sorry. I'll let you go." He's slurring his words and I can hear a slight echo.

"No. It's okay!" I respond quickly. "Are you okay?"

"Yes. No."

I feel my body tense. "Where are you?"

"In the bathroom of my hotel room," he admits. "Contemplating a cold shower."

I smile. "Are you alone?"

"Loops is passed out in the hotel room," he replies, still slurring. "But yeah. I'm alone. You're still the only girl I take cold showers with."

I laugh. "What happened, Dev?"

"Ashleigh called. And I told her…" He takes a deep ragged breath. "I think we're going to get divorced."

"I think you are too," I reply honestly.

"So I failed."

"She failed you. You failed at nothing," I argue softly.

"I failed Conner," he mumbles in a whisper, and I know he's close to tears.

It breaks my heart and I feel tears prick the corners of my own eyes. "Failing Conner would be staying with a woman who doesn't think you are the single most amazing human being on the face of this earth. Because that's what that kid believes you are and he would want whoever you are with to believe it too."

He says nothing. I hear nothing but his uneven breathing.

"And Conner deserves to have two parents who are loved

just as much as he is, even if it's not by each other," I explain
and roll onto my side and curl into a ball, the phone wedged
between the pillow and my ear. "Conner will survive divorced
parents. You and Ashleigh both love him. And his uncles and
aunts love him. And his grandparents love him. As long as he
is loved—and you love yourself enough to do what's best—the
kid will not feel like a failure and not think of you as a failure.
I promise."

"You're amazing," he whispers.

"I am," I say with a smile. "And I didn't even have parents!
Remember that."

He laughs. It's tiny and weak but it's better than nothing.
"You had my parents. They love you like a daughter."

"I know. And I'm eternally grateful."

"You deserve it, Cal," he replies quietly. "You deserve love."

I feel suddenly panicked. I don't like where this conversation is headed. It feels like it's taking a turn I'm not going to
like. "You going to take that cold shower or what?"

"Not as much fun without you," he murmurs. I think he
may be starting to fall asleep.

"Devin, honey, go to bed."

"Mmm…are you in bed?"

"Yes."

"Are you wearing those cute pajamas? The ones that get see-
through when they're wet?"

Oh my God. I go from zero to completely turned on so fast
I should have whiplash.

"No. I'm wearing a T-shirt and pajama pants. It's cold tonight,"
I reply quietly. "And there's no one here to warm me up."

"I wish I could warm you up," he mumbles.

I have the distinct feeling he may not even remember this conversation tomorrow—but I will. "Well, maybe I should just warm myself up and think of you while I'm doing it."

There's a pause. "Yeah. You should," he agrees in a husky voice.

"Go to sleep, Devin," I command again.

"Mmm. 'Night, Callista." He uses my full name and it feels intimate and special. No one ever uses it. I had no idea he even knew it.

"'Night, Devin."

I hang up.

Holy shit, what are we doing? I sit there reeling, trying to calm down and ignore the dampness in my panties. Fifteen minutes later I give up the fight and let my mind wander to thoughts of him as my hand slips into the front of my pajama pants to work myself to a release.

Chapter 26

Devin

As I walk up the driveway, I feel like I might throw up from nerves and embarrassment. When I woke up this morning, my head was pounding and my brain was foggy, but as I got ready to meet the team and get on the bus to head for the airport, my memories became clearer.

Last night after Ashleigh's phone call I got obliterated at the bar. There were puck bunnies everywhere, as is usually the case in Canadian towns, and a short, perky redhead was following me around like a puppy. I talked to her a little bit and a part of me wanted to take her back to the hotel and fuck her senseless. But I didn't.

Both Loops and I stumbled back to the hotel room with just each other and looming hangovers. He pulled off everything but his underwear, left it in a heap on the floor, and was snoring loudly before his head hit the pillow. I stripped into my underwear and I took my cell and headed into the bathroom to call Callie.

I didn't remember much of the conversation when I first woke up this morning. I could recall talking about maybe getting divorced. As I showered I started to remember what she said about Conner. Her words made sense and they alleviated a lot of the guilt I was feeling—not all of it, but enough that my chest no longer felt like it was in a vise and my shoulders weren't so tight.

And then I remembered the end of the conversation. As soon as the words replayed in my head—*"I wish I could warm you up"* and *"Well, maybe I should just warm myself up and think of you while I'm doing it"*—a wave of desire rippled through me and I was instantly hard.

I envisioned her lying in my guest room, her hands in her panties playing in the wetness caused by thoughts of me...I had no choice but to jerk off right then and there in the middle of my morning shower or I would have had to get on the team bus and the airplane with a rock-hard cock. Blue balls at twenty-five thousand feet? No, thank you.

Now I'm freaking out at the prospect of seeing her again. I feel like she'll know what I did—and I don't know if I can look at her innocently and not think about what she might have done last night. And the more I think about it, the more my dick twitches in my pants, which does nothing to keep me calm.

I hold my breath and open the front door to the brownstone. I'm greeted by the sound of music. Old music—seventies music. I leave my suitcase in the hall and follow the sound into the kitchen.

It's a band my parents used to listen to on actual records

in the den when they were feeling nostalgic. Fleetwood Mac. "Don't Stop," I think the song is called. I turn into the kitchen and stare at the sight before me.

Callie and Conner are dancing around the room. She's singing along with the chorus of the song at the top of her lungs, barely in tune. He is humming along completely out of tune. They're both holding wooden spoons that are dripping with remnants of cake batter. Full cupcake tins are sitting on the counter by the oven and a dirty mixing bowl is on its side in the sink.

There are globs of batter on the counter and the floor where they are dancing, but neither of them seems to notice or care. I don't either. I happily take it all in unnoticed. She's smiling brighter than sunshine at Conner, who is clearly having the time of his little life.

Finally she notices me and her smile gets even brighter. "Hey! Daddy is here!" she tells Conner. He spins, drops his spoon with a splat on the floor and runs to me. I bend down and let him climb into my arms, not at all concerned about the chocolate batter his fingers are smearing across my suit. If it were Ashleigh, she would freak out and tell him to stop. But I don't care. I have other suits. This moment is once in a life-time.

"Daddy, we bake cupcakes and lick batters and dance!" he tells me in an excited rush.

"I see that," I reply and kiss his sticky cheek.

The song starts to fade out as Callie bends and picks up his spoon. She's in a pair of yoga pants and a gray tank top with the Rolling Stones tongue on the front, and her long wavy hair is pinned up on her head in not one but two knots. It makes her look like a punk Princess Leia or something. She smiles sheepishly at me, hurries to get the cloth from the sink and starts wiping up the mess.

"Ashleigh dropped him off. Said she wanted to save you the trip," she tells me with a look that says it's way more than that. "I promise to clean up the mess. Sorry we got carried away."

"Don't mind in the least," I tell her honestly and walk over to where she is about to put the cupcakes into the oven. "What flavor?"

"Devil's food cake." She winks.

"Of course." I laugh. It was her favorite flavor when we were younger and my mom always made it for her for her birthday.

She dips the tip of her spoon in one of the cups of batter and lifts it to my mouth. I taste it but don't take all of it and she promptly bops me lightly on the tip of my nose with the spoon. A dollop of batter splatters across the bridge of my nose.

I give Callie a mock scowl but Conner squeals with laughter. The beginning chords of Journey's "Don't Stop Believin'" start to rift through the stereo. She places the cupcakes in the oven and then she closes her eyes and sighs.

"Best song ever!" she declares and spins away dancing by herself and singing again.

I put Conner down and he runs to join her. I can't believe how happy I am in this moment. I don't honestly remember the last time I ever felt this content. Callie Caplan is the best thing that ever happened to me.

Chapter 27

Callie

Devin!"

It's been happening all night. It's what is supposed to happen at these things. Rich Brooklyn Barons fans drop a ton of money on tickets to hobnob with the players and get drunk on free booze and fat on free appetizers. Well, maybe they weren't doing the second part, but I sure was.

I grab a cream cheese crab puff off a passing tray and wash it down with a swig of Champagne. Devin asked me to come to the Annual Barons Winter Mixer and keep him company because all the players were bringing their significant others and he didn't want to stick out. Plus, he said he needed the positive reinforcement. I agreed because I love a party, and if Devin needs me, I'll be there.

Devin smiles brightly at the large man with a ring of fuzzy gray hair who called his name. He's marching toward us with an overly primped woman with giant Southern belle gray hair and dark red lipstick on her thin lips. When they reach us, the man shakes Devin's hand powerfully and grins.

"Good to see you again!" he says to Devin.

"You too, Mr. Kensington." He turns to the woman and smiles even more brightly. "And you, Mrs. Kensington, are looking more beautiful every time I see you!"

I'm amazed at how comfortable he seems to be in this role of being on display and schmoozing these people. All night he's been relaxed and friendly and he's never had to ask a single person's name, even though I know he only sees these rich hockey fans maybe twice a year at events like this. And all his inner turmoil, which I know is still brewing, is not at all evident. On the cab ride over here, he told me he told Ashleigh he's hiring a divorce lawyer. When I asked how she took it, he said there was crying and accusations. Apparently now he's the one ruining everything. I wanted to get out of the cab, walk to Ashleigh's and kick her in the teeth. That woman was beyond delusional.

I know that's the hardest decision he's ever made. I know he thinks it means admitting failure even though I keep telling him repeatedly it doesn't. But I also know that he knows, failure or not, that it's the best decision possible.

Mrs. Kensington is delighted with the compliment and she giggles like she's twelve. "Oh, Devin! You are too sweet. Isn't he too sweet?"

She's looking at me now. I swallow my mouthful of Champagne and nod. "Yes. He is pretty fabulous."

You can tell by their expressions that they are trying to figure out who I am. They've probably seen Ashleigh at these events in the past and there is no mistaking I am not her. Besides the fact that Ashleigh is blond and taller than I am, she would also never wear this dress. I'm in a black, one-shouldered micro-mini dress with a layer of gauzy black chiffon that also goes over the shoulder and hangs off one arm, creating a sort of wide sleeve effect. It's Zac Posen and it cost me an entire paycheck, but I love it. It's a total Callie dress. An Ashleigh dress would be high-necked and to the floor.

"Where is your wife tonight?" Mr. Kensington finally asks.

"She wasn't able to make it," Devin says without a moment's awkward hesitation. "This is Callie Caplan. She's a family friend."

They both shake my hand but I can see skepticism in their eyes. I pull out the secret weapon that has been quelling everyone's doubt all night.

"I grew up with the Garrisons in Silver Bay." I smile softly with wide, honest eyes. "And my sister is marrying Devin's brother Jordan this summer."

"Oh! How delightful!" Mrs. Kensington says and I'm not sure if she's delighted by the fact Jessie is marrying Jordan or by the fact that I'm clearly not the husband-stealing whore she thought I was a second ago. Either way I honestly don't care. We chat with them for a few minutes more and then politely slip away when Mitchell and Tara Lupo start chatting with them.

"This is tiring," I whisper to him as I grab two more Champagne flutes off a waiter's tray and pass him one. He takes a big gulp and crinkles his nose as the bubbles overpower him. I smile because he looks freaking adorable.

He notices my grin and gives me a quick, soft smile that makes him look like a kid, not a man who has just gone through some of the roughest stuff anyone could go through. "You're making it manageable, though, Callie. Thank you."

"Anytime you need me to throw on a hot dress and drink and eat for free, I'll be there for you," I joke, and he chuckles. "It's actually kind of fun. I had a fun conversation in the bathroom with two women about which NHL players wear the best suits. And earlier, when this other guy found out who I was, he gave me a long list of things Jordan has to do in order to improve his game."

"Really?"

"Oh, yeah. I typed it all into my phone so I could recite it to Jordy later and annoy the crap out of him." I grin evilly and Devin bursts out laughing.

"Ashleigh never had a minute of fun at these things."

"I can find fun in anything," I remind him and wink.

"You need to teach me how to do that," he murmurs.

"I tried once…" I whisper back.

His eyes lock on mine and I know we've both got memories of the tractor and the barn in our heads. He smiles a small, incredibly sexy smirk.

"Devin!" a Barons management guy whose name I can't remember calls for him. "Time to announce the silent auction winners."

He leaves my side and heads to the front of the room. I admire the way his expensive suit hugs that strong, athletic ass of his. Wow. I should probably stop with the Champagne. It's making me dangerous.

Chapter 28

Devin

She's giggling beside me, her head tipped back and her hand in front of her mouth like she's embarrassed. Her shoes are on the seat between us and her fancy, sexy little black dress is hitched up, exposing more of her beautiful, toned legs, which are curled up onto the seat as well. Her feet are kind of pressed into the side of my thigh. I could probably sit farther over on the seat and give her room, but I like the contact too much.

"Cole?!" I say again. We were reminiscing about Silver Bay and she just told me she had kissed my youngest brother. I had no idea.

"It was a total dare and I honestly didn't think he would do it," she says, still giggling at my initial reaction, which was to let my jaw hit the floor of the cab we're in.

"Why wouldn't he do it? Did you think he was gay or something?"

"No. But you know Cole—he's such a goof. I figured he'd just make a joke and blow me off," she responds. "But, man, oh man, he can be serious, because it was a seriously good kiss."

"I had no idea you used to have a crush on him," I say, trying not to think about my brother kissing her. It makes me feel bad and I'm sick of feeling that way.

"Cole is an adorable-looking ginger, don't get me wrong, but I've never been even remotely attracted to him," she says breezily. "I just wanted to see if he would do it."

I stare at her and she stares back. We're both walking the line between tipsy and drunk thanks to copious amounts of Champagne. It's a good feeling. I have been drunk a lot in the last few months but it never felt good like this. I decide I should drink Champagne more.

"Like what you did with me in the barn," my tipsy brain deduces. "You wanted to see what you could make me do."

She bites her bottom lip and her lids lower so she's looking up at me through her lashes now. "The thing with you in the barn was not at all the same thing."

The cab pulls up in front of our brownstone, and as I reach for my wallet, she scurries out and up the driveway. I toss the driver forty dollars and chase after her. She's unlocked the front door and left it open for me. Her shoes are on the floor at the foot of the staircase and I worry for a minute that she might have gone up to her room to pass out. I want so badly to keep hanging out with her right now.

I make my way down the hall into the kitchen and find her lying on the wicker couch in the little glassed-in porch that's attached to the kitchen and has French doors that lead onto the back deck. Her eyes are closed.

I wander to the fridge. "I'm hungry."

"That's because you were too busy being Mr. Perfect Beautiful Hockey God to chow down on all those yummy appetizers," she tells me without opening her eyes.

I smile. "Mr. Perfect Beautiful Hockey God?"

"Oh, shut up. You know it's true," she replies in a flat tone. "You should be the face of the NHL. They should put you on billboards in Times Square. You're hot and your charm levels are through the roof."

I'm laughing now as I grab an apple out of the fruit bowl and start devouring it. She falls silent and I worry she's going to pass out. I don't know if she's just tipsy or full-on drunk.

"Callie?"

"Mmm?"

"How was the barn thing different than daring Cole to kiss you?" I want to know. "I mean in both cases you were testing our limits."

"Uh-huh," she agrees in a sleepy voice. "But like I said, I've never been attracted to Cole. I've thought you were drop-dead gorgeous since I was ten."

I feel like someone dropped a piano in the center of the room. Or even more accurately, in the center of my brain. It's like something just went *boom* and all my thoughts were blown clear out of my head.

She's been attracted to me since she was ten. Me? The sexiest, wildest, craziest, strongest woman I have known in my life—the very essence of everything I never thought would ever want anything to do with me—has been attracted to me for over thirteen years.

Wow.

She's quiet again. I put down the half-eaten apple, walk into the little glassed-in room and stand above her. Her eyes are still closed. Her arms are above her head, hanging over the arm of the couch. Her hair is fanned out on the cushion she's got her head on. The pale pink eye shadow on her eyelids is glittering in the dim light and her lips are pink and glossy like she recently licked them.

"Callie," I start softly. "That night I was on the road trip…did you do what you said you'd do?"

Her lids flutter but she doesn't open her eyes. "What are you asking me, Devin?"

"Did you warm yourself up to thoughts of me?"

"Did you take that cold shower that night?" she questions back, eyes still closed, body still motionless.

"No," I reply honestly. "I took a warm one the next morning and jerked off to thoughts of you."

I blame the Champagne. I blame the bold, dirty words and the inability to stop them from coming out of my mouth on the Champagne.

"Then we're even because I did it too." Her eyes flutter and her lips twitch, almost smiling. "And for the record, I'm going to do it again tonight."

Her eyes finally open just enough to peer up at me as I crouch down beside her.

"You won't have to tonight," I tell her and press my lips to hers.

She makes a little sound—a cross between a moan and a sigh—and reaches out and touches the sides of my face, letting her hands slide backward over my ears and into my hair. I lose my grasp on my self-control and deepen the kiss. My lips move, hers move, our mouths open and our tongues connect, and electricity darts down my spine.

The kissing goes on forever. It never loses its intensity. My hands get lost in her long, silky hair; she runs her fingertips through mine. Our tongues explore each other's mouths needily. I can't stop touching her or tasting her. I wonder crazily if I will ever have the power to stop.

She starts to sit up. I move with her, so our kiss doesn't have to break. She holds on to the front of my suit jacket and starts turning me. I reach out with my hand and find the edge of the couch as she pushes me back. Without ever taking her lips off my lips or her tongue out of my mouth, she manages to get me to sit on the couch and she's straddling my lap. The barn memories race through my brain.

She pulls away from my lips just enough to speak.

"Feel familiar?" she whispers with a tiny smile and grinds her hips over my hardening dick.

"Feels fantastic," I whisper back and kiss a hot trail up the side of her neck.

She tips her head back, exposing more of the soft skin of her throat, and grinds into me again. I bite down lightly. She shudders. It's mind-blowingly hot knowing I can make her react like that.

"Are you going to finish what you started?" I whisper the challenge in her ear as my hands slide up her thighs and under the hem of her dress.

"Do you want me to?" she counters back, pushing my suit jacket off my shoulders.

"More than anything," I reply.

She wraps a hand around my tie and gives it a tug, pulling my lips to hers again. Our tongues battle for dominance. It's the best battle I've had in my life. Her hand that isn't wrapped around my tie reaches in between us and starts undoing my belt, and then the button on my pants, and then the zipper.

My hands are buried under her dress and I let them slide over her inner thighs. My fingers skim along the soft fabric of her underwear, which covers her soft folds. It's damp. I push my fingertips into it—pressing her panties into her—and the fabric gets wetter.

"You're wet."

"Your fault."

She tugs on my bottom lip with her teeth and pushes her hand into my underwear in response. Her hand holds my dick and starts pumping—jerking me off slowly but firmly. I kiss her hard and hook my fingers under the fabric of her underwear. Without hesitation I push two fingers into her. She's silky, soft and slippery.

"Devin." She gasps my name and pushes herself onto my hand, losing the grip on the control she insists on keeping.

I smile in victory but then she pulls herself off my lap and out of my reach. I feel panic and disappointment. I make no attempt to hide it from my face. She smiles reassuringly at me.

"Don't worry," she promises in a throaty whisper. "You'll get what you want."

She reaches down for her purse, which she had dropped on the floor beside the couch when she came in. She opens it, takes something out and tosses it at me. The condom hits me in the chest and drops into my lap.

"Put it on." The exact same words she uttered at eighteen leave her lips again, and once again I do as I'm told.

I pull my aching cock out through the front flap of my underwear the same way it was exposed to her years ago, take the condom from the wrapper and roll it on.

As I look up, her underwear is sliding down her thighs and falling to the ground at her feet. She steps out of them, places her knees on either side of my lap and hovers there, kissing me passionately. Her tongue dominates my mouth and I don't even try to stop it. Fuck it, she owns me.

She reaches down, takes hold of my cock, and starts to lower herself. I break the kiss and push her dress up over her thighs and hips and watch as my tip slips between her folds and her body welcomes me in.

Chapter 29

Callie

The minute I feel his lips, it is like someone put a match to a puddle of gasoline inside my body. Everything is on fire. I don't think about whether this is right or wrong. I don't think at all. I just feel—and he feels incredible. I knew from that first kiss that we'd be finishing what we started in that barn in Silver Bay—and now we are.

"Still so fucking big," I whisper faintly, more to myself than to him.

I close my eyes and revel in the feeling of my body expanding around him. It's exactly the way I remember it. He is filling me up, and just when I think it's impossible to take any more of him, my body magically makes space.

"Fuck, Callie," he whispers through a rush of breath that escapes his lungs. "You're incredible."

His words make me tingle. His dick makes me quiver. Holy fuck, this has barely even begun and it's the best sex I have ever had. How is that even possible? He's completely inside me now and I can feel it in every part of my body. I want to come hard and fast so I start to ride him, moving up and down in a steady rhythm. His hands hold my hips but don't try to control my movement. I wrap my hands around the back of his neck and hold on.

He starts to move his hips a bit, bucking in time with my movements. His sexy, full lips part and he grunts. I curl my torso and touch my lips to his. I want to kiss him but suddenly I can't bring myself to do anything—his hand has moved from my hip to under my dress again and his thumb presses against my clit. The friction is the last straw and breaks my control in half. I push my lips onto his and moan into his mouth as my hips move faster, more erratically.

"Come," he demands in a raspy whisper.

Normally if some guy ordered me like that, I would make it my mission to not come for him—ever—no matter what. But with Devin, I wouldn't be able to hold out even if I wanted to, which I don't. I don't want to fight it. I want to come for him.

Chapter 30

Devin

Her eyes flutter closed and her eyebrows pull together. The whimper that escapes her as her orgasm hits is the most addictive sound I have ever heard in my life.

Her pussy tightens, which I would never have thought possible—and although her hips keep moving, my dick can barely move. Between that and the warm rush of her orgasm, I lose it and come harder than I ever have in my life. I pull her into me, holding her tightly to my torso, and press my face to her neck and let out a sound even I can't describe.

As she slows her hips to a stop, I feel her thighs trembling. I hold her even tighter and I can feel her pulse hammering in her neck under my lips. We stay like that, motionless and wordless, until we both regain our senses. Finally she takes a deep, cleansing breath and runs her hands seductively over my head, ruffling my hair.

"Well, that was worth the wait," she decides in a low, satisfied voice.

I smile. "Definitely."

She carefully lifts herself off me. I slide over on the couch and she drops down beside me, flopping back in exhaustion.

"I'll be right back," I murmur and kiss her cheek.

She smiles sleepily as I tuck myself back into my pants and get up off the couch to head for the bathroom to dispose of the condom.

In the bathroom I clean up and catch my reflection in the mirror. My cheeks are flushed and my lips are swollen. My eyes are light and bright. You would never know I had been broken and crying a little over twelve hours ago while looking up divorce lawyers. Even more shocking is that not only do I not look like that Devin Garrison, I don't feel like the Devin Garrison who was broken anymore, either. I smile at my reflection and head back to Callie.

She's exactly the way she was before we reenacted the barn moment. Stretched out on the couch, arms above her head, hair feathered across the pillow—only this time, she's fast asleep.

I don't want to leave her down here. This wicker couch is only a two-seater; she will wake up tomorrow with aches and pains. I bend down and scoop her up into my arms.

When I get upstairs, I hesitate in front of the guest room she's been using. I don't want to put her to bed in there. I want her with me—in my bed. So I walk past her room and push open the door to mine with my foot.

I lay her down on the side I usually sleep on because the sheets are already tossed back from when I got up this morning. She curls onto her side immediately and lets out a big breath. I pull the duvet up over her.

I walk around to the other side of the bed and get undressed. I slip under the sheets beside her and curl myself into her back. My arms circle her waist and I let the smell of her spicy citrus perfume and the feel of her warm body lull me into a blissful sleep.

Chapter 31

Callie

When I wake, I feel like I am coming out of a coma. I had been in such a deep, glorious sleep. I have no idea what time it is or where I am, but I don't care. Life is good. Great. Amazing. I have a total feeling of euphoria—but I have no idea why.

I stretch like a cat and smile into my pillow. It smells amazing—why does it smell so good? What is that? I inhale again, turning my face into it. It smells like the ocean and mint and…what is that familiar elixir?

Devin.

It smells like that heady mix of cologne, deodorant and hair product that makes up Devin Garrison. My eyes open. The room is still relatively dark; just a little bit of morning dawn is sneaking through the California shutters that are three-quarters closed.

I'm in Devin's bedroom. In Devin's bed. I roll over quickly but lightly. I'm in Devin's bedroom. In Devin's bed. *WITH Devin!*

My heart starts to hammer its way out of my chest as I go from euphoria to panic in a millisecond. He's dead asleep on his back, one hand over his head, the other across his exposed midsection. He's shoved the covers down to his waist and that sexy cut of muscle by his hip and the thick trail of hair that starts at his belly button and leads to the promised land.

I scurry as quickly and lightly as possible out from under the covers. As soon as I stand up, my head starts to reel—from the panic and the bucket of Champagne I consumed last night. I bolt for the door and slip across the hall and into my room. I toss myself face-first onto the bed and run through the night before.

The party was good—and kind of fun. Devin was amazing—smiling and chatting and charming the pants off every person in the room. He looked devastatingly handsome too in his light gray suit, crisp white shirt and blue-and-gray silk tie. As I started to drink more free Champagne and eat fewer free appetizers, I got tipsy, and that last thought started to consume me. He was *gorgeous*. He was charming. I was horny.

I remember coming home and almost passing out on the couch and then he kissed me and I was already so ridiculously hot for him there was no way I was stopping it. I wanted to finish what we'd started so many years ago. I needed to get it out of my system. That's all it was. And now we could go back to being buddies. It should be easy.

So why the hell did I wake up in his bed? He must have put me there. Why would he do that?! You don't do that to a girl you were just scratching an itch with! You do that with a girlfriend or a wife or whatever.

I am not that. I don't want to be that. I will *not* be that. No. No. No.

"Damn it, Devin!" I whisper to myself.

I'm still exhausted and it's still stupid early but I can't sleep. Not with my heart hammering like this and my mind filled with images of riding him on the couch downstairs. I sigh and drag myself into the bathroom. Might as well go to work.

An hour later, my assistant Sam walks into the office and looks startled to see me. "Hey! You're here early!"

"Couldn't sleep," I mutter as I sort through the wardrobe items for the next week of shooting.

Sam's great. He's smart and quick and has an amazing sense of style, which is needed for this line of work. He's also nosy and in my attempt to keep all of Devin's secrets from my sisters, I've found myself confiding in him. He puts his stuff down on his desk and stares at me. "How was the party last night?"

"Fine."

"Fine?"

"Fine."

My phone starts to buzz. I walk over to where it's lying on top of my desk. It's Devin. I send it to voicemail and walk back over to the clothes racks. Sam's got his eyebrow in the air now. "Something is not fine."

"Everything is fine," I argue back.

I have to tell someone and I can't tell my sisters. They will lose their minds and tell their silly boyfriends and then this will become a big, huge deal. I am trying to avoid the big, huge deal.

"I fucked Devin."

"Yes!" He literally starts to jump up and down and reaches out to high-five me. I stare at him and cross my arms over my chest. His face gets serious. "Was it horrible? Please do not tell me he is horrible in bed! I Googled him and he's gorgeous. I'd be so devastated if he wasn't any good."

My glare softens. "Best sex of my life."

"Yes! So what the hell is the bitch face for?" Sam wants to know, giving me a look that says he thinks I'm insane.

"We had sex on the couch," I start to complain.

"Not that classy, but whatever. It's Devin Garrison. If he asked me to do it in a gas station restroom, I would," Sam blurts out and I laugh. "More details, please."

"Well, afterward I kind of passed out and he took me upstairs and put me in his bed instead of mine," I complain.

I drop down into my desk chair and look up at him. Sam is staring at me blankly from behind his thick-rimmed black glasses that he wears because "hipster is in" and not because he has vision problems.

"Does he cuddle?" he wants to know. "I bet he's a rock star at cuddling."

"I do not want to cuddle my one-night stand," I say in slow, overpronounced words so he gets the point. Sam stares at me for a long minute, blinking cluelessly, and then he bursts out laughing. It's such a weird response that I can't help but laugh a little too.

"Have you lost your mind?" I ask him with a giggle. "What is so funny?"

He holds his sides and wheezes through his chuckles. "That you think Devin is a one-night stand!"

I stop laughing.

"Why wouldn't he be?!" I demand and feel that panic attack from earlier trying to make another appearance.

"You really believe that?" he asks me skeptically.

"Why shouldn't I?"

"Hmm, well, let's see," He scratches his chin and stares up at the ceiling pretending to be lost in deep thought. "Because you've known him forever and he's one of your best friends. Because you've been helping him through a really emotional time in his life. Because you talk about his kid like you gave birth to him. Because you LIVE together. Oh yeah, and because you CARE about him."

"That doesn't mean this can't be a one-time thing," I insist as the panic attack erupts inside me again. I put a hand to my heart to make sure it doesn't crack through my rib cage. "I mean the friendship part is forever, but the sex thing was a one-off."

He says nothing, just stares at me with a smug, knowing smirk that makes me want to run screaming from this building, from Brooklyn and from Devin Garrison.

"Stop looking at me like that!"

There's a knock at the door and Matthew is standing there holding something wrapped in foil that smells delicious. His eyes find me and he grins.

"Brought you a breakfast burrito from the craft services cart." He offers it to me.

I step around the clothes rack and gratefully take the burrito. "You're awesome. Thank you."

"I try." He winks at me. "Hey, are you busy tonight?"

"Yeah. With you. We're going out," I reply and I give him a minute to absorb the shock. "I'll text you my address. Pick me up at eight."

"Great!"

Matthew leaves and I bite into the scrumptious scrambled eggs, cheese and salsa mixture inside the whole-wheat tortilla. As I swallow, I glance over at Sam, who is still staring at me but his expression is no longer bemused; it's unimpressed.

"What now?" I ask sharply.

He shakes his head and gives me a disapproving stare. "You're going to regret that, Callie."

Chapter 32

Devin

I wake up just after seven and find my bed empty. Where did she go? Did she have to be at work early today? She hadn't mentioned that. But then again we hadn't given ourselves much opportunity for small talk last night.

I smile at the memory. It was amazing. Sexually I swear I'd never been so turned on or come so hard. I'd slept with my fair share of women in my life prior to Ashleigh. All of them were attractive with hot bodies and pretty lips and bedroom eyes and lots of things that Callie had, physically, but something about being with Callie was just...better. She was unbelievable.

I lie back in bed and call her. But when she doesn't answer, I feel concern sprout up in the pit of my stomach. I decide to send her an email, but when I open that on my phone I see a message from Doris, our team counselor.

I had called her yesterday while I got ready for the charity event and asked her to recommend a divorce lawyer. This was her getting back to me. I open the email with a heavy heart. Duthie, McLennan and Partners was the name of the law firm she was recommending. She said they were used to the privacy needed for high-profile clients and were very quick and efficient. What else did I need from a divorce lawyer? I had no idea. She also expressed her sincere apologies and wanted me to know that her door was open to talk any time.

I really wish I could talk to Callie right now. My day was starting to look like hell on earth. I twist my wedding band, which is still on my finger for some reason, and then dial my parents' number.

My mom answers on the second ring and sounds relieved to hear my voice. She listens as I explain everything—from Ashleigh cheating on me to my decision yesterday—but I don't mention sleeping with Callie. That's something I will keep to myself, at least until Callie and I discuss what it meant.

Although I can tell my mother's heart is breaking at the thought that ending my marriage is the choice I intend to make, she also makes it clear she knows it's my only choice.

The rest of the day is long and strenuous. I have practice, which is grueling, and then stay late with the trainer to work on my hamstring, which has been bothering me. Then I have an appointment at the law office. Walking into that law office is the hardest thing I have ever done in my life. The appointment runs almost two hours. By the time I get home and step into the townhouse, I'm emotionally exhausted. I walk into the living room and drop down on the couch.

The house is empty. Callie isn't here. The other thing weighing on my brain is that she seemed to be ignoring me. I had called her again and once again got her voicemail.

I thought last night was…well, it was fucking epic. Did she not feel the same way? I was certain she enjoyed it as it was happening and that she wanted it as much as I did. So…what is the issue? I lie down and close my eyes. I must have fallen asleep, because the next thing I know the doorbell is ringing. I sit up and rub my tired eyes as I hear footsteps on the stairs.

I walk to the front hall in time to see Callie, looking model-beautiful, coming down the stairs. She has on a shimmery shirt that hangs off one of her shoulders, leaving the pale, perfect skin exposed, and jeans that hug her perfect ass and these open-toed, totally sexy little high-heeled ankle boots. I've always been a shoe guy. A sexy pair of heels on a sexy woman does something for me.

I wonder when she got home and am about to ask her when her brown eyes catch mine almost guiltily. "It's for me. You can go back to your nap."

I can't help but give her a confused look. She hesitates with her hand on the door handle. It's like she doesn't want to open the door with me there.

"Are you going out?" I can't help but ask, even though I'm not sure it's my business.

"Umm…yeah." She clears her throat and turns her gaze to the marble tile under her feet. "I have a date."

"A what?"

The doorbell rings again. She turns away from me and opens it. There, on our front step, is a lanky guy with his brown hair pushed up into a fauxhawk. He smiles as soon as he sees

Callie and it reminds me of a slobbery, horny teenager looking at his first *Playboy*. Gross.

"Hey, Matthew, let's go!" she says hurriedly.

I cough. *Loudly*. His eyes turn to me and he looks shocked. I give him a hard smile.

"Hey," I say, stepping forward. "I'm Devin."

"Uh…I'm Matthew." I walk across the small hall and move in between him and Callie to shake his hand. He's wearing a ton of leather cuffs and bracelets on his arm and about seven long silver chains around his neck. It's ridiculous.

"Are you Callie's brother?" he wants to know.

"No," I say flatly and his eyes grow more confused.

"He might as well be," Callie pipes up a little too loudly. "I've known Devin forever. He's from my hometown. He's letting me stay here until I get my own place. His brother is engaged to my sister. And his friend is dating my other sister."

Matthew starts blinking so furiously I think his eyelids might be having seizures. I smile again and this time it's because I'm completely amused.

"Oh," is all he says because Callie has buried him so far under a giant pile of useless information I don't know how he will ever find his way out.

"Later, Devin," she says as she takes Matthew by the elbow. "Don't wait up."

She shuts the door with a small click and I'm left alone.

Chapter 33

Callie

As Matthew's lips crash down on mine, I decide that I hate Sam. The little shit was right but I would rather fire him than ever admit that to him. It was bad enough I had to admit it to myself. I regret this.

This "date" with Matthew has been a disaster since the moment I opened the front door. As if Devin being there weren't enough, Matthew had then taken me to some quaint little Italian restaurant and forced me to sit and eat and make ridiculous small talk over candles, wine and dinner. I never understood why couples did this as part of their mating ritual—just sit there and eat in front of each other and ask each other stupid questions like what music do you like or whatever. So annoying and tedious.

Finally, after dinner, I convinced him to head to the bowling alley across the street. I am not a big bowler but it would give me something to concentrate on rather than just him and his silly questions, like what is my favorite color and did I eat a lot

of lobster growing up in Maine? I ordered us two beers and we
rented some shoes and started a game.

With two balls he only managed to knock down three pins.
We played three games and I won all of them easily. I became
even more bored. No competition. I guess I have been spoiled
hanging out with the Garrison brothers, who are impossibly
good at every sport. On the drive back to my place he started
talking about Devin again, asking why he lived in Brooklyn in
such an expensive brownstone. I explained he played for the
Barons.

"That's a hockey team, right?" Matthew questioned.

"Yeah."

"I don't watch hockey," he told me.

"You should. It's awesome."

"Maybe your buddy can get us tickets," Matthew suggested.
I tried not to scrunch my nose up at how much that thought
did not appeal to me.

I just shrugged my answer and prayed he would drive faster
so I could get to bed and end this day. And I had been so close
to escape as he pulled up to the curb in front of Devin's townhouse. I had my hand on the door handle and everything, but
before I could get away, he grabbed the back of my neck and
kissed me.

And that's where I am now—stuck in the middle of a horrible kiss. Nothing about it makes me feel good. I don't know
why. It's not like he's overly sloppy or forceful or anything, but
when I feel his tongue move and graze my lips I want to puke.
I pull back suddenly and am out of the car before he realizes
what's happening.

"See you at work!" I call and hurry up the stairs to the front door.

The house is dark and silent. I kick off my shoes and climb the stairs. My body feels heavy and so does my mind. I'm borderline depressed, but I don't know why. What the hell is wrong with me?

When I reach my door, I can't help but glance over toward Devin's room. His door is open and there's a dim light pouring out. I can see his bare feet at the bottom of his bed, on top of the duvet. I know I probably shouldn't, but I walk over to his room anyway. He's sitting up wearing nothing but gray-and-white-checkered pajama bottoms and he's reading a book. His dirty-blond hair is kind of matted down like he'd been wearing a baseball cap earlier or something. His heavy brow looks even heavier as he concentrates on whatever it is he's reading. He must sense me standing there, because he looks up and doesn't seem surprised. I guess he heard the front door.

"How was the date?" he wants to know, only you can tell by his voice that he really doesn't want to know.

"Honestly?"

"Are you ever not honest with me?" he questions back. We look at each other. I don't need to answer that because he knows I'm always brutally honest with everyone.

"It was atrocious," I reply and run a hand through my hair, pulling it forward over my shoulder as I sigh. "The kid doesn't watch hockey and he took me to some romantic dimly lit restaurant and he can't bowl to save his life."

Devin's face bursts into a giant grin. "Bowling ability is a must for you in a mate?"

"At least an ounce of athletic ability is," I counter and smile. "And all that combined with what I already knew were deficits—like that he has the fashion sense of a hipster douche bag—and I guess it just became one giant deal breaker."

Devin just nods, still smiling.

"Anyway, I'm going to bed," I tell him and wave. It's awkward but then again everything about tonight has been awkward, so whatever.

Ten minutes later I've changed into my pajamas, washed my face and finished brushing my teeth. When I head back into my bedroom from the bathroom, Devin is standing in my door. I freeze. Something in me starts to flutter with excitement and something else starts to flutter with fear. Overall it makes me feel light-headed and weak.

"We haven't had a chance to talk about last night," he says quietly.

"I don't want to talk about last night," I reply firmly. I walk closer to my bed but hesitate before getting into it. He still hasn't left. I hate to admit that part of me is glad.

"Okay, then, let's talk about your date again," he offers and his dark eyes stare right into me with an intensity that takes my breath away. "If you wanted someone tall and athletic who knows about hockey, you didn't have to leave the house."

I don't want to smile at that, but I can't help it. I turn my face away from him and let my hair make a shield, hoping he doesn't see it. I start to fluff the pillows on my bed.

"Did you kiss him?"

"Does it matter?" I challenge.

"Did you like it?"

"No."

I turn back to face him and he's right in front of me now. I'm shocked I didn't hear him move. He towers over me, his eyes heavy with lust, and his lips in a full, sexy smirk.

"Why?" he wants to know.

"I don't know why," I snap back. I shake my head but I'm smiling again. It's sheepish and unsure and I don't know why. "What's with the questions?"

He touches the back of my head with his hand and leans down and presses his lips to mine. The kiss isn't hesitant. It isn't shy. It's powerful and dominant. His tongue pushes its way into my mouth, not like he's exploring or claiming territory but like he already owns it—owns me. I'm so turned on by that I could pass out.

"Did it feel like that?" he asks me.

"Of course not," I respond in a throaty, breathless sigh.

"Then that's why you didn't like it."

Before he can say anything else and before his smirk can grow any wider, I wrap my arms around his neck and kiss him back. I lower us both onto the bed. His body hovers over mine. His forearms and biceps are tight and hard beside me as they hold his weight. I move my lips from his lips to his neck and run my tongue up to his ear.

He lowers his body slowly onto mine and pushes his hips into me at the same time. I wrap my legs around his waist and hold our groins together. My hands are on a mission, roaming over his bare back and chest and shoulders and arms—they touch every part of him, and still it's not enough.

I have wanted men in the past—*really* wanted them—but

never have I been this overwhelmed with desire for someone. And the fact that I have already had him and still want him more than before I had him—that scares me.

"We should stop," I say as his hands start to tug my tank top off my body. "We did this already."

Despite my words, my hands, which no longer seem to be listening to my brain, slip down his back and under the waistband of his pajama pants. His ass is smooth and hard under my fingers.

"Last night was about the past," he murmurs in a heated, hoarse voice against my collarbone. "Tonight is about the future."

I don't like that. There is no "future" for us. There is no "us." I want to tell him this—I need to—but he's pulled my tank top over my head and is now sucking my left breast into his hot, wet mouth and his long fingers are pulling the waist of my tiny pajama shorts down.

Unfortunately the need to fuck him far outweighs the need to set him straight at this point. His lips move to the other breast and he's gotten my shorts down to my knees and I'm not wearing any underwear. Completely exposed, he moves his hands between my legs and pushes them farther apart. I start to push his pajamas off his hips.

My back arches and my head rolls back against the pillow as he teases me, running his fingers through my wetness and flicking my clit lightly. My fingers dig into the flesh on his ass. He growls into my neck and pushes two fingers into me at once. I can't control the moan rolling out of me and my hips buck against his hand.

"You're so beautiful," he whispers into my hair as his fingers move in and out of me slowly. I reach between us, wanting to grab his dick and make him as out of control as I am, but he tilts his hip, pushing it down against my thigh and making it impossible for me to reach between us. He knows he's got all the control right now and he wants to keep it that way.

His fingers keep pumping in and out of me, his thumb pushing and rubbing my clit with every thrust. My breath is ragged and my spine is arched and then he curls his fingers and touches my G-spot and my eyes snap shut and he starts whispering in my ear.

"You're fucking amazing, Callie. So hot. So sexy. I see you and my dick gets hard. I want you so bad. All the time. I want to make you come so hard. I want to..."

I move my lips to his, shutting him up with a kiss. He hits my G-spot again, pressing into it for a long glorious moment. My body melts and my orgasm rolls over me like a tidal wave. Devin rides me through it with his hand.

As it ends, I struggle for breath and he moves his hand from me. I feel his rock-hard cock against my thigh. I fight the urge to grab him and guide him into me; I have never wanted anything more in my life but I'm not on birth control. That's always been enough motivation to stay the hell away from an unprotected guy, but somehow with Devin, I have to remind myself of the danger.

"Suitcase," I pant and point to the mostly empty hard-shell zebra-print suitcase against the wall at the side of my bed.

He gets off the bed, flips it open, grabs the box inside and pulls a condom from it. I sit up, kick my pajama shorts fully off my body and snatch the condom from him. His pajama bottoms fell off when he stood up and now he's standing naked in front of me as I kneel on the bed, naked, in front of him.

I lick his penis as it stands at attention in front of me from base to tip, sucking the wetness off the head as my hands tear the package open. I carefully roll the condom onto him. As soon as I'm done, his hands are on my shoulders pushing me back and he's on top of me, sliding into me gently.

He is looking down at me intently. His eyes are clear and soft. His full lips are bent into a small, satisfied smile. As he moves inside me, his hips pulling up and pressing down with a fast and steady rhythm, one thought takes over my brain—I have never seen a more beautiful man in my life.

And then he lets his lips graze my forehead and he catches my eye again and I can see something there—something I haven't seen before—and it makes me uncomfortable. He is looking at me like he is thinking the same thing about me.

It's too much. I can't do this like this.

I buck my hips and put my hands on his chest and push him. He rolls over and takes me with him so I'm on top. I let him slide out of me and turn around.

"Callie…" he says in protest and reaches for my hips, trying to turn me back to face him.

I ignore him and slide down on his dick, my back facing him. As soon as he's inside me, the air rushes from my lungs. I've done reverse cowgirl before but with Devin being so big it's a completely different feeling. He must love it too because his protests stop and he makes that growling moan sound he does when he's close to coming. Devin puts one hand behind him and pushes himself up so he's sitting. He nips the back of my shoulder blade as his other hand wraps around my waist.

He's helping lift me up and down and the extra force makes me feel him in every part of me, but it's not uncomfortable. And then I lean forward a bit and he pushes me down hard and the tip of his cock hits my G-spot where his fingers had been before, and I whimper.

"Come with me," he commands. "Come, baby. Please."

"Fuck, Devin," I say and bite my lip to try and hold in another whimper as he hits that sweet spot again. "Fuck yes."

My body tenses, then breaks open around him. I feel him slam up into me and grunt and collapse behind me as his dick twitches and spills its release. I fall back gently onto his chest and he wraps his arms around me and holds me.

I feel his lips in my hair, pressing into my temple.

"That was unbelievable," he whispers in a raspy voice.

"Yeah," I manage to sputter out as a response as I struggle to come to my senses.

What's with this hugging shit? My brain starts screaming. I push his arms off me and carefully roll off him. He lets out a little groan of protest. I force myself to get up and start putting my pajamas back on.

He watches me, lying across my bed completely naked and exposed and not the least bit insecure about it. I guess if you look like that—like a perfectly muscled sex god—there's nothing to be insecure about. And to be honest, I have to fight my natural instinct to just stand there and admire him. His lips are pulled into a sexy smile.

"What are you doing?" he asks me.

"Getting ready for bed," I explain. "You need to head back to your room."

"This is my place so, technically, all the rooms are mine," he retorts snarkily.

"Ha. Ha. Seriously. Thanks and everything," I say firmly and matter-of-factly, "but I need to sleep. Alone."

He stares at me for a minute, like he expects me to say "just joking" or something, but when I don't, he gets up and walks to the bathroom. I'm fully clothed now. I reach down and pick up his pajama bottoms and hold them out to him as he walks back into the bedroom after disposing of the condom.

"Devin, that was fun," I say calmly. "More fun than last night, which I didn't think was possible. But we're not doing this again."

"It was more than fun; it was amazing. It got even more amazing the second time," he surmises, giving me a stare that says I'm nuts. "And you know what else is fun? Spending the night in the same bed and waking up together. And morning sex. That's fun."

"The sex will start to become more than sex if we keep having it," I explain tersely.

"Oh." He thinks about that for a second. "It'll *become* more…"

I know what he's implying. He's implying that it already *is* more. And it angers me a little that he would think that. And that I think he might be right.

"I don't fuck guys I like, remember?" I tell him.

"So you don't like me?"

"Of course I like you. You're the best." I shake my head,

growing more frustrated. "And because of that I never should have slept with you. And I won't do it again. I'm not Ashleigh. I don't want a husband and a picket fence."

"I don't want you to be Ashleigh."

"But you still want a wife," I argue back, and my chest feels tight. "So we can't keep having sex. In the end, the orgasms won't be enough, Devin. And I want to stop this before you start wanting from me what you wanted from Ashleigh, because I can't do that."

"You can't do kids?"

"I could. I will one day. On my own," I say and smile at the thought. "That's been my plan since I first learned what the term 'sperm donor' meant."

He stands there motionless for a long minute. I can't watch him watching me anymore. It makes me feel like shit, so I turn my back and start to pull back the covers.

"Good night, Callie," he says simply, and by the time I turn back, he's gone.

Chapter 34

Devin

She's out on the back deck when I come downstairs at around eleven the next morning. I can see her lying on one of the two loungers on the cedar deck. She's wrapped in her winter coat, jeans and Uggs and she's got big dark sunglasses on, a coffee mug in her hand and her laptop on her lap.

I don't go out and say hello. I don't know what to say to her. I can't say what I want to say, which is "What are you so afraid of?" and "We should see where this goes." I just go about my morning routine pouring my own coffee and poke around for something to eat. So I decide to just stay silent and get out of here and head to the airport early. I'm suddenly grateful for my three-day road trip. As I'm pouring my morning coffee and trying to decide whether to have cereal or toast, I notice the tray of muffins on the stovetop.

"I made them fresh this morning." Her voice comes from behind me. "Banana nut."

I nod and sip my coffee. "No work today? And aren't you cold out there?"

"Night shoot. And I'm trying to force myself to get used to the cold," she explains. "Have a muffin."

I want to say no, reject her the only way I can, but I'm hungry and they look really good. I reach over and pop one out of the tin. It's still warm. I bite in and almost groan. It's delicious.

"I had no idea you were such a good cook," I mutter and finally for the first time look up at her.

She smiles, happy with the compliment. "Well, Jessie kept us in line and Rosie kept the house clean, but I kept us fed."

I think back on her childhood. I don't know as much about it as Jordan or even Luc because I was drafted around the time their grandma dumped them to go to Florida, but I know it was hard. I know my parents and my brothers really worried about them.

"When do you leave?" she wants to know.

"I have to be at the airport for twelve thirty," I explain and take another giant bite of the muffin.

"Who are you playing?"

"Los Angeles, Sacramento, San Fran, then home," I reply.

"Kick their collective asses," she requests with a smile. As I nod, her eyes fall to my hand holding the muffin. "You're not wearing your wedding ring anymore."

I glance down at my bare left hand. There's a slight tan line where the solid platinum band used to be.

"Yeah. I met a lawyer yesterday," I reply, trying to sound casual. "He said if Ashleigh doesn't argue any of my terms, it should be done in a few months."

She looks surprised. "You didn't tell me you went to a lawyer."

I give her a long stare for a second and then shrug as I finish the muffin and sip my coffee. "I was going to, but you went on your date. And then afterward, I got distracted."

She looks flustered at that. She almost blushes. "Right. I want you to know you can talk to me about that, the lawyer stuff, if you need to. We're friends. I want to help you through this."

There's that word again. *Friends.* I try not to frown, and remember what she said last night. She didn't want what I wanted. I should be lucky she's up front about it now so I don't actually fall in love with her.

"It's fine. I talked to my mom. Told her everything. She made me feel okay about it," I explain and finish my coffee. I put the mug in the sink and turn back to her.

I have an overwhelming urge to just lean in and kiss her. God, I wish I could just kiss her. I sigh.

"Later, Callie," I mumble and give her a pat on the shoulder as I walk past.

My suitcase is already in the hall and so I just grab my keys and slip into my suit jacket, which I had left on the end of the banister. She's leaning against the doorway into the kitchen staring at me with a look I can't quite read.

I give her a wave and head out the door.

Chapter 35

Callie

I curl up on the couch. It's been snowing all day so I've been stuck inside and the townhouse feels cavernous and depressing—because I'm lonely. I think about calling Sam and inviting him over, but as lonely as I am I don't want company. Then I think about calling Jessie or Rose but, well, they're going to want to talk about Devin and that is the last thing I want to discuss.

So I turn on the gas fireplace, curl up under the blanket on the couch and turn on the TV. I don't want to watch Devin's game—I really don't. I didn't watch every single game he played before I moved here so I shouldn't watch them now. After all, nothing has changed. I'm still just his buddy. I don't need to see every single game he plays.

I sigh. Unfortunately, because it's the middle of a Sunday afternoon, all the channels are filled with infomercials and bad movies. So I end up on the Thunder-Barons game by default.

I make myself feel better with the fact that I didn't watch the Tigers-Barons game the night before.

It's the middle of the second and the Barons are down 2–0. The game seems overly intense. This isn't a franchise rivalry so I don't know why there is so much aggression on the ice. Also, the San Francisco Thunder aren't known as an overly physical team—and neither are the Barons—so why are there so many hits and penalties?

When I tune in, Devin is in the penalty box. He's never in the box! The camera focuses on him, his jaw clenched sternly and his eyes dark and narrowed. He's rocking back and forth with pent-up aggression. The caption says "Devin Garrison, two minutes for boarding." *BOARDING?!* What the hell is he doing?

I fight the urge to text him.

The game goes on and they kill off his penalty and manage to even get a goal, but the third period turns into a slugfest. There are three fights before the halfway point. And then one of the Thunder players flat-out slew foots Tommy Donahue—using his own leg to hook Tommy's from behind, wrenching his knee. Tommy goes down in a heap on the ice and Devin goes after the guy who does it. His gloves fly across the ice and he gets off two solid right hooks before the Thunder player even knows he's being challenged.

"Devin Garrison, calm the fuck down!" I yell at the TV. The linesman starts grabbing at the back of Devin's jersey, trying to pull him away, while the ref tries to get in between them. Before the fight can be dismantled, the Thunder defenseman gets a solid shot off, clocking Devin across the jaw.

I jump off the couch. Devin teeters backward but the linesman keeps him upright and drags him to the penalty box. They break for a commercial as the trainer runs to the ice to deal with a still unmoving Tommy.

I pace the living room until they show Devin again in the penalty box. He's pressing a towel up to his left cheek. When he pulls it away, there is blood on it from a small cut and I can see his cheek is already swelling.

"What the hell are you doing?" I whisper to his image on the flat screen.

The game ends in a 2–1 loss for Brooklyn.

I want to text him and see if he's okay or call him and yell at him for fighting, but I don't let myself do it. It's not my place. I'm not his wife or girlfriend. It's not a big deal. He'll be fine.

Chapter 36

Devin

I open the door at one in the morning and carefully and quietly lift my suitcase into the hall. The house is dark and silent. I slip out of my shoes and start up the stairs, leaving my suitcase downstairs in order to avoiding making unnecessary noise.

Her bedroom door is closed. I pause in front of it. I want to see her so badly. I know—even though it makes no sense—that just seeing her will make me feel better. And she'll have some opinion or rationale about the game that will be bold and crazy yet completely logical and it will make me smile. But I can't. She's not my wife or my girlfriend. She's just my...roommate? At least that's all she wants to be, so I leave her sleeping and head into my room.

I strip out of my clothes, leaving on just my underwear, and head into the bathroom. I study my face in the mirror. There is a small cut—it only needed two stitches—but the welt forming is pretty big and angry looking.

I head back into my room and stop dead. She's sitting on the edge of my bed. She's in gray capri sweats and a baby-pink T-shirt that says "Bar Star" in pink glitter across the chest. Her hair is pulled up in a sloppy half ponytail–half bun thing that girls do. In her hands she's got what looks like a washcloth with something wrapped in it.

"Did I wake you?"

"I wasn't sleeping," she replies and motions me over. I walk to her and sit down beside her. She reaches up and touches my cheek with what's in her hand. It's cool and damp against my puffy cheek. I realize it's ice wrapped up in the washcloth.

"Does it hurt?"

I nod. "A little. The freezing they gave me when they stitched it is wearing off."

"Devin, what the fuck were you thinking?" she demands in a quiet but firm tone. "You don't fight."

"I can fight if I'm pushed, and they pushed us," I argue back calmly. "Tommy is probably out for the season. It doesn't look good at all."

"It was a crazy game," she whispers and shakes her head. "I was so freaked out watching it I was yelling at the TV. I'm surprised the neighbors didn't call the cops."

I smile at that. "I thought you liked hockey fights. Didn't you once say that they turned you on? 'Hockey fights are hot' were your exact words."

She laughs self-consciously. "You remember that?"

I nod and smile. She had said it one year when Jordan, Luc and Cole were still on the Silver Bay Bucks and they had made the play-offs. I was already at home, my first Barons season over. We ended up at the same house party and the girls were talking about the Silver Bay game earlier that night. Jessie was recounting Jordan's two goals in detail, much to her boyfriend Chance's dismay, and Callie was recounting every single fight with a giant smile on her face.

"Luc sure can throw a punch. It's totally hot," is what she had said, and I repeat it to her now.

She looks up at me in mock anger as she stands up. "Yes, I used to love hockey fights, but now thanks to you that's ruined. No longer hot."

"Why?" I ask, not wanting to let this go. "Was it that bad? I thought I got some good shots off."

She pauses as if replaying what she saw on TV in her head. "Devin, when he hit you, you looked like you might collapse on the ice. That was not hot."

"Sorry I don't make you wet when I throw punches at assholes on the ice," I snap. I am not a fighter. I don't like to do it, but I don't think I'm bad at it.

She puts her hand on my shoulder and gives it a small squeeze. "I wasn't worried about how you looked, dumbass. I was worried you were hurt."

I look up and our eyes meet. I swear to God it takes my breath out of my lungs. "You were worried about me?"

She almost frowns but nods a confirmation anyway. I can tell it's painful for her to admit.

"I'm fine."

"Are you sure?" she counters. "Do they know for sure you don't have a concussion?"

"He didn't hit me that hard," I reply.

She starts for the door but hesitates. "Are you sure? Because you hockey players have pretty soft heads."

I smile. "Well, you're welcome to stay in here and wake me up every hour."

"That's concussion protocol?" she asks and I nod with a smirk.

"And you can wake me up any way you want," I add and wink.

She laughs out loud at that but she's blushing. "Don't give me any ideas, Devin."

"Ideas are a good thing, Callie."

She just smiles and stares at me for a long moment. I know there's a battle raging inside of her—probably between her libido and her brain. I really hope her brain loses.

"I have to go," she says and my heart sinks.

"If you say so…" I reply, not bothering to hide the disappointment I feel.

She walks to my door but doesn't quite leave. We stare at each other and then finally I stand up and pull off my underwear. Her eyes go wide as I'm standing there naked in front of her for a second and then I pull back the sheets and slide into my bed.

"I sleep naked, remember?"

"Yeah. Hard to forget," she mumbles with a grin. "But thanks for the reminder."

"So…?"

I can see the eternal battle rage on inside her head. Sadly, her brain wins out.

"Sweet dreams, Devin," she tells me before closing the door behind her.

So close. Dammit. I almost won that.

Chapter 37

Callie

When I walk up to the brownstone a few nights later, I see a rental car parked in front—right next to Wyatt and Donna's truck. I'm confused. Should I be panicked? Is something wrong? I rush up the stairs and fling open the door. The first thing I hear is chatter—lots of it. It's coming from the back of the house. I drop my bag and my coat, kick off my boots and rush toward the noise.

The kitchen is filled with people and through the French doors, past the deck, I see even more people in the snowy yard. Donna is sitting at the breakfast bar next to my sister Rose. Luc is on the other side of the breakfast bar holding a freshly opened bottle of wine and Devin is standing in front of the stove, stirring something that's cooking in a giant pot. Outside Conner is building a snowman in the yard with Wyatt.

"What's this pleasant surprise?" I ask, excited to see everyone.

Rose jumps up at the sight of me. Her coal-colored eyes are bright with excitement. I get a panicked flash that she's going to tell me she's engaged. She straightens her small shoulders and grins.

"Luc's been traded!" she announces and she jumps up and down. "HERE!"

I cross the short distance to her and hug her. My eyes find Luc over her shoulder. He's smiling happily. This potential trade has been hanging over his head since last summer, and judging by the look on his face, he's happy about where he landed.

"You'll look good in the red jersey," I say with a proud smile. I can't believe I missed this news but I was so busy at work I hadn't even checked my Google alerts for the day—which were all related to these guys and my show. "Better than that crappy yellow and black Vegas wears."

He just chuckles at that.

"Tommy needs knee surgery. He's out for the season," Devin explains, turning away from the pot on the stove. "Our GM told me they were talking to Vegas already anyway, but the injury made it happen more quickly."

I break my hug with Rose and hug Luc. Then I hug Devin because I know he's excited about having one of his hometown "brothers" on his team. Jordan, Luc and Devin have never played together professionally but when they were kids, that's what they dreamed of doing. They all wanted to be on the same team. Plus, he got really close to Luc this summer when Luc was going through problems with his team and problems with Rose.

Devin wraps his free arm—the one not holding a ladle coated in chili—around my waist, buries his head in the crook of my neck and hugs me back so hard he lifts me off the ground for a second.

"This is so great," I whisper in his ear. "I mean, not for Tommy, but…"

He laughs at that.

I break the hug reluctantly and move to Donna. She's smiling at me with a bit of a knowing look. I just don't know what it's for but I hug her anyway.

"You must be thrilled to see them together on one team," I say jokingly.

"Now we just have to get Seattle to trade Jordy," she jokes back.

Wyatt is climbing the deck stairs and Conner is following. I can hear him repeating my name excitedly as they open the French doors and step inside.

"Callie! Callie! Callie!" he sings and I reach down and scoop him up. He feels like a plush, damp pillow in his puffy snowsuit. He wraps his little arms around my neck as tight as he can and it makes my heart swell. I kiss his cheek and pull off his hat, ruffling his hair.

"Hey, sport," I say. "Did you congratulate your uncle Luc? He's going to play hockey with Daddy!"

"Yay, Lu!" he bellows.

Everyone laughs. I kiss Conner's cheek and he gives me a tiny but strong hug.

"Chili's ready!" Devin calls out. "Let's get you out of your snowsuit, Con."

"I'll do it. You serve up dinner. I'm starving," I tell Devin and start unzipping Conner's jacket.

The dinner is amazing. It's not the food; it's the company. All of us squeezed in around the kitchen table laughing and teasing each other brings back the only warm and loving memories I have from childhood. It makes me feel happy and content and safe.

Devin is sitting on one side of me and Rose is on the other. Conner is moving from my lap to Devin's and back every ten minutes or so as he eats his chili and corn bread. We pass him back and forth wordlessly with an unspoken, comfortable rhythm.

The talk is pure hockey. I glance up and notice Donna watching me as I help Conner hold his spoon properly. As Conner climbs back over to his dad, who wipes his son's face and hands him his sippy cup of milk, I smile at Donna and she smiles back. It's different than her normal smile. This one is deeper and softer and she almost looks like she might cry. I guess having Luc and Devin play together has got to be overwhelming. I know that Luc has been taking a lot of criticism in the last year or so, being called a failure, and although she never said a word, I think Donna and all the Garrisons were bothered by it as much as Luc was.

"So you're coming to the game with us tomorrow night?" Rose says, giving me a little hug.

"Of course."

"We're bringing Conner too," Donna tells me.

"It's a big deal," I reply and smile.

After dinner the boys head into the living room but Rose,

Donna and I stay in the kitchen and finish the wine. I look at Rose and pull the parental role because someone has got to do it. "Have you applied to graduate programs yet?"

"Not yet," she answers as she refills my wineglass. "I still have time. And now I'm focusing on schools in New York, obviously."

I give her a cautious glare. She stares back unblinking, not backing down. I sigh.

"Excuse me for a minute. Bathroom break," Rose announces.

When she's disappeared down the hall, I look over at Donna. "I love Luc and Rosie together but I worry about her. She's so caught up in the romance, it's like she's willing to throw her own goals away."

Donna thinks about that for a minute but she shakes her head. "I don't think you give her enough credit. I know that she's making her relationship with Luc a priority, but she's still got her head on her shoulders. She's just adapting her life to make it all fit."

I don't respond to that, but my brow stays furrowed and she sees that. I sip my wine.

"It's like what you're doing," Donna tells me quietly. "You're adapting your life to fit Conner and Devin into it."

I am? I wonder silently. Sure, I don't go out to bars or party as much as I did in Los Angeles, but my job is more strenuous and leaves less time than my other jobs in the past. To be honest, I would rather pick up Conner and hang out with him and Devin than get drunk at one of the local pubs anyway. And, yeah, I don't eat takeout every night like I used to in L.A. I cook for Devin and Conner, but I worry that if I don't, they won't eat properly, and I like cooking and having people to cook for again.

"I appreciate it too, Callie. More than you know," Donna tells me, and she reaches over and puts her hand on top of mine on the table. "I worry about Devin all the time but it helps to know you've been here for him. And Conner."

"I'm not adapting," I argue back. "It's not like it's a hardship. I love hanging out with Devin and Conner. We have fun. And it feels good for me to have someone here too. I would be all alone in New York if it wasn't for him."

I glance at her. Her big blue eyes have that look in them again like she might cry. It makes me nervous. "Conner is pretty much in love with you, Callie."

"Good, because I love him to bits."

"And Devin is pretty much in love with you too."

That statement is like an atomic bomb going off in the middle of the kitchen. My head spins to look at her—glare at her, actually. She squeezes my hand tightly, as if she's worried I might jump up and run away and she wants to keep me still.

"I know that scares you to death. And I'm fairly certain at this point in his life, with what Devin has gone through, it probably scares him too," Donna explains to me in a confident, calm voice. "But I can't take my eyes off you two tonight. You work like a team. A family. It looks so natural. I always saw the struggle with Ashleigh and Devin. Maybe that's why this looks so breathtaking."

"Donna…" I swallow down the rest of my wine in one fast gulp and pull my hand from hers. "Please don't."

Devin comes walking into the room with Conner, who is in his pajamas holding his daddy's hand.

"He wants Callie to tuck him in," Devin announces and smiles at me. "Apparently Daddy doesn't tell good bedtime stories."

I try to ignore the smile that spreads across Donna's face. I know this is proving her point and I want to just get up and walk—or run—away. But I can't deny the little blond angel. So I stand up and take his hand from Devin's. I take a deep breath and try not to look as distressed as I feel.

"That's because you read from books," I explain to Devin. "I make the stories up."

"Well, aren't you little Miss Creativity?" Devin rolls his eyes in mock annoyance. "Thanks for showing me up with my own kid."

"My pleasure," I joke back with an easy wink and then stiffen. This is the exact thing Donna was talking about. Without another word, I lead Conner through the house to say his good nights to everyone one by one and then I take him upstairs. I weave a tale about a purple dragon and a green bull who become friends. Before I can get to the part where the dragon and bull meet a giraffe, he's out cold.

I smooth his wheat-colored hair from his forehead and sneak out of his room. Devin is coming up the stairs as I pull Conner's door almost closed, leaving it open an inch. I raise my hands to my lips to indicate we have to be quiet.

"He's out?" Devin whispers.

"Yeah," I reply and pause for a second. "Listen, I found a place."

"What? What place?" He looks completely baffled.

"I found my own place to live," I tell him and his hazel eyes look instantly devastated. I move my eyes to the carpet.

"Why?"

"It's time," I reply, trying to sound confident. "You and Conner are settled. And I can't live here forever."

He doesn't say anything to that. He doesn't have to, because I can tell by his face that he's upset. There's nothing I can do about that. If I stay here a minute longer, it will just get worse. Donna made it clear Devin and I aren't on the same page about our friendship.

As I start down the stairs, he reaches for my hand. "When are you leaving?"

I feel a flutter at the feel of his long, powerful fingers around my wrist. My brain fights to remain calm. I have to figure out an answer.

"Friday," I blurt out. It's only two days away and hopefully I can find a place by then, even if it's just a hotel room. "It'll be great. You can have your place back to yourself."

"I don't want my place to myself."

"Then invite Luc and Rose to live with you for the rest of the season. He's going to need a place too and he's your family," I rationalize and try to smile lightly like I don't have a care in the world—like I don't feel sick about leaving him, which I do. "But I have to warn you that Luc and Rosie are loud in bed."

I pull my wrist from his grip and continue down the stairs. There. Done. Everything will be better now.

Chapter 38

Devin

When I walk into the dressing room to get ready for the game, my eyes scan the room until they land on Luc. They've given him a locker directly across from mine. He's sitting below the nameplate, "L. Richard," and pulling on his Under Armour. His number on the Vipers was 4 and I see it's still going to be 4 here—that means Dmitri Kortin, our rookie who was wearing it, offered it to Luc because he's a veteran. I smile at Dmitri as I pass him and tap him on the shoulder. He nods and smiles.

Luc's jaw is set in a hard line and he's got his brow pinched together like he's concentrating really hard on something. I walk over to my locker and hang up my suit jacket. Then I head toward him as I start to loosen my tie. He glances up and nods, his face still stern, but I can't help but smile. I can't wait to play with him.

"I just did twenty minutes of pregame interviews with

everyone from *Wake Up, Brooklyn* to *Hockey Night in Canada*," I tell him, not hiding the amazement in my voice. "*Hockey Night in Canada* flew their asses out to Brooklyn, Luc. And it's not even a Saturday or a play-off final. You're big news."

He shakes his head and shrugs. "They're all eager to see me fail here like I did in Vegas."

I smile lightly at that. "It'll be fine. You're skilled, Luc. Forget the past and play the way you know you can."

He nods and continues dressing. I walk back over to my stall and get ready. The PR coordinator for the team, an uptight woman with frizzy red hair named April, comes in and tells Luc to sit next to me when he's tying up his skates. The NBC Sports crew wants to get footage of us together. Luc just nods curtly and switches places with Loops.

"Are you feeling confident with the plays?" I ask because I know Coach gave him a playbook yesterday.

He nods. "Can we talk about anything but hockey? Just for a minute?"

He's bordering on terrified. I can see it in his dark eyes. I try not to frown in concern. I can't make this worse. I have to talk him off the ledge. I glance around the room. The TV crew hasn't come in yet and the other guys are busy with their own pregame chatter. I hold Luc's eye for a second and then reach down for one of my skates.

"So I'm sleeping with Callie."

I glance back over to him and his jaw is hanging wide open. "You're fucking kidding me, right?"

"Nope. Not only are we sleeping together but I'm kind of,

well...how should I say this?" I pause and shove my right foot into the skate. "I think I really like her."

"Callie? Caplan?" he questions, and I nod and chuckle.

The camera crew comes in and starts setting up. He shakes his head and reaches for his skate as they start to film. We glance at each other again. There is no sound on this. It's one of those B roll locker room pieces they'll splice in as the announcers blab on about Luc's debut as a Baron.

"Dude," Luc mumbles barely above a whisper but with a smile on his face for the camera's sake. "That's the worst possible thing you could do right now."

I tug on my skate laces, glance up and smile. The camera is sweeping by us now and then the light above it goes off. They're done.

"Oh, I know," I tell him once I know we're not the center of attention again. "I didn't plan it. But she's been there for me, you know? She's helped me through everything. And she's Callie. Funny, adorable, sexy as hell Callie."

"Callie will be your best friend," Luc surmises and stands to pull on his shoulder pads, which he dragged over from his cubicle earlier. "You should see her with Rosie. She's always checking up on her. She sends her money even though Rose never asks for any. She offered to fly to Vermont and punch a professor that gave Rose a bad grade."

I can't help but laugh at that. Luc does too for a minute but then he gets serious again. "Callie is a warrior. When she loves you, she'll do anything for you."

I swallow and try not to let the dark feelings in my heart

take over. "But she doesn't love me. She doesn't love anyone. She doesn't want to—that's the problem."

"Nah, man, that's all an act." Luc shakes his head. "She loves everyone."

He walks back over to his locker and I try to make sense of his words. Callie loves everyone. Including me? That makes no sense. Or does it?

Chapter 39

Callie

I meet Rose at the hotel the Barons have put Luc up in until he finds something more permanent. She comes bounding off the elevator full of energy and kisses my cheek.

"Donna and Wyatt are picking up Conner and meeting us there," I inform her as we jump into a cab in front of the hotel. "Are you nervous?"

"No. I'm excited. He's nervous," she explains happily.

"He'll be great," I assure her, even though she doesn't need it.

"So…" she starts, letting her sentence trail off.

"We're not having sex anymore so you don't need to lecture me," I blurt out, knowing that she's been dying to talk about Devin and me since she got here yesterday. "And I'm moving out, so it won't happen ever again."

I glance over at her and she looks disappointed, which confuses me. She pulls out her phone and starts to dial. I don't ask what she's doing but then she hits speaker and I hear Jessie's voice fill the car.

"Hey, Rosie! Are you with her?"

"Yep. You're on speaker."

"Seriously?" I roll my eyes and glance at the cabbie, who is trying to act like he's not paying attention, but he's smiling ever so slightly. "Are you guys holding an intervention here?"

"Pretty much," Jessie confirms.

"I just told Rosie it's not going to happen again," I repeat firmly as we stop at a red light. "I'm moving out and then we'll go back to being friends."

"Callie, I hate to break this to you, but take it from two girls that know," Jessie announces through Rose's iPhone. "Once you've had the monkey sex, you never go back."

I laugh out loud at my sister using my personal term for crazy, hot sex. It just bursts from my lungs and it sounds more nervous than amused.

"You two are crackheads," I announce and try to contain my giggles. "I did Devin when I was eighteen and I walked away. I can do him at twenty-three and walk away too."

"How, exactly, can you say you walked away when you came back?" Rose wants to know, a small smile on her face. "It may have taken five years, but you ended up in his bed again."

"Technically, it was on his couch…and then my bed, but never *his* bed," I correct her snidely because I don't know what else to say. Rose is right. Technically, I slept with him and came back—two nights in a row. And now I have to fight the urge to do it again every waking minute of every day.

I glance at the cab driver again in the rearview mirror and he rolls his eyes. I shrug as if to say "whatever." I honestly don't care what this old guy knows about my sex life. He's a New York cab driver. I'm sure he's heard worse.

"Couch sex," Jessie says longingly. "Couch sex with a Garrison is good sex."

"Back on track here!" Rose commands, sounding like the schoolteacher she's studying to become. "I don't care if you sleep with Devin a hundred more times."

"Rosie! We're supposed to be on the same team here!" Jessie argues. "Remember? The Don't Touch Devin Again Because You'll Break His Heart team?!"

"It's too late for that, Jessie," Rose tells my sister, turning her pink-glossed lips toward the phone she's holding up. "You should have seen them yesterday! They touch each other without even knowing it. And they give each other little looks and smiles and they share Conner. And Conner loves it!"

"Oh my God," is all that comes through the phone.

I feel my whole body get rigid. "Okay, wait a minute! Do NOT bring Conner into this."

The driver pulls to a stop in front of the Barons arena. I throw twenty dollars toward him and scramble out before he can give me change. Rose scurries to join me, slipping a little on the icy sidewalk. She's still got the damn phone in her left hand, with Jessie on the other end, and so she grabs my arm with her right one.

"Callie, he looks at you like you're his second mother. And Devin looks at you like you're the love of his life," Rose says in a low, soft tone. "And I hate to break this to you, big sister, but you look at Devin like...like you're in love with him."

I stop dead, fans in Barons shirts bustling by us, and spin to face her so fast my knitted hat flies off my head.

"Rose, you're completely delusional," I say in a heated, angry growl. "I'm not kidding. You want to be a romantic fool, fine. I have always supported you and loved you anyway, but don't you dare try to make me one too. I know better."

"Callie!" Jessie yells through the phone. "What are you afraid of?"

"Afraid?" I repeat like she's an idiot, because right now she fucking is. I yank Rose to a less busy part of the area outside the arena. "I'm not afraid. I'm smart. You two think it's all shits and giggles? Look at Mom. She died alone. The man who was supposed to love her—our dad—left her. And us. Lily was supposed to love us. Excellent grandma she turned out to be, huh? She cared so little she left us alone as soon as she thought she could do it and not get arrested."

"Luc and Jordan would never do that," Rose states in a flat, firm voice. She's completely one hundred percent confident in her boyfriend and Jessie's future husband.

"They both fucked up," I remind them heatedly, which I know is harsh, but I'm furious. I'm shaking, raging, furious. "You spent half your life pining after Luc before he figured out he loved you, and Jessie…Jessie spent years with her heart in pieces. I barely got through both your heartbreaks, which is why I don't want to go through my own. Devin wants this perfect little family, and I'm far from perfect. If Ashleigh couldn't live up to it, how can I?"

"Devin seems to think you're pretty perfect," Rosie comments calmly.

"Shut up!" I bark and take a deep, ragged breath. "I'm going to watch my *friends* play hockey now. And if either of you bring this up again, I swear to God I will disown you. Bye, Jessie."

I don't wait for a response. I just start storming toward the entry gate as my vision blurs with hot, angry tears. I can hear Rose calling my name and it makes me walk faster. Damn them. I'm so upset with my sisters. I feel betrayed. I've always had their backs. I've always supported what they wanted, even when I didn't think it was the right thing to want.

"Callie, please!" Rose grabs my arm and forces me to stop walking. She turns me to face her and I snap my eyes shut. My cheeks are damp, and she makes a whimper at the sight of my tears and pulls me into a hug. "We're sorry."

"When Jessie was still clearly in love with Jordan after all he did to her, after all those years, I supported her," I say in a shaky, whispery voice. "I talked to him. I told him he had to go for it. I wanted her to be happy."

"I know. And we want *you* to be happy," Rose promises in an earnest voice. "That's all we want."

"I am happy. I'm happy not ever putting myself in the position to be heartbroken. I don't need a guy. I don't need Devin."

"But do you *want* him?" Rose asks me in a small voice.

I hesitate. Do I want him? That's a loaded question and I know it. She hands me a tissue from her bag and I snatch it from her and wipe at my eyes.

"Because he wants you," Rose states flatly. "I would bet my life on it. And I know you think love is just a way for stupid people to inflict pain on themselves. But it's also pretty fucking awesome and completely worth the risk."

"Are you done?" I ask, regaining my composure. "Because I'm done talking about it."

"One last thing," she says simply, as she loops her arm through mine and guides me toward the building entrance. "You have always seemed happy with your life. But I have never seen you look or sound happier than you are around Devin these last few months. Thought you should know."

I give her a hard stare but say nothing. She just smiles and kisses my cheek.

Chapter 40

Devin

We won 4–0. A shutout, so Loops is thrilled. I scored a goal and not only did Luc not score on his own net, he assisted on my goal and got one of his own. Definitely a great debut as a Baron. I was grinning ear to ear when we headed back into the locker room after it was over.

I keep glancing over at him and smiling while I talk to reporters. I can barely see him, as his own wall of microphones and digital recorders surrounds him. When the reporters are finally ushered out, before we even have a chance to shower, Luc and I head into the hall. Rose, Callie, Conner and my parents are there. Everyone looks exactly how I feel—proud, excited and relieved. It couldn't have been a more perfect game.

Mom and Dad both hug Luc, but his eyes are on Rose the whole time. She's got tears in her eyes. She wants to be the big girl but she's so thrilled for him she's like a kid who got a brand-new bike for Christmas. When my parents stop praising him, Luc and Rose grab each other and hold on for dear life. It's ridiculously touching and I suddenly long for that kind of deep relationship—again. I want that. My heart aches just a little bit.

"Daddy!" Conner calls, pulling my focus away from Luc.

Callie has scooped him up in her arms and he's smiling and reaching for me. I walk over and take him. He hugs me for a second and then his face wrinkles up. "Daddy, you stinky!" he proclaims and reaches back for Callie.

She lets out a belly laugh and takes him back into her arms again. I give her a smirk and she winks at me. I'm overwhelmed with the urge to reach out and hug her, so I do.

"Great game, Hockey God," she whispers in my ear, and kisses my cheek softly before adding loudly, "You ARE stinky!"

Conner giggles and claps his hands.

"Fine! I'm showering. Relax!" I hold my hands up and walk backward to the locker room.

My parents drop Conner back at Ashleigh's and meet us at a local pub to celebrate. A few teammates come out too. It's a relaxed but joyous night. Everyone is so happy. I can't believe how good I feel, and as I watch Callie joking with my teammate Alex and my dad, I know that she's the only thing that would make me feel even happier.

A few hours later my mom and dad decide to call it a night. I head to the restrooms as Callie is making her way back from them. We cross paths at the edge of the dance floor as the music changes to something slower. Spontaneously, I grab her wrist and pull her onto the floor and into my arms.

"We're doing this now, are we?" she asks with a cocked eyebrow.

"Why the hell not?" I counter and give her my best cocky smirk.

She laughs and her fingers deliciously scrape the back of my neck. "Why the hell not?" she repeats softly.

I pull her closer. She feels just as fantastic as I remember. My thumb makes lazy circles on the small of her back.

"So about this moving thing…where is your new place?" I ask casually.

"Soho," she mutters.

"What street?"

"I don't remember."

I pull back a little and look at her. She looks over my shoulder. "Don't move out."

"Devin."

"Don't move out."

"I have to." She shakes her head as if arguing with internal voices as well. "Jessie texted me during the game. I guess the NBC crew focused on us a few times during the game."

"Yeah." I nod. When a player's family is at a game—especially their first game on a new team—it always makes the telecast, and usually the Jumbotron in the arena too. I had seen them up there on a TV time-out.

"They said it was the Garrison family, including Luc Richard's girlfriend and Devin Garrison's wife and kid," she says and pauses. "You have to fix that."

"It's over with. No one probably even paid attention," I say with a shrug. "It's okay."

"But Ashleigh is going to freak out," Callie insists.

I assume she would be concerned that people think she's my wife because she hates the idea of it for herself, but her concern is Ashleigh, which shocks me.

"It's all good," I assure her and smile. "I'll tell them you're my hot nanny."

"Oh, yeah, that's much better," Callie retorts, unamused. "So when news of your divorce gets out, they'll think I'm the skank who did it."

"Cal, Ashleigh is the one with the boyfriend, remember?" I counter calmly. "You're not the skank."

She settles down a little bit at that and goes back to grazing her fingers against the back of my neck. It's making me hot for her. What else is new?

"You don't have a place yet, do you?"

"Do we have to talk about that again?"

"Yes," I reply curtly. "Because until you have a place and I see it for myself, and approve of it, you aren't moving out."

"Excuse me?" She stops moving with me and stands perfectly still, her body rigid. Her hands drop from my shoulders and land on her tiny hips.

"You're a part of my family and have been for years," I tell her and grab her hands, pulling them from her hips and holding them tightly. "You aren't moving into some crappy hotel or some sketchy rental because you were too scared of your feelings to find a proper place. You want to run scared, fine. But be smart about it."

She opens her mouth to speak but nothing comes out.

"And for the record," I add softly, leaning in so our faces are inches from each other, "you can run all you want. I'm pretty fucking irresistible, and even if you're not across the hall, you'll still have trouble staying out of my bed."

I kiss her cheek softly and slowly; then I let her hands go and walk away.

Chapter 41

Callie

I barely had an entire drink all night, but as I walk home from the bar with Devin, I have to question my mental state right now. I feel pretty fucking intoxicated. That's what being horny as hell does to me, I guess. What the fuck was that on the dance floor? He's so fucking cocky and full of himself—and it's the hottest thing ever. It's one of the things—besides the physical height, muscle, hazel eyes with flecks of amber and gray and thick, dirty-blond hair—that attracted me to Devin even as a teen.

He has this air about him…a strong confidence. Like he's not as great as he appears, he's actually better. It wasn't there when I first moved to Brooklyn, thanks to Ashleigh. He was still attractive in a different way then. I can honestly say that seeing him vulnerable was a turn-on and I've never thought that about a man before. But now—on the dance floor—was the first flash of that other quality he's had his whole life. And it was so sexy and manly and just…He left me standing there in the middle of the dance floor with wet panties. He barely talked to me for the rest of the night and now I'm following him back to the townhouse and I'm completely and utterly on fire for him.

Tonight is going to be hard to get through, knowing he is right across the hall. I try not to stare at his perfect round ass as I follow him wordlessly up the path. He opens the door and allows me in first. We both kick off our shoes and I drop my purse and head upstairs. He goes into the kitchen.

In my room I shut the door and peel out of my clothes. I hear his feet on the stairs and walk to my door. I lean my head against it and wait to hear his bedroom door open and close, but the sound doesn't come.

Where did he go?

Suddenly every part of my body and soul is praying silently that he's about to come into my room. *Oh God, Devin, please do it*, I think despite the fact I know I shouldn't. *Please just barge in here and rip my thong off, pull your perfect dick out and fuck me blind. Please.* I crack open my door, unable to control my overwhelming need to figure out where the hell he is and what the fuck he's doing.

He's standing with his back against the railing of the stairs directly across from my door. Our eyes connect.

"Tell me to come in," he demands in a low, gravelly voice filled with lust.

I don't say anything. I just slowly pull the door wide open so he can see me standing there in nothing but my black lace push-up bra and matching black thong. His eyes sweep over me slowly and fully before holding my gaze again.

"Tell me," he demands again.

"Come in." It's barely a whisper and it quivers with need.

The next thing I know, our lips collide and he's pushing me back onto my bed, his long, muscular body on top of me, and his hands everywhere. His tongue controls my mouth—owns it. Oh God, it feels amazing.

"Devin, I fucking missed this," I admit shamefully.

"Your own fault," he whispers back as his full, wet lips move to my throat and down my chest. "I would deny you nothing, Callie."

He's licking and kissing the flesh on my bare stomach now. It's a glorious feeling and as he keeps heading south, I tangle my hands in his hair. I feel his long fingers hook the sides of my thong and slide them down as he circles my belly button with long strokes of his tongue.

As soon as I'm naked from the waist down, his torso falls in between my legs. I glance down at him; his beautiful face is turned toward my thigh, kissing the inside of it softly, his eyes closed.

He opens them and looks at me as he turns, face inches from my core, and juts his tongue out. It softly licks my center and my head automatically bends back, pushing into the mattress beneath me.

"You taste incredible," he murmurs into me, creating a vibration that makes me gasp. His tongue slides over me again and again before pushing past my folds and into my middle. The breath is sucked out of my lungs.

"Ohmygodyou'rekillingme," gushes from me in one long word.

"I can stop if you want," he whispers and then his tongue moves upward and takes a long, soft swipe at my clit.

"Don't you fucking dare," I murmur and my lower back arches. I feel his hand move and a finger plays with my outer lips teasingly as he sucks my clit into his mouth and rubs his tongue over it. I whimper.

"You want my fingers inside you, baby?" he asks before delving back at me with his tongue.

"Fuck, yes," I moan. "Touch me, Devin."

He pushes a finger into me and my back rises even higher off the bed. I tug hard on his hair in my hands. He seems to like that. His tongue moves faster and harder over my clit and another finger pushes into me and pumps me hard and fast.

I can't feel anything but his hot, wet mouth and his strong, long fingers. My body is wound tighter than a guitar string about to break. A warmth builds in my abdomen and then his fingers curl in just the right way and his tongue licks up and down and around and…

I let out a loud gasp and my spine curls and I pant his name as my orgasm rips through my body. I feel my pussy squeeze his fingers and he just keeps going, never stopping his tongue or pulling away.

Finally, after what feels like forever, my spine lays flat against the mattress and Devin pulls his hand from me and I feel him move up. He kisses my cheek and my ear. I can do nothing but whimper and reach for him, but he pulls away. By the time my eyes open, he's off the bed and walking toward the door.

"Where are you going?"

He turns back and smiles softly. "To my room."

"What?! Why?" I'm shocked. I want desperately to make him come as hard as I did.

"You want me, Callie, then you're going to have to admit that you want all of me," he tells me in a riddle my orgasm-slammed brain is having trouble understanding. "I'm done with the casual sex."

I try to argue but he closes the door before I can think of something to say.

Chapter 42

Callie

When I get home from work two days later, after a night shoot, I brace myself in case he's already up. I've been able to avoid being alone with him since that night. My work schedule has been crazy and the only time I saw him was after a fourteen-hour day. He, Donna and Wyatt were on their way out to dinner with Luc and Rose. I used exhaustion as my excuse not to join them.

The shoot I'm coming back from now went from ten at night until ten in the morning. I sigh and open the front door. At least, after an all-nighter, it won't be odd if I beeline straight for my room. But as I enter the hall I hear a familiar voice coming from the kitchen. And then a different, equally familiar giggle. I head straight for the sounds.

"Cole!" I scream and rush over to where the youngest Garrison brother is leaning against the counter. He puts his coffee mug down and wraps his long arms around me.

"Hands off my husband," his wife, my childhood friend

Leah, says as she stands up from her seat at the kitchen table, and then she laughs. "I have always wanted to say that!"

As we pull apart, my eyes land on Devin. He's looking at me with a small smile on his face and his soft hazel eyes seem to have more gray flecks than normal. I look away like the coward I've become. I feel weird after our last encounter. I mean it was *amazing*, but he had all the control and I had none. And I hate ultimatums. I always do the exact opposite of what someone who challenges me wants me to do, just to spite them. To prove no one can tell me what to do. But…something about Devin's ultimatum makes that knee-jerk reaction I usually find instinctive impossible. The problem was giving in to what he wanted…that was impossible too, wasn't it?

"I'm so excited you're here!" Leah says with her usual beautiful warm smile. "I knew you were in New York but I didn't know you were living here with Devin."

"Yeah," Cole pipes in, shooting Devin a quick, hard stare. "Somebody forgot to mention that. Among other things."

"It's only temporary," Devin replies lightly. "She wants to get a place of her own."

They all look at me. "I was thinking about it." I shrug and change the subject. "So what's with the visit?"

Cole nods. "We came to see Jordan get his ass kicked by Luc and Devin."

"Ah, yes, the Garrison-and-Richard-against-another-Garrison game." A huge yawn overcomes me suddenly. "Sorry. Long night."

"How was work?" Devin asks.

"Good." I stifle another yawn.

"When does the show start?" Leah wants to know. "Is it already on the air?"

"No." I shake my tired head. "It airs tonight for the first time. They were going to wait until January but one of those shows they debuted in September tanked so they're putting us in their spot."

Devin looks shocked. "What? Why didn't you tell me?"

"I don't know. It's not that big a deal. I was just going to order pizza and watch it." I shrug and yawn yet again. "I have to sleep before I fall into a coma."

"You'll come to the game tomorrow night, right?" Leah asks hopefully as I hug her again.

"Are you kidding me? Wouldn't miss it. I'm gonna make a 'D. Garrison Is Better Than J. Garrison' sign and get myself on national TV!"

Devin laughs at that and I can't help but wink at him with a small smile before heading up to bed. I peel out of my clothes and nose-dive into my bed, sinking immediately into a deep sleep.

I wake up panicked. The show starts in ten minutes. I almost missed it! I run my hands through my hair and grab a pair of black leggings and an oversize shirt as I rush down the stairs. I should have the place to myself. Devin had mentioned the family was going out to dinner.

I look up as I hit the landing and see Wyatt standing in the middle of the living room. He's grinning at me as he waves excitedly. He's surrounded by Devin, Rose, Luc, Donna, Cole, Leah, Jordan and Jessie. There are plates of cheese and crackers and bowls of chips and dip all over the coffee table. Everyone is holding a glass of wine or a bottle of beer. I freeze and can do nothing but blink.

"Surprise!" Rose squeals and everyone laughs except me. I'm still frozen.

"Devin told us your show was airing tonight," Wyatt says, walking over to me and hugging me tightly before guiding me into the crowded living room. "We wanted to watch it with you and celebrate!"

I look over at Devin. He looks nervous, like he's scared I might get mad. How could I be mad? This is amazing. I wish I could tell him that but I'm still in shock. Rose hands me a glass of wine. I take a big gulp, which makes everyone laugh, and then grab Jessie in a bear hug. I had no idea she was even in town again.

"Why didn't you tell us, silly?" Jessie wants to know.

"There's so much else going on with everyone," I say, finally finding my voice. "I just didn't want to add another thing to everyone's plate."

"This is just as big as me being traded," Luc notes and I give him a grateful smile. I can't believe he just said that. He's proving once again why Rose loves him.

I hug him tightly and kiss his cheek. "Thank you for saying that, French Disaster."

The oven makes a loud *ding* sound from the other room. Devin jumps and puts his beer down on a side table. "That's my wings!"

I watch him hurry by me and head for the kitchen. "His wings?"

"He is cooking for you," Cole notes with a look that says he's amazed too. "I don't know who he is anymore."

I laugh.

Devin comes back with a platter filled with piping hot teriyaki and buffalo wings, and a few minutes later we all settle down to watch the show. I'm ridiculously nervous. I want them to like it. More important, I want America to like it. If the show doesn't do well and it gets canceled, I have to leave New York, which means leaving Devin and Conner, and the thought of that makes me feel sick.

I sit on the edge of my seat for half of the hour-long drama. Devin is beside me and Rose is on my other side on the couch. All the outfits look as good as I'd hoped and that's all that matters to me. One of the main actors, the youngest girl in the cast, is a little stiff in her dialogue and then the main guy actor delivers a cheesy line to his love interest and everyone in the room groans. I raise my hands. "I don't write it, people!"

As we reach the commercial break midway through, Devin places a hand casually on my lower back and leans forward.

"I'm not hating this teen angst as much as I think I should," he whispers jokingly. "And the clothes look amazing."

"Thank you," I reply with a small laugh.

When it's over, everyone claps.

"For a teen show, it's actually kind of intriguing," Donna says. "I mean, I actually like the story line. It's smart and there were some witty lines."

Everyone nods in agreement. I'm relieved they didn't find it too goofy.

"Okay, that purple slip dress that Tasha character wore to

the dance." Leah grabs my hands. "Please tell me you found that here and I can pick up my own one before I leave."

"A store in Tribeca," I tell her happily. "I'll take you there before the game tomorrow night."

"Great," Cole says in mock annoyance. "Just what our bank account needs, a shopping trip."

Everyone laughs. Later that night I glance around the crowded living room and can't find Devin. I sneak into the kitchen in search of him. He's loading some dishes into the dishwasher. I walk up behind him and touch my hand to his hip.

"Thank you," I say shyly.

He grins at me. "I was worried it might freak you out, but there was no way we were not going to be a part of your special moment. You are such an important part of all of ours."

His kaleidoscope eyes look so warm and inviting and filled with love. And…it's not freaking me out. It makes me feel…good. Great, actually. So why do I want to cry?!

"Callie," he whispers my name and reaches up and cups the side of my face. "Are you going to cry?"

I shake my head, scared my voice will betray me with a quiver or a crack. I try to take a deep breath. I wrap my arms tightly around his neck and pull him to me and hoarsely whisper, "You're the best person in the whole world, Devin."

I pull back, but only enough to touch my lips to his. The kiss is soft, subtle and tender. Even when he opens his mouth slightly and slips his tongue past my lips, it stays gentle and sweet. And I fucking love it.

"Oops!"

We leap apart and find Cole standing there holding an empty chip bowl. His cheeks match his red hair color. He stares at me and then at Devin and then back at me. I don't say anything; I just walk by him and head back to the living room. I don't know what to say anyway, so I'll just let Devin handle that. Rose walks over to me as I reach the living room.

"You okay?" She must see something in my expression.

"I feel like I might have a heart attack and die," I tell her bluntly and take a shaky breath. "And I think I don't even care if I do."

She grins, her dark eyes gleaming excitedly. "Yeah. It's awesome, isn't it?"

"No. Yes. I don't know." I shake my head and grab her wineglass from her hand and drink the rest of it.

"Yeah. That's part of it too," she assures me happily.

"A part of what?" I swallow hard. "On second thought, don't answer that. I don't want to know. Just get me more wine."

Chapter 43

Devin

When we enter the bar, Callie jumps to her feet and yells, "Go, French Disaster, the Hip Check King!"

Everyone bursts out laughing and I can't help but join them. Jordan shoves me angrily. "Thanks, bro."

"Hey. He's on my team, you're not," I remind him. "And besides, you looked fucking hysterical flying ass over helmet."

"Fuck you."

Rose runs over and leaps into Luc's arms, wrapping her legs around his waist, and she kisses him wildly. He keeps one hand under her butt and wraps the other one in her hair. The two stay like that so long even the whistles from our friends and teammates stop.

"Hey!" Callie barks loudly. "PDA overload."

Rose breaks the kiss and drops to her feet. "That hit was the hottest thing I have ever seen."

I chuckle. "What is it with you Caplan women and your violence? If I'd known it would get that kind of reaction, I would have hip checked Jordy myself. Twice."

The bar is packed and there is a large contingent of both Barons and Winterhawks players there. I notice Avery Westwood slide into the chair next to Callie smiling brightly, and Cole's bachelor weekend comes slamming back into my brain.

Ashleigh and I were already solidly on the rocks at that point. I didn't want to admit it then, but deep down I knew. She hadn't even wanted to go to the weekend in Atlantic City but I had forced her. I thought that it had done us good. She got drunk the first night and confessed how bad she felt for not being happy and we'd actually had sex for the first time in four months that night. But the next day she was standoffish and cold to me, and then she ended up not even showing up for Cole and Leah's wedding. We said to everyone she went to see a sick aunt in Jersey, but she told me she had gone back to Brooklyn because she needed time to herself. What I know now is she was probably seeing her boyfriend. Yeah, the summer had been a nightmare of personal drama, but what I hadn't missed that weekend in Atlantic City was that Callie had slept with the Winterhawks' captain.

At the time I hadn't thought twice about it. Now, the thought makes me feel like barfing. Avery looks up at me and raises his glass. "Good goal, Garrison."

I had beaten him on a face-off and immediately taken a shot on net, whipping it past their goalie. Still, we'd lost the game 2–1. I nod and force myself to smile at him. Luc shoves a beer into my hand.

"Thanks, Hip Check King," I say, and Jordan hears and flips me the bird.

"That is going to make the highlight reel for years to come," I warn Jordan. "Get used to it."

"It's already on YouTube!" Chooch, the Winterhawks' goalie, announces and places his cell phone on the middle of the table.

Everyone leans around it to watch the clip. Luc has the puck and he's skating quickly up the boards. He's got Dmitri slightly in front of him near center ice. Jordan is coming at Luc full force. As Jordan turns his shoulder toward Luc, readying himself to check his lifelong friend backward onto his ass, Luc turns sideways and shoots the puck up ice to me. It was a risky pass but because of that no one expected him to make it and no one was ready to intercept it. Just before Jordan and Luc collide shoulder-to-shoulder, Luc crouches down and the center of his body hits Jordan in the side of his hip. Jordan flies over Luc, cartwheeling through the air skates above his head, before landing hard on his side on the ice. It's a totally legal, perfect hip check.

"When the fuck did you ever even learn how to do that?" Jordan snaps as everyone cheers at the image of him flailing.

"Oh, I have tricks you wouldn't believe." Luc lifts his beer toward his best friend and winks. "Can't wait to show you more next time we play."

"Please don't break my fiancé before the wedding," Jessie says to Luc, and everyone laughs loudly at that.

As we all move on to talk about other things, I turn and see Callie whispering something in Avery's ear. He smiles smugly and laughs lightly. His arm is around the back of her chair. I tighten the grip on my beer and force myself to turn away.

She doesn't do repeats. She's made that her very public life motto. She won't sleep with him again because she broke that motto for me and me only...Right?

Chapter 44

Callie

This quirky little pub that the players like to frequent is having a country night, and trying to teach Avery Westwood how to line dance is amusing and adorable all at the same time. I know he has rhythm—I danced my ass off with him in Atlantic City this summer—but country is clearly not his thing. He keeps tripping over his own feet and can't figure out right from left. We turn with the group doing the line dance on the floor with us, but Avery double-steps to his right instead of his left and bumps me hard, almost knocking me over. I laugh.

"Aw, fuck this," he says in a bit of a growl as he grabs me and starts swinging me around, holding my body to his and dancing *his* way.

I burst out laughing. "I guess maybe two-stepping is genetic and clearly you weren't born with the gene!"

"But I was born with many other abilities and skills," he murmurs in my ear, still holding my body to his as he guides me around a small corner of the dance floor.

"Yes, you were," I confirm, because it's true. He'd been great in bed.

"I'd like to show you my skills again, Callie," he says softly and lets his lips graze my cheek.

"Umm…" I can't help but murmur, but find myself shaking my head without hesitation. "Sorry, Avery. I'm a one-night-stand type of girl. And the key to one-night stands is they're once."

"Really?" he questions, not buying it. His hands around my waist slip a little to rest at the top of my ass. "Can't you make an exception?"

"I can and I have…" I reply. "But that never ends well."

"That's too bad…"

I look over his bulky shoulder and see Devin standing by our table. Luc is sitting across from him talking to him but Devin's eyes are on me. He's holding his beer glass so tightly I can see that his knuckles are white.

It makes me angry, but not as angry as it should. The anger is being diluted by desire. Once again, I want him so badly I can barely stand it—even though he's clearly itching to get me away from Avery and any other guy I might possibly want to fuck. That, in the past, would make a guy so unattractive to me, but not with Devin.

The song ends and Avery and I break apart. I take his hand and lead him back to the table. Devin's narrowed eyes are burning a hole in me but I refuse to even look at him.

"I think we need some shots!" I announce and head to the bar.

I'm a foot from the bar when his hand grabs my arm. I don't

even have to turn around to know it's him. I can tell by the way he feels against my skin. He pulls me off toward the corner of the bar.

"I slept with Avery, remember?" I snap before he can open his mouth. "I've slept with a lot of guys. If that bothers you, then fuck you."

He doesn't even seem bothered by my words. That perturbs me. He should be furious. He should be repulsed. I yank my arm out of his grip.

"And he's not the only NHL player," I announce belligerently, shoving my hair off my shoulders and crossing my arms over my tight, lacy purple top. "When I was living in Los Angeles, I ran into a bunch of Milwaukee Comets at a bar who were in town for a game and I slept with Jude Braddock."

"Braddock? That dude's a total tool." He rolls his eyes. He doesn't look angry, just unimpressed with my selection. I glare at him. He stares back with serious eyes. His full lips are straight, not smiling but not frowning, like he doesn't know how to react yet. God, I love those lips.

"Are you going to sleep with Westwood again tonight?" he asks point-blank.

"That's none of your business," I snap back, instead of telling him the truth, which is no, I have absolutely no intention of touching Avery ever again. All I want is you, Devin Garrison.

"Don't."

I sigh and uncross my arms.

"I'm not going to, but it has nothing to do with you," I explain swiftly before he can look triumphant. "It's who I am. I don't do relationships. Even casual ones. I get what I want and I move on."

"Not always," he counters and takes a step toward me.

I take a step back and put my hand out to keep him from coming any closer. "What do you want from me, Devin?"

"I want you to stop."

"Stop what?"

"Stop having flings. Don't move on from ours." His hazel eyes are leveled on me with such a clear, focused stare that I get goose bumps. "I'm your final move."

I suddenly can't make my lungs work. I can't take a breath. I feel light-headed and dizzy and angry and confused. He takes another step closer to me despite my hand in front of me trying to block his way. He just simply reaches out and moves it down, out of his way. And then he wraps an arm around my back and pulls me into him so our bodies are flush against each other. It does absolutely nothing to help me regain my composure. In fact, my pulse starts to race even faster and my knees get weak.

"I have never felt the way I feel with you with anyone else. Not Ashleigh. No one," he whispers against my ear. "And you'd feel it too if you let yourself. I'm not asking for marriage. I'm just saying—don't move on."

My body goes into full-on panic mode. I push him back, turn and walk away without even looking back. I head directly into the women's restroom, into a stall and slam the door.

I can't do this. I can't do this. I can't do this.

I don't know how long I've been in there when I hear the bathroom door open and close.

"Callie?" It's Leah. "Are you okay?"

"Fine. Thanks!" I call back, and it's too loud and completely strained.

"Can you come out?"

I take a deep cleansing breath and open the stall door. She's leaning against the sinks, her almost white blond hair swept off her face with a side braid. Her eyes are friendly and warm and she's wearing a bit of a smile. She hands me a glass of water she must have gotten from the bar. I take it and take a sip. My hand is shaking.

"So I guess this is the first time you've been in love," she says softly and I glare at her. "Don't get mad at me. It's not my fault you're so obvious about it."

"I never said I..." I shake my head. "I don't want to be yet another Garrison victim. No offense."

She laughs at that. "Hey, if having a beautiful, smart, funny, talented man love me unconditionally for the rest of my life makes me a victim, then that's what I am."

I take another sip of water. The door to the bathroom opens again and Rose and Jessie slip in. Rose sidles up to the sinks and stands next to Leah, facing me. Jessie leans against the closed restroom door.

"Look, I fell in love with Cole when I was just sixteen," Leah tells me. "I didn't know any better. So I'm not judging."

"I've been in love with Luc almost as long, but I *am* judging," Rose tells me flatly.

"Thanks a lot," I snap back at her. "So much for that unconditional love siblings are supposed to show each other."

"Shut up." She rolls her eyes and gives me a half smile.

"I love you no matter what happens with Devin. But Callie, I don't get it. The exact same people in life abandoned us both. I've been there too. Jessie has as well. But we never ever thought it meant that all love was evil."

"I'm not you," I say lamely and put the glass of water down beside Leah and look at my reflection in the mirror. I'm a little pale and my eyeliner is a little smudged. I wipe at it carefully with my finger.

"No, you're stronger than both of us," Jessie announces and gives me a small smile. "You're the one that has always been the strongest. You handled Mom's death the best. You handled Grandma Lily leaving us the best. You kept us from falling apart when things went sideways with Luc and Jordan."

"You know why I'm strong enough to do that?" I question, and before they can answer, I tell them. "Because I don't let myself get hurt like you do."

I catch Jessie's eye in the mirror. She is staring back at me with an unwavering gaze. She really doesn't get it. I can tell looking at Rose that she doesn't either. How can they forget how destroyed they got over Luc and Jordan? How devastated Mom was when Dad took off?

"How is that so damn easy for you?" I rant and spin to face them. "How can you all just give up everything and just become a part of them and their lives without even blinking?"

"See, that's your issue right there," Leah interrupts with a bright smile and a bit of a jump, like she's just figured out a cure for cancer or something equally important. "You think falling in love with someone means losing yourself. Giving up who you are for someone else."

"Not falling in love. *Being* in love," I correct hastily and sip down the rest of the water. "Falling in love feels like jumping out of a plane without a parachute and somehow landing safely and then wanting to do it again the next day."

Jessie suddenly gets teary eyed. "So you admit you're falling in love? With Devin!"

She hugs me. It's lopsided and sloppy and so tight she's just about cutting off my air supply. I untangle myself from her. "Stop putting words in my mouth."

"Callie, I haven't given up any part of me to be with Cole," Leah assures me. "Cole complements who I am."

I say nothing. I just stare at her looking for signs she's lying. She's not. Damn her.

"I've only been here forty-eight hours, Callie, but you look like you're enjoying the life you've worked out here with Conner and Devin," Leah tells me.

"I do. I love it," I confess in an embarrassed whisper. "It's so fun taking care of Conner and cooking for them. I forgot how much I love cooking. I may actually take some courses. I want to learn how to make homemade pasta."

"And, by the way, you don't seem any different. You're still the same cantankerous, blunt freak you always were," Jessie says and winks at me. "Only now you have this warm smile on your face all the time."

"Well, except now. Now you look like you might throw up," Rose explains, her dark eyes narrowed with concern.

In a way I guess I can see how it might seem stupid. But then I remember waking up in our tiny San Diego apartment after our parents separated and hearing her sob. Every single night

I woke up for that short time between their breakup and our mom dying, I could hear her cry. Love did that to her. Love wrecked her. He never came to see her when she was sick but yet the last time I was allowed to see her, two days before she died, I remember she murmured his name as she floated in and out of consciousness on her pain meds. I never understood it before and it made me angry. But right now I feel like I would murmur Devin's name if I were on my deathbed.

"Because what if I fail? What if Devin and I fail?"

"Please." Leah smiles brightly and laughs. "Have you not met the Garrison brothers? They fail at nothing."

Chapter 45

Devin

Are you about to just storm right in there?" Cole asks me cautiously. "Because you look like you might and you don't need an arrest charge."

"I'm not going to storm in there," I reply calmly. "I just want to talk to her as soon as she gets out. Before Jordan's shitty captain can get to her."

"He's the best player in the entire NHL," Jordan mutters and then shrugs as I glare at him. "But let's just call him Shitty Captain anyway. I'm good with that."

"So, like, what the fuck is going on, Dev?!" I glance at Cole quickly. He looks completely pissed off and confused. I realize that, although I finally talked to him about the whole divorce, I never mentioned the Callie stuff to him.

"Devin and Callie are banging," Jordan pipes up helpfully as he hands both of us fresh beers and sips his own.

"You're kidding, right?!"

"You saw us kissing."

"I know. I just thought she was being Callie."

"It wasn't Truth or Dare, Cole. We're not fourteen."

He gives me the bird. "When did you start sleeping with her?"

"Long after my marriage fell apart. I promise."

"But Callie doesn't do relationships," Cole reminds me.

"See, that's the problem." Jordan nods and points at me. "This one here is hell bent on changing that."

"Wow…" Cole shakes his head sadly and sips his beer. "You'd have a better chance at winning a wrestling match with a polar bear."

"Thanks for the vote of confidence, asshat," I bark.

Leah, Rose, Jessie and Callie all emerge from the women's restroom. I start toward Callie but Jessie cuts me off by standing in front of me and putting a hand on my chest.

"Give her some space, Dev," she insists, so I just stand there helplessly and watch her make her way back to the table of NHL players.

An hour later I can't stay away from her. I've been watching her the entire time. She's been smiling and chatting with everyone but she looks guarded and tense. Avery is sitting beside her again and his arm is across the back of her chair again. And it's making me lose my mind *again*.

I walk up to the table and stand across from her. Avery looks up at me right away but I ignore him and wait for her to acknowledge my presence. She finally turns her chocolate-brown eyes on me, batting her long, thick eyelashes.

"I'm going home," I tell her, trying to sound calm and unaffected, even though inside I'm tense and quite frankly freaking out at the possibility that she'll sleep with Westwood again just to spite me.

"Okay. Drive safe." She turns back to Avery. I lean on the tabletop in front of her.

"Are you going home with him?" She looks back at me with shock. Avery also looks stunned. Neither of them say anything so I just keep talking. "Because if you go home with him, Callie, then we're really done. I won't play those games. And if you come home, you better be coming home to me. Not to my house. Not to my guest room. To me. Those are your two options."

I turn to Avery. "If she chooses you, I will fucking wreck you next time we play each other, so sorry in advance."

Before anyone can pick their jaws up off the table, I turn and storm out of the bar.

Chapter 46

Callie

Cole and Luc find me pacing on the sidewalk in front of the bar. They both walk right up to me and stand in front of me like a wall while Leah and Rose continue past us.

"I love you, Callie!" Rose is looping her arm through Leah's and wandering down the sidewalk back toward the hotel they're staying at. "Do the right thing!"

"That's Devin, by the way!" Leah adds as she waves, blows me a kiss.

"Did my wife just call my brother the right thing to do?" Cole makes air quotes around the words "right thing" and "do" while making a horrified face.

"Yeah. Sucker," Luc jokes back. Cole pretends to shiver in horror and then turns to me and puts his hands on my shoulders to stop my incessant pacing.

"He told me that if I went home with Avery then we were over," I explain in a helpless voice.

Cole nods. "Makes perfect sense."

"And then he said that if I don't go home with Avery and I go back to his house—where I freaking live—then that means I'm coming home to him and a relationship. Like I have to start dating him if I want to sleep tonight."

"If you're dating him, I doubt you're sleeping tonight," Luc pipes up with a goofy grin and his eyebrows wiggling.

"Shut up, French Disaster," I snap.

"Wow." Cole laughs in amazement. "I gotta give you credit, Callie. The brother I thought I knew would be hate-fucking his way through women for years after having his wife rip his heart out. But a few nights with you and he's not only willing to hurl himself back into a relationship, he's willing to do it with the most commitment-phobic woman in the history of the universe. You must be something in bed."

"If she's anything like her sister, she totally is," Luc adds.

"Shut up, French Disaster!"

"So what are you going to do?" Cole wants to know.

"Get a hotel room," I inform him quietly. "And then quit my job and move back to L.A. and change my phone number. Maybe dye my hair or get plastic surgery. Change my name."

Cole laughs and hugs me. "Or maybe you should do something *really* crazy like start dating a great guy who is crazy about you and makes you happy."

"I hate you," I tell him.

He lets me go and Luc comes over to hug me. I cuff him upside the head.

"Ow! What the fuck?!"

"We live in the same city now and if you hurt my sister, I will be able to do that to you every day for the rest of your life," I inform him and then hug him as he's still rubbing his head. "She better not regret moving here. You better be serious about this, Luc Richard."

"She's not just a roommate, Callie." He shrugs off his winter coat and then lifts the hem of his shirt underneath until his well-defined torso is visible.

I see the tattoo that he got a couple years ago, except now it's finished. Before, in the top half of the large, ornate fleur-de-lis was an intricate drawing of four boys playing hockey on the frozen lake in Silver Bay. In the middle were the French words for "More Than My Own Life," but the inside of the bottom of the tattoo was empty. I once teasingly asked him if he'd decided it hurt too much halfway through. Now it wasn't empty. There was a flower—a rose—inked in that space and the word *Fleur* in script at the bottom.

"That's about Rose." I blink and suddenly feel teary. "Fuck, Luc! That's going to be with you forever."

"So will she. That's my plan at least," Luc assures me seriously as he puts his coat back on, then gives me a wry smile.

My mouth hangs open as they both kiss my cheeks and follow their significant others down the street. I stand there alone, leaning against the building for support, and watch the snow begin to fall. I close my eyes and try to take deep, calming breaths. I'm fairly certain almost an hour goes by and I still don't move.

People come and go from the bar. No one seems to notice me, until Avery walks out of the bar with Chooch. They both hesitate when they see me.

"Hey." Avery smiles. It's warm, inviting and completely

ultimatum-free. He says something quietly to Chooch that I can't hear and then walks over to me as Chooch walks the other way and starts dialing his phone.

"So, you and Garrison have something going on?" Avery asks tentatively.

"Sort of," I admit. "It's complicated."

"Considering he had a wife a few months ago, I can understand that." Avery reaches out with both hands and rubs my shoulders soothingly.

"They broke up before I got involved with him," I blurt out quickly.

"I figured," Avery assures me in his sexy, soothing baritone. "You're too honest a girl for that nonsense. And Devin is like Cole—he's too good a guy for that."

I nod and almost smile. Devin really is an amazing human being. And he wants me. Me. How the hell did that happen?

"So are you going to Devin's house?" he asks me with a sweet, sexy little smirk. "Or are you coming back to my hotel room?"

Avery doesn't want me to change. Avery doesn't want me to be in a relationship. He just wants me for simple, clean, fun sex. Avery is the easy answer.

Chapter 47

Devin

As the clock hits two a.m., I let the realization hit me. She's not coming. I don't know if I should punch something or cry. I want to do both. I sit up in bed and grab my cell phone off the bedside table. I want to call her and scream at her. She healed my heart just to fucking break it again. Why the fuck would she do this to me?!

I close my eyes and bump the back of my head gently, over and over, against the headboard. I'm so angry I spend the next half hour just sitting in bed thinking of all the things I want to scream at her. *You're a coward. You just gave up the best thing that will ever happen to you. I hope you're happy alone. What the fuck is wrong with you?*

Eventually that anger turns to defeat. It's over. She doesn't want me. I pushed her too far and it's done. I can't be mad at her. I mean, I *am* angry at her, but I shouldn't be. She doesn't *have* to love me just because I love her. I just…God, I wanted her to so badly.

And at almost four in the morning the sadness and self-pity hit. What the hell is wrong with me that I can't get a woman to fall in love with me and stay in love with me? And Callie…I had no idea how much she would mean to me. Yeah, there is no denying she's gorgeous and I've always found her attractive, but I never thought she would be what I wanted in a life partner. She's bold and assertive and sometimes downright blunt and abrasive. I always wanted a demure, sweet, loving woman. But now…the thought of losing her…it's killing me. Callie is blunt but that means there's no mind games and her abrasiveness only comes out when she's protecting someone. She may not be demure but she's sweet—watching her with Conner is proof of that. And she's incredibly loving in her own way—she may not come out and say she loves you, but she takes care of you, which is proof enough. And in bed…she's so sexual and not at all shy. When I was younger, it was a little intimidating, but now…it's the hottest thing I have ever experienced in my life. I could honestly see a future with her. If only she wanted one with me.

My thoughts are interrupted by the sound of a car engine coming down the street. I strain to hear it and fight not to get my hopes up. It's Brooklyn. There's traffic all day and all night, but because it's a little less bustling than Manhattan, it does tend to quiet down at this hour. Still, that doesn't mean it's Callie.

The engine noise gets louder and then slows and idles nearby. It sounds like it's right outside my house. My heart is jackhammering in my bare chest. I stupidly consider crossing my fingers. I'm a fucking idiot.

I wait and…Nothing. No footsteps. No front door. Nothing.

After about five minutes, I hear the front door open. I have to stifle the impulse to yell YES at the top of my lungs. After all, she could have already been with Avery tonight. It's almost four in the morning. Maybe she's just coming to get her stuff.

I hadn't bothered to close my bedroom door when I got home. There was no need. I was sure she was coming to join me. At least I figured if I did that, it would make me feel more sure and calm my nerves.

A second later I see her as she walks right past her own bedroom door and right to mine. She leans on the doorframe and her eyes find mine. In the dim light from the lamp beside my bed I can see she may have been crying.

"Where have you been?"

"Walking around, trying to find a way to do this without dying of fear."

She wasn't with Avery. She didn't pick him. She came to me. She's picking me. Us. She wants us.

"Callie…" I whisper her name and smile softly as my emotions do a complete one-eighty. "Come here."

She obeys my command and walks into the room, stopping at the side of my bed.

"Get undressed and come to bed," I whisper to her.

Again, she does what I tell her. It's a beautiful sight, watching her peel away her shirt and her jeans and then her bra and finally her underwear. She's so fucking beautiful and sexy even now when she's so vulnerable. Especially now.

I slide over to the other side of the bed and pull the covers back, not at all embarrassed that she can see me naked now too. She crawls in and lies on her side, facing away from me. I inch closer to her until I'm pressed right up against her back; my thighs curve against hers and my groin is flush with her perfect, perky ass.

After a minute I gently push her hair up on the pillow and kiss the back of her neck. For the first time I notice a neat, tiny black-inked Asian symbol tattooed there. I never saw it before and I wonder when she got it.

She sighs and I finally feel her body relax. Her left hand moves to rest on top of the one I have draped over her midriff. I only let myself sleep when I'm sure she's asleep and won't disappear on me.

Hours later…I don't know how many…I wake up again. My arm is still around her middle, fingers dangling below her belly button, skimming the top of the tiny, narrow patch of hair that leads between her legs. I can't see her face but I think she's awake too. That hunch is confirmed when she gently pushes her perfect ass back into my growing erection.

I brush my lips against her neck, over the dark ink, and whisper sleepily, "What does the tattoo mean?"

"Family," she whispers back and curls her fingers around my hand at her waist and guides it lower.

I take the hint and slide my fingers between her legs. She's wet. I slip a finger into her pussy and she pushes down, tilting her ass back into my cock again. She makes a little circular motion with her hips, causing my palm to rub up against her clit and her ass grind into my erection again. We both let out soft moans.

"I will never get sick of this," I find myself confessing.

I push myself into her and slip a second finger inside her. I move my lips over her skin, trailing kisses across her neck and shoulder. She reaches back, putting a hand on my hip and grinding against me harder than before. I pull my fingers from inside her and grip her toned thigh, pulling it up and spreading her legs. This time when she pushes back against my cock it slips past her ass, toward her core and slides over her opening. Then she reaches down between her legs and grabs it, rubbing it and holding it against her wet opening. I clench and fight the urge to push inside of her. I want to feel more than just a little of her wetness on my tip. I want to be surrounded by it.

"I want to be inside you so badly, Callie," I murmur as my tip slips ever so slightly into her again.

"Condom," she commands, almost regretfully.

"Right. Drawer."

She reaches out, opens the drawer to the nightstand and digs into the open box, pulling out a foil packet. I take it from her and quickly roll it on. A second later I gently tug on her shoulder, trying to turn her around so she's facing me, but she resists.

"I want to see you," I tell her, but she ignores me and wraps her hand around my now-shielded cock, repositioning it at her entrance.

I don't know what her defiance is about, but I'm too overcome with lust to really push this right now. I'll take her any way I can have her. If she wants it from behind, so be it.

"Please just fuck me, Devin," she whispers, her tone dripping with need. How can I deny that? I push forward and my dick slips inside her. I groan as her body slowly makes room for me from this new angle. Once I'm completely inside her I start to move. It's a bit awkward but that just makes it impossible to go fast, and I'm okay with that.

I lift up on one elbow, place my other hand on her hip and rhythmically slip in and out of her warm, tight, soaking-wet pussy. The measured pace makes it so I can feel everything—every muscle she tightens, every shift of her pelvis. Everything.

I think this is the quickest I'm going to come since I was sixteen.

I move my hand from her hip to her clit and press down on it, rubbing it with my middle finger until she shudders.

"Yeah, just like that Devin," she praises and shudders. "Devin…Devin…"

"I'm going to come, Callie. I can't stop." I push into her—deep and hard—and groan as I come.

I collapse, my body pushing her over onto her stomach and I pump into her on top of her, my body flush with hers, a couple more times riding out my orgasm as hers erupts too. She comes on my hand, the only thing wedged between her and the mattress.

"The monkey sex better not stop just because we're…a couple," she cautions into the pillow.

"Monkey sex?" I repeat, confused. "Why do you always call sex monkey sex?"

She giggles. "Not all sex, just Garrison sex. Well, and Luc too. You boys are wild sex machines. Anywhere, any time, any way. It's epic."

"Oh, really?" I gently slide out of her and carefully dispose of the condom in the wastebasket next to the bed.

"Yep. Caplan consensus," she replies sleepily.

I touch her shoulder and gently roll her over and into my side. She's tense for a second but relaxes into me, her head nuzzled just above my shoulder on the pillow and her hand splayed across my bare chest.

"Well, then, you would have been crazy to walk away from the chance to have unlimited monkey sex," I joke lightly.

"Yeah, that's totally why I relented," she kids back. "The monkey sex."

I kiss the top of her head. "Whatever it takes, Callie. Whatever it takes."

We're silent for a while, both dozing off and almost drifting back to sleep as the morning light starts to filter through the windows.

"If you hurt me, I swear to God I will kill you with my bare hands," she warns in a tiny, vulnerable whisper.

"Fair enough," I whisper back and hold her tighter.

I want to tell her it's impossible to hurt her because I love her too much. But tonight…well, her being here, giving in to a relationship with me—that was victory enough. I don't want to ruin it by scaring her with the L word. So I keep silent and hold her close and fall back asleep.

Chapter 48

Devin

Bang! Bang! Bang!
Ding-dong!

I'm so lost in sleep I forget where I am. Who the hell in Brooklyn would be waking us up so early? Oh wait…We flew into Silver Bay last night for a quick Christmas trip. Callie groans beside me, rolls over and puts her pillow over her head. I snuggle deeper under the thick down duvet and closer to her warm naked body.

Bang! Bang!
Ding-dong!

"Fuck!" I groan.

"Do you own a shotgun?" Callie mutters sleepily from under her pillow. "Because we should invest in one. People like whoever is at our front door need to be shot."

I grin at the fact that she just said "our" front door. In the last two weeks she's been using the words "our place" a lot when referring to the Brooklyn rental and it makes me fucking blissful. It's even more appealing to hear her say it about my house in Silver Bay. I was worried that because this is a house I used to share with Ashleigh, unlike the Brooklyn place. Callie could feel uncomfortable but she seems to be fine with it. I take it as a huge sign she's really getting comfortable with the whole relationship. It's amazing and it makes me feel that way too.

"Devin! Get up, asshole!"

I recognize the voice instantly. Callie must too because she groans again and says, "The Winterhawks have a lot of really good players. They wouldn't even miss Big Bird if we shot him."

I grudgingly roll out of bed and look around for something I can put on. I can't exactly open the front door buck naked with a semi-hard cock. I find my boxer briefs and jeans from the night before and throw them on.

Callie doesn't move. I walk down the hall and down the stairs to the front door. When I swing it open, I see Jordan but also Jessie, Cole, Leah, Luc, Rosie and my parents on my front stoop.

"About time," Cole barks, but he's smiling as he pushes past me into my house.

"Welcome home!" Rosie says and kisses my cheek as she pushes past me, her arms carrying two bags of what looks like takeout from Rosa Linda's, a local restaurant we like to go to for breakfast.

"Merry Christmas!" Leah almost sings as she passes by me after Rose, kissing the same cheek.

Jordan gives me a shove and raises one blond eyebrow suggestively. "Late night?"

I glance at my dad and mom, who are right behind him, and blush my answer. My mom pretends not to notice and my dad chuckles but says nothing as they both walk into the house.

Jessie rocks up on her tiptoes and kisses my cheek. "Let me guess. Callie is still in bed?"

I nod. She laughs. "That girl will sleep for a week straight if you let her."

"I don't let her sleep much, trust me," I say quietly so only she and Jordan hear.

Jordan slaps my shoulder. "Attaboy!"

Jessie just shakes her head and laughs. "I'm going to go wake her up."

"I'll go with you," Rose pipes up. "She usually doesn't throw stuff if there's two of us."

The two disappear up the stairs. I pad barefoot into the kitchen where everyone has congregated. Leah is pulling take-out containers of pancakes, fruit salad, breakfast burritos and home fries out of the bags Rose was carrying and my dad is making coffee.

"I'm so glad you're all here for the second Christmas in a row! I feel spoiled!" my mom gushes and she cups my face in her hands and kisses my cheek. It's been four weeks since I last saw my parents in Brooklyn, but my mom always acts like it's been years. "You look good, Devin. Really good."

I smile at her. "I am good. I'm great. I'm…just really content, you know?"

For a second I think I see her bottom lip quiver but she pulls it into her mouth and nods. "It really shows."

"You look like you gained weight," Jordan observes with

a smirk. "You better watch it. A fat hockey player is a bad hockey player."

I flip him the finger. "I'm not fat, jackass."

"Language!" my dad warns.

"Callie is just a great cook. But it's healthy," I explain and rub my hands over my bare, muscular chest and stomach. "The trainers say I've actually improved my muscle mass. So up yours, *Big Bird*."

Cole and Luc chuckle at Jordan's expense.

"She really is rubbing off on you. Fantastic," Jordan replies dryly.

My mom puts a hand over my arm and I glance at her. She looks worried about something.

"Ashleigh has brought Conner by the house a few times since she got here for the holidays," she says carefully, her blue eyes clouded with concern.

My heart almost stops. "Is he okay? Is something wrong?"

"Oh, no, honey, he's great!" she assures me with a smile. "Your dad's been taking him out on the rink to skate."

"He's going to be faster than all of you lugs," my dad pipes up with a proud grin as he starts handing out mugs of coffee.

"Ashleigh and I have been talking," my mom continues in a lower voice meant only for me. "You know…while Dad and Conner skate."

She just stares at me for a long minute like she's trying to find something in my face—in my expression. I don't know what she wants, but I'm fairly certain I look guardedly indifferent.

"She's having a hard time, son," my mom finally confesses.

I stare at her for a long moment.

"I'm going to go find a shirt to put on," I say simply and walk out of the room.

I stand in the hall and try to not get angry with my mom. But I can't help but be upset and confused. My mother loves Callie. She loves Callie and me together. She told me that point-blank just a few weeks ago when I told her we'd decided to date. A few days alone with Ashleigh and all of a sudden she wants me to what? Take on responsibility for Ashleigh screwing up her own life? That's not my problem—and my mother shouldn't think it should be my problem.

As I start up the stairs, Callie, Jessie and Rose are coming bounding down them. I catch Callie's eye. She looks slightly sleepy but beautiful and happy. She loves being with her sisters even more than I love being with my brothers. I smile lovingly at her.

We meet on the landing halfway up, where the stairs change direction. She holds up a pale gray long-sleeved T-shirt. "Looking for this?"

I wrap an arm around her waist and pull her to me and kiss her. She tastes like toothpaste. "I was actually looking for you. Morning, baby."

"Morning, baby," she repeats back with a beautiful smile as she kisses me again.

When we pull apart, I see tears in Jessie's eyes and a big smile spread across her face. She quickly looks away and starts past us on the stairs. Rose follows.

"Get dressed, Devin, or Callie might jump you in the middle of brunch and ruin it for all of us," Rosie kids and reaches back to grab Callie's arm, pulling her down the rest of the stairs and completely ruining my idea of sneaking back upstairs with her for a quickie.

I snag the shirt from Callie and pull it over my head, walking back downstairs after the girls. As soon as I hit the landing, the doorbell rings again. I furrow my brow. Everyone is here. I have no idea who it could be. I glance into the kitchen as Callie is hugging my mom and then my dad, and then reach for the door handle and swing it open.

Ashleigh and Conner are standing there bundled up in their winter coats. As soon as I see Conner, my eyes light up and so do his. He raises his little arms and yells, "Daddy!"

I pick him up and hug him. His red winter coat is so puffy that it feels like hugging a stuffed animal. He gives me a quick peck on the lips and wiggles in my arms. My heart swells and I squeeze him. Past my shoulder he glimpses everyone in the kitchen. "Unkie Jordy! Unkie Lu! Unkie Cole!"

His excited little voice gets everyone's attention and my family starts spilling into the hall. I put my son down and he runs over and Jordan grabs him and throws him in the air before hugging him.

I glance at Callie as she wanders into the hall with everyone else. Her big brown eyes look apprehensive. I turn back to Ashleigh, who is still standing awkwardly on the front stoop.

"He knew you were coming home today and I just couldn't keep him away any longer," Ashleigh explains with a sheepish grin. "Sorry. I should have called."

"It's fine. I'm glad to have him, obviously. I missed him a ton," I reply with a small smile.

She hands me a little suitcase. "This is his stuff for the next couple days. And some gifts from me and my family for him to open on Christmas Day."

I nod and take it from her. She hugs Conner and tells him she loves him and to be good for Daddy. He promises he will be and asks if she'll be there when Santa comes.

"No, baby, I'll be with Pappy and Nana," she says to him, referring to her parents. "But I'll see you the very next day."

"But you're always here when I open my Santa gifts," he whines.

"You'll have Daddy and Grandpa and Grandma and all your unkies and aunties and your friend Callie," Ashleigh points out, and I feel uncomfortable that she calls Rose and Jessie Conner's aunties but Callie is just Callie. If only she knew how much more Callie really is. She *should* know.

"I'll walk you out," I suggest and shove my feet into what I think are Jordan's boots at the door. I grab my coat out of the closet and as I meet her on the porch, I glance back and see Callie looking at me nervously. Outside, the air is freezing but the sun is out and glinting off all the piles of pristine white snow. It makes my eyes instantly water. I lift a hand to shield them so I can look at Ashleigh.

"He'll be fine," Ashleigh assures me, talking about Conner. "If he really freaks out, just call me and maybe I can come by and hang out for a little bit until he calms down. I don't want you to have to bring him back to me."

I nod. "Listen…"

She looks at me intently, waiting, but I have nothing to say. How do I start this conversation? I scratch my head and realize I probably have fuck-me hair from the night before. Callie and I hadn't been able to stop ourselves the minute we got in the door. We fucked on the stairs, with her riding me. We got to the bedroom and fucked in the shower, doggie style. And then when we finally hit the bed, still damp from the shower, she sucked me off. Half an hour later, just before she succumbed to sleep, I went down on her and made her scream so loud I think she might have woken up the neighbors. Why do I feel guilty? Maybe I should have told Ashleigh about Callie as soon as we decided this was a relationship, but the last four weeks have been perfect and I didn't want anything to wreck that. I'm fairly certain Ashleigh won't be happy about this. Not to mention I know Callie is still skittish—I can feel it and see it on her face. She wants me—she wants this—but she's still terrified. I wanted to keep things smooth and simple.

"Have you talked to Andrew?" I ask, hating the fact that I have to say his name. "Is he here for the holidays?"

She shakes her head. "We're…not talking right now. I don't know if I want to work it out."

"Why?"

She hesitates, biting her thin bottom lip for a second. "The relationship started in lies. I lied to you. I lied to myself. I just…I regret it."

I swallow. Hard. She looks at me with tears in her eyes. "I should have tried harder with you. I should have worked at my marriage."

"Ashleigh…" I sigh. "Yes. You should have. But…you can't undo what you did. Or where it's landed us now."

"I know. But maybe we can move on."

"I did. I—"

"I mean move on *together*," she interrupts.

Her blue eyes are hopeful. I feel like I might throw up. She takes my hand in hers. Her fingers are cold. I guess mine are too. I don't know. I can't seem to feel my body at this point. I think I may be in shock.

"I don't want you to answer me. I know you'll tell me it's over. It's because you're hurt. I did something horrible to you. I get it." She takes a big breath and purses her lips for a second before carrying on. "But Conner deserves two parents who love each other. We were that. And I still love you, Devin. I know if you let me, I can make you forgive me. I can. Please think about it."

I open my mouth. I want to speak. I just…can't. She kisses my cheek, squeezes my hand and disappears down the icy walkway to her car in the driveway.

Chapter 49

Devin

Five hours later, I've just flipped on the gas fireplace and am alone in the living room when I hear the front door open and close. I smile and dart out into the front hall. I can't help but chuckle at how bundled up Callie is as she peels out of her big parka, mitts, scarf and hat. She hears me, turns around and smiles sheepishly. "You know I hate winter here."

"I know." I watch her hang her coat.

I walk over to her and wrap my arms around her neck. I pull her to me and kiss her.

"Didn't you get my text? I wanted naked Devin," she whines with a smile.

"Conner is napping upstairs but could wake up any minute," I reply apologetically. "Or else I would be naked and you would be too."

She smiles into the kiss and it makes my heart sing and ache at the same time. She is not going to be smiling when I tell her about Ashleigh. I've spent all day thinking about what Ashleigh said. It was impossible not to. Now I wish I could just shut my brain off—by losing myself in Callie—but I have to tell her. She deserves to know.

"How was the mall with your sisters?" I ask as we walk back into the living room and sit on the couch.

"Cold. I almost killed myself on the ice in the parking lot."

We say nothing for a long minute and I just wrap my arm around her and enjoy the feel of her up against me as we both watch the gas flames dance behind the glass of the fireplace. The sun has started to set for the night and the room is in shadows.

"What time do we have to be at your parents'?" she asks softly.

"In about an hour," I respond and take a deep breath. "So…Ashleigh is having a hard time."

She doesn't say anything for a second and I can't see her face to tell how she is reacting. Her body doesn't go slack or get tense. "A hard time with what?"

"That douche she cheated with, I guess." I'm trying so hard to sound casual so it's coming out forced. Great. "And the divorce."

"Does she not like the settlement you're offering?" Callie asks. "Does she…not like the idea of living in New York?"

I pause. "No. I guess maybe she doesn't. She wants me back, I think."

"What?"

And there's the reaction I knew was coming. Her voice is pitchy. Her body tenses. Her eyes dart sideways up to mine and she looks completely rattled. She cares. Callie Caplan cares about me. It's written all over her face—finally!

"She asked me to give her another chance," I say, feeling sick.

"I see." Callie's face suddenly slips into a neutral expression. She pulls herself off me and slowly slides over to the other side of the couch. "Okay."

"Okay?" I repeat, confused. "Okay what?"

"Devin, she's your wife. She's the mother of your child. She's still in love with you." Callie's voice is weird. It's vacant of the usual warm tone and strong emotion it normally holds. It's almost robotic. And gone is any trace she cares about me—or anything else, for that matter.

"I didn't say she was still in love with me," I reply tersely and run a hand through my hair in annoyance. "I said she wanted me back."

"Same difference."

"Not really."

Conner's little voice calls for me from upstairs and the conversation ends there. I get up but hesitate. He calls out "Daddy" again and this time it's strained.

"Go to him," she urges. "I have to get ready for dinner at your parents' anyway."

"We'll talk more later," I say, and she just looks away.

I turn and take the stairs two at a time as Conner's call develops into a near wail. When I get to his room, I try to smile reassuringly at him. It's hard because I'm so incredibly tense from that conversation downstairs.

"Daddy!" Conner says and reaches for me.

I sit on the edge of his bed and hug him. "You okay, Con?"

"I was comfused," he says. He still gets his *m*'s and *n*'s mixed up. "I thought I was at Pappy's and Nana's."

"No, Mommy brought you here, remember?"

He nods. "Is Mommy here?"

"No, Conner. I don't live with Mommy anymore, remember?" I say. He hesitates, then nods. I pause and make a split-second decision. "I live with Callie now."

"Callie!" He sings her name and claps his hands. "Is Callie here?"

"Yep. She's getting ready to go to Grandma and Grandpa's house with us," I say cheerfully.

"I love Callie," he tells me as he untangles himself from his sheets and starts to climb from his toddler bed.

"I love Callie too," I tell him and grab his hand so he can't run to his toys and get distracted. "I love Callie so much she's going to live with me for a long time."

"For how long?" he wants to know, blinking curiously. "For a billion years?"

I chuckle. "I hope she lives with me forever. Is that okay? How would you feel if Mommy lives somewhere else and Callie lives with Daddy forever?"

He thinks about that, scrunching up his tiny little perfect face. "I wish we could all live together forever."

"Unfortunately, that can't happen, son," I say calmly and give him a small smile. "But you'll always get to live with me and Mommy, just on different days."

"When I live with you, I get to live with Callie too?" he asks hopefully.

"Yes. You definitely do."

"Yay!" He claps his hands and jumps.

I laugh and feel relieved. Callie has been so good to him—so loving and so thoughtful—of course he's okay with her being with me. That's all I can ask right now.

Now that Conner knows, I have no choice but to tell Ashleigh the next chance I get. That will put delusional reconciliation thoughts out of her head and hopefully change Callie back from the robot she just morphed into downstairs.

Chapter 50

Callie

The ride to Donna and Wyatt's place for Christmas Eve dinner is blissfully taken over by Conner, who is chattering excitedly about Santa and Christmas and Rudolph. I keep silent in the passenger seat and listen as he begins his own rendition of "Rudolph the Red-Nosed Reindeer." It hits me like a ton of bricks how much I am going to miss hearing his little voice on a regular basis. The snow is falling slowly in big, fat flakes outside. Not a storm, just a picturesque sprinkle to make it even more festive. I wish my heart wasn't breaking and I could enjoy this.

We open the front door to the Garrison house without knocking.

"We're here!" Devin calls out, and bends to help me get Conner out of his snow gear. I unzip the tot's jacket while Devin tugs off his boots. When we stand up and Conner is left in just his jeans, socks and flannel shirt, Donna is standing in the entrance to the kitchen beaming at us.

"Come on up here and let me hug you all!" she demands, and we climb the three stairs up from the entrance landing to her. She hugs Devin and then me, squeezing me tightly. For a second I wonder if it's wrong to think she's on Ashleigh's side. Conner hugs her tightly and then runs into the adjacent living room, where all the Garrison men are hanging out with beers in their hands and glued to the television as Wyatt shows them all the highlights he's kept on the DVR from the season so far. They're all joking and insulting each other's clips. Wyatt looks overjoyed. All the boys are having great seasons, even Luc since he was traded, and Wyatt is beaming with pride.

For the first time in my life, I feel like an intruder being a part of this. I'm not their friend anymore. I moved past that when I started dating Devin. And I'm not his wife. He has one of those and she wants him back. So now…I'm nothing. At least that's how it feels.

Wyatt jumps up as we enter the room. Conner runs to him and hugs him before running over to the couch and climbing all over Cole and Jordan, who are sitting side by side.

Wyatt grins at Devin. "Get yourself a beer and join us."

Devin nods and heads for the beer fridge in the garage. I turn to wander into the kitchen but Wyatt grabs me into a big hug first. "I'm always glad to have you here, Callie. And it's even more special this year."

I pull back and catch his eye. He looks so…happy. He clearly has no idea Ashleigh and Devin are getting back together. I feel an overwhelming need to cry but I fight it off. I just give him a tight smile and nod and head for the kitchen. Leah is hovering over a serving tray she's filling with steaming hot green beans. Rose is at the stove making gravy. Donna is peering into the slightly ajar oven door.

"Roast is almost done," she announces happily.

I glance through the opening off the left side of the kitchen and see Jessie setting the table in the dining room. I wander over to her. She smiles happily as I walk up beside her and take the pile of forks from her hand and begin to lay them out. She kisses my cheek and grabs a pile of napkins and begins folding them, placing them next to the plates. I notice we're using Donna and Wyatt's good wedding china.

"Are you and Jordan going to get wedding china?" I ask absently.

"Are you kidding?" Jessie asks back, laughing lightly. "He breaks at least one dish a week. He's a klutz. Besides, all our big family dinners will likely be here anyway."

I nod. That makes sense.

"What about you and Devin?"

I snap my head up and catch her eye. She's smiling lightly but I can tell she's fucking serious.

"Devin and I will never be married, Jessie," I respond in a quiet, deathly serious voice, and busy myself laying out the cutlery.

"Callie." She puts down the pile of napkins and reaches for my hand. "Talk to me."

I shake my head, refusing to look up from the pretty plates and glasses decorating the table. "It's not the time."

"Screw that. Something is wrong," she replies in a heated whisper. "Tell me."

I finally put the last fork in place and look up into her pretty green eyes. I've always envied that she ended up with our dad's eyes. They're this unique, beautiful mossy green color. I got my mom's brown ones and Rosie got an even darker version of that. At least Rosie's look exotic. Mine are just plain old cowshit brown.

"Nothing is wrong," I say firmly because it's the truth. A wife wanting her husband back isn't wrong. It's right. The vows finally mean something to Ashleigh and she wants to fix her mess. That's what she should have done months ago. "It's fine. But you know me—I'm not the marrying type."

She isn't buying it. Sometimes I wish I wasn't so close to my sisters. It would make lying easier. She won't let go of my hand.

"This afternoon at the mall you would have been okay with that china joke. So what is going on?"

"I'm never going to marry Devin," I repeat and the words feel like razor blades slicing through the center of my heart as I speak them. "He's married and he's going to stay married and that's okay. That's how it should be."

She stares at me in complete stunned silence for a long minute.

"Are you drunk?" she says finally, her voice dripping sarcasm.

Before I can answer, Donna calls out that dinner is ready. The boys jump up from the living room and scurry toward us like starving wildlife. Jessie and I jump back to let them push and shove for places at the table.

I feel a tug on my pant leg and look down. Conner is peering up at me. "Can I sit next to you, Callie?"

I should say no. I have to say no. He has to detach himself

from me. I'm not going to be around like I was before. I glance at the table. Devin has left two spots next to him open. I pick Conner up and carry him around the table.

"How about you sit next to Daddy and I sit on the other side next to Daddy?" I ask as Leah and Rose start placing piping hot bowls of green beans and roasted potatoes and baby carrots with dill on the table.

Wyatt is in the other room carving the roast beef under Donna's watchful eye. I plop Conner down in the chair to the left of Devin, who has already put his booster seat on it. He looks up at me and scrunches his perfect little face in disappointment.

"You don't want to sit next to me?"

"Of course I do, but you should sit next to Daddy and Unkie Jordy," I say. "They're your family."

Devin shoots me a strange look at that and I see Jordan's blue eyes glance up too. Jessie is flat-out glaring at me as she slips into the chair at the end of the table next to Jordan.

"Hey, Con, if you sit next to me, I'll eat your carrots for you," Jordan promises in a low but totally audible whisper.

"Okay. I hate carwits," he announces firmly in his baby accent.

Everyone chuckles as Wyatt brings a platter full of perfectly cooked roast beef into the dining room. I slip into the seat next to Devin and take the bowl of green beans from him, using the serving fork to place a few on my plate before passing the dish on to Wyatt, who is sitting at the end beside me.

"You're family too," Devin says in a soft whisper as he hands me the dish of carrots.

I say nothing.

Dinner is upbeat for the most part. Devin keeps staring at me, though, and every glance makes it harder and harder to breathe. As soon as we start clearing the plates after dinner, I excuse myself to use the bathroom. I pace the small room for a moment before splashing some water on my face.

When I pull the door open, Devin is standing in the hallway waiting for me.

"I told him," Devin says flatly. "Earlier today. I explained to Conner that you're going to be with me. Living with me. Forever."

"What?!" I feel like he's suddenly the biggest idiot in the universe. "Are you trying to fuck your kid up? Because if so, good job!"

He shakes his head and points down the hall. Conner's giggles can be heard clearly from here. "Does that sound traumatized to you?"

"You're going to confuse him, Devin!" I blurt out.

"So you're not in this forever?" he questions, his eyes narrowing accusingly. "What's going on, Callie?"

"Your wife wants you back," I remind him. "That's what's going on."

"Here's a news flash that shouldn't be a news flash," he snaps, and I can literally see the anger bubbling up in him. "I don't care what my wife wants."

"Don't be petty about this, Devin," I say in a voice that has the slightest hint of a wobble, damn it. "Put your wounded ego aside and think about this. You made a vow to this woman. She wants to honor it. You might not think this is cheating, and it wasn't when she wanted the marriage over too, but now she doesn't. Now you're the only one keeping your family apart."

I push past him and march back into the living room.

I avoid him the rest of the time we're at Wyatt and Donna's. I don't want to finish this conversation in front of our families. I was on the verge of tears and they did not need to see that.

Conner falls asleep in the car as we drive home. Devin is silent but it's a tense, angry silence. I try to ignore it and stare at the snowbanks gleaming in the moonlight as we drive along. When we pull into the driveway, Devin starts to gently undo Conner from his car seat and I head to the house to unlock the front door.

He walks past me with his beautiful, sleeping angel in his arms and I feel a lump in my throat. I wish Conner were mine. Ours. I always knew I wanted children; I just never thought I'd want a man to have them with. But…that changed. I had begun to fantasize about having a baby with Devin. Our own child. There'll never be an "ours" now.

He heads up the stairs with his son and I follow but turn left into the guest room where my luggage is already waiting, still packed. I sit on the edge of the bed and stare at my hands in my lap. I wish I'd never agreed to come home with him for Christmas. I wish I had never agreed to date him. I wish I had never agreed to work on this show in New York. I wish had never even met the Garrisons. I wish I had never even been born. I wish…

"We need to talk." His voice is low and even.

I look up and he's standing with his arms crossed in the

doorframe. The light from the hall is framing his silhouette, which is taking up the entire doorway.

"Did he wake up or is he still sleeping?" I ask softly and stand up.

"Sleeping," he says before adding, "What the fuck is going on with you?"

"Close the door."

He hesitates but does what I say. I walk up to him and without a word I just grab his face in my hands and kiss him with every emotion brewing in my heart. It's the most intense kiss I have ever given anyone in my entire life. It embodies everything I ever felt for him and everything I'll never get to feel.

His response is swift and complete. He grabs my waist and pulls me to him roughly and pushes his tongue into my mouth and attacks me with just as much passion. I'm overwhelmed by the need to have him—be close to him—just one more time. I know it's the worst possible idea. I know it will make this that much more impossible, but I can't stop. I can't deny myself. I *need* him.

I start undoing his pants. He starts undressing me too and within minutes we're both standing there in the semi-dark naked, still kissing and groping each other. I turn us and lean my back against the wall and then pull him against me. His bare skin against my bare skin is warm and smooth and makes me dizzy with lust.

I suck greedily on his neck as he scoops up my left thigh and hitches it over his hip. He pushes his pelvis into me, his solid dick slipping across my wet slit. Oh fuck, I want him. Right now. Like this.

I push down on him and his tip slips into me. His body trembles as he fights the urge to push deeper. I bite my lip to keep myself from telling him to just do it. Take me. Fuck protection.

If this were twenty-four hours ago, I could have said it and it would have been okay. If I got pregnant twenty-four hours ago, I would have been shocked and scared but I would have felt, without a doubt, that it would end up okay. Because twenty-four hours ago I would have been spending my life with this man. But now…Ashleigh had taken that option away.

"I want you too, but we…"

"I know," he says in a husky thick voice. He bends down and picks up his pants and digs through his pockets. A second later the condom is covering him and this time I push down on him all the way as our lips meet in another fiery kiss.

He pushes into me slowly but it's clear I'm soaking wet and completely ready for him, so as soon as he's completely buried he starts thrusting fast and hard. I can't do much more than balance on one foot as he holds my other leg up around his waist and presses me into the wall.

He breaks our endless kiss and pulls back slightly. Our eyes lock on each other. He keeps pumping into me, his full, gorgeous lips slightly open. And I see it. The look on his face—the look that says he wants me. He needs me. He *loves* me. I know I'm mirroring it and I fight the urge to turn away and hide. I keep one hand wrapped around his shoulders and move the other to his cheek, cupping it softly. He pushes into it. I feel his five o'clock shadow tickle my palm.

"Devin…" I whisper and tilt my pelvis. I start to feel that euphoric feeling pooling in my abdomen.

"You're so beautiful," he whispers, his dark eyes still focused on mine. "Callie, I love you so much."

"Devin," I pant out his name again. "Please…"

I want to say please stop. Please stop loving me. This is too hard. It's just going to hurt more. But words are unreachable as my orgasm starts. I break the stare and drop my head back against the wall behind me. My eyes close as that euphoria explodes, rippling through me, making my knees weak. Devin grabs the back of my other thigh and wraps it around his back. The only thing holding me up now is the wall and Devin. I quiver and shake as he grunts and gasps and explodes into me, slamming me back against the wall one more time.

We stay there, me wrapped around him up against the wall and him leaning into me, for minute after minute. We're both breathing hard but not saying a word. Finally his hands move from under my thighs and I put my feet down on the floor again.

He pulls back and brushes his lips against mine. "Come to the master bedroom with me," he whispers. "It's okay. I promise."

"It's not," I argue back. "Not on Christmas. He'll be up at the crack of dawn. Let him adjust bit by bit."

"I don't sleep well without you," he mumbles back, resting his head on my shoulder.

"You'll be okay, Devin. I promise," I say solemnly and mean that in ways he does not understand.

He pulls back and kisses my lips softly before turning and

pulling the condom off. He tosses it into the plastic trashcan by the desk in the corner of the room and pulls on his jeans and underwear. Gathering the rest of his discarded clothes, he kisses me again.

"We still need to talk about all this," Devin says firmly. "I'm not keeping my family apart, Callie. At least I didn't think I was. I thought I was starting a new one—the right one—with someone who wanted it too."

I swallow and stare at my clothes scattered around my feet.

He lets out a frustrated huff of breath. "I know you hate ultimatums, Callie, but at some point you have to give me another sign that you're still in this too."

With that, he opens the door and slips into the hallway, closing it behind him.

I sink to the floor and cover my face with my hands, fighting the devastatingly powerful urge to cry. I don't cry. I won't cry. I can't.

A little while later, when I'm sure I can control my emotions and I'm sure Devin is fast asleep, I put my clothes back on and grab my suitcase. I make a careful, silent descent down the stairs and out the front door.

Chapter 51

Callie

I'm exhausted. I'd walked the ten minutes it took to get from Devin's house to Jordan's last night, by myself in the pitch-black tranquil Silver Bay night. It was freezing and I couldn't feel my fingers by the time I opened the door to the apartment Jordan built last summer in the renovated barn. I sat on the couch staring at nothing for I don't know how long and then I'd moved to my bedroom and stared at the ceiling until the sun came up. My eyes had continually watered but I refused to give in to tears. I did this to myself. I would not become one of those sad, lovesick, pathetic messes both Jessie and Rose had turned into thanks to Luc and Jordan. I didn't deserve the chance to cry. I did this to myself. I never should have let myself care. I knew this was going to happen. Maybe not Ashleigh, but something or someone would make him leave me. It always happened to me. My parents, my grand-mother—everyone left. He was bound to do the same.

This morning, as soon as I know they're awake, I walk into

Jessie and Jordan's kitchen. They're sitting across from each other at the kitchen table and both look stunned to see me.

"Devin and I are ending things," I announce, my voice oddly calm. "I'm grabbing a flight back to New York this afternoon."

I turn and leave, marching across the snowy ground back to the barn. Jessie chases after me in her slippers and robe. "Callie, talk to me. Now!"

I open my mouth to speak but I can't. So I shake my head and run up the stairs to the apartment and stumble into my bedroom and slam the door. My chest hurts so much I think I might die. I wish I would die. Tears fill my eyes but I refuse to let them fall. Why the fuck did I ever break all my rules for Devin? Why? What the fuck was I thinking? I'm an idiot. I deserve this.

Jessie barges right into the room and sits down next to me on the bed.

"Ashleigh wants him back. She's his wife. I'm not. I'm giving him back," I blurt out and my stupid voice cracks. She just grabs me and pulls me into a hug without saying a word.

I wiggle out of the hug when I realize it's just going to make me cry. She gives me such a sad, disappointed look. "I can't believe he wants to give her another chance after what she did."

I sniff. "He should. It's the right thing to do. I'm just…"

I was going to say, "I'm just a fling," but before I can finish the sentence Jessie does. "You're the best thing that ever happened to him. I know he knows that."

"I'll take the train to Boston. I could only get a flight from

Boston to New York—there aren't any leaving from here today—so if you could drive me to the train station, I'd appreciate it," I say and she nods. "Thanks."

She looks almost as sad as I feel as she stands and walks to the door. "I'll be back in fifteen minutes; just let me throw on some clothes."

Ten minutes later, as I'm wheeling my suitcase into the living room, the front door of the apartment swings open and Devin is standing there. His hair is askew and he's wearing his pajama bottoms under his black parka. I can see his bare chest under the parka because it's not done up. He must have literally gotten out of bed, found me missing and stormed over here.

"Where's Conner?" I ask.

"When I found you gone this morning and you wouldn't answer your cell, I called my mom and she came over to watch him and I borrowed her car to come find you," he says in a low voice, thick with anger.

I just nod. I know I have a passive, unaffected look on my face because if he saw how upset I was, it wouldn't help anything. He has to go back to his wife. I won't be a home wrecker, and besides, she's what he needs. She's a better fit.

"I want a woman who is strong, capable, independent and fiercely passionate—not just about me but about life and everyone she loves," he says in that same dark, deadly tone. "That's not Ashleigh."

"It was. It can be again."

"Shut up!" he barks and I bristle. He takes a deep, heavy breath and continues. "But I also want a woman who is fearless and trusts me and is confident in her love for me and my love for her. And that's not you."

He turns and walks out of the apartment as Jessie rushes back in. She calls out to him but he ignores her and continues down the stairs. She turns to me, her green eyes wide. "What the hell just happened?"

"Nothing," I croak. "Let's go. I don't want to miss the train."

I lug my suitcase down the stairs, still reeling from his words. As we exit the barn Devin's borrowed car is just turning onto the road and Jordan is standing on the porch glaring at me.

"I don't know what your plans are this summer, but if you're coming back to Silver Bay, you'll have to find another place to live," Jordan tells me in a deep, low, angry tone. "This is my house and you're not welcome here anymore."

Jessie erupts like a volcano. "You can't do that, Jordan!"

"I'll come for the wedding and stay at the motel in town," I tell her and give her a quick hug. "I won't miss it. I promise. It's going to be the best day of your life."

I mean that with all my heart. No matter how much Jordan hates me right now, he loves Jessie in a way that terrifies the crap out of me. When you look at him looking at her, he looks like he couldn't live without her. Like she literally supplies the light and air and warmth he needs to live. The look in Devin's eyes last night as we made love against the wall of the guest bedroom was almost that exact same look. *Almost.*

"I'm not going to marry him if you aren't here all summer to help me," Jessie announces in a shaky whisper as a tear trickles down her pale, freckleless cheek. "I won't do it. Not without you."

"What?!" Jordan bellows in shock.

She turns on him with heartbreak plastered all over her face. "I love you, Jordan. But she's my sister. My only family! If you keep her from me, then I can't…"

"He's my brother! She fucking destroyed him today!" Jordan yells back.

"Ashleigh did that! Ashleigh is *still* doing that!" Jessie yells back.

"STOP!" I scream.

Everyone turns to me.

"Jessie, you're going to marry Jordan. Jordan, you have every right to hate me," I tell them all in a firm but distressed tone as I straighten my shoulders, trying to look calm, sure and in control, and everything I am not. "Devin *will* get over this and he *will* be fine. I promise you that. In the end, we'll both be better off."

Jordan takes a step toward me, shaking his head. His blue eyes have gone from menacing to disheartened. "It's ridiculous that I ever thought of you as someone I respected. You're a sad, selfish mess who is letting her own stupid insecurities ruin my brother's happiness. You should be pitied, not admired."

"Jordan!"

He ignores Jessie's indignant cry and just turns and storms back into the house. I grab Jessie's shoulders and force her to look at me. "You are going to marry that boy. Don't you dare let my mistakes fuck this up, do you hear me?"

"I can't believe he would be so cruel!" Jessie whispers.

"He's angry for Devin. He's a good brother," I tell her honestly. "It's amazing because it shows he loves Devin just as much as Luc and Cole, which means all that rivalry and tension we see between them means nothing after all. This is a great thing, Jessie. Please just cut him some slack on this. Let him hate me."

She takes a deep, ragged breath and runs her hands through her perfect auburn hair. Our eyes lock and she tears up instantly again. The look of pain on her face makes me hold back my own tears. I never cry when my sisters cry. It's been like that since we were little. When they lose it I need to hold it together. Be their rock. Get them through it; even when it is killing me as much as them, I can't let them see it.

"Let me leave so I don't ruin your Christmas completely," I say as I pull my cell out of my pocket and shakily dial the number for the one cab company in Silver Bay.

I can't wait to get the hell out of here.

Chapter 52

Devin

The doorbell rings just as I'm packing the rest of Conner's stuff into his little suitcase. I hurry down the stairs with Conner right behind me and open the door. Ashleigh is standing there smiling. For the first time in a long time she's got some color back in her cheeks. She's got on lip gloss and tight skinny jeans under a new white parka with faux fur trim. She looks pretty.

"Hi," she says shyly. "Is he ready to go?"

"Mama!" Conner squeals as she bends and picks him up, hugging him and peppering his cheek with kisses.

"I missed you so much, baby boy!" she coos. "I hope Santa was good to you!"

"He was," Conner confirms and hugs her hard. "I wish you were there."

My chest tightens with guilt on that one.

"Maybe next time," Ashleigh replies calmly and catches my eye. I look away.

"Hey. Umm...I need a favor," I say quietly as I hand over Conner's suitcase.

She looks stunned but nods. "Okay, sure. What can I do?"

"Can you drive me to the airport?" I ask hopefully and run a hand over my messy hair, which I haven't bothered to style. "My parents are driving Luc and Rose and I didn't want to squish in with them. If you can't, I can just take a cab."

"No, of course I'll drive you!" Ashleigh says with a bright smile. "You can tell me all about Christmas. I want to know how it went."

No, you really don't, I think to myself. Or at least I don't want to relive it. I give her a tight smile and a nod instead of saying my thoughts out loud. And then I grab my suitcase and jacket and lock the front door.

As Ashleigh pulls out of the driveway she peppers me with questions. What did Conner get? What did Cole get Leah for their first married Christmas? What did Jessie get Jordan for their last unmarried one? Did my mom make her pecan pie?

"Remember when you wrapped up that vacuum cleaner box?" She laughs at the memory and her big blue eyes glint in the sun bouncing off the snow and through the windshield. "And everyone was so horrified that you would buy me a vacuum for our first married Christmas."

"Yeah." I can't help but smile at the memory. "I thought my mom was going to slap me upside the head until she saw the car keys hidden inside."

"Remember as soon as we got back to our house the car was sitting in the driveway with a big bow and we took it for a long drive out to the middle of nowhere?" Her smile turns softer and pink rises to her cheeks. "And you convinced me to christen the car out on that deserted dirt road."

I laugh, remembering how nervous she was about having sex in the car on that deserted road. "Yeah, and you kept freaking out, saying that this is how people get killed by murderers."

She bursts out laughing. "Well, it's true! In the movies the people doing *you know what* in the woods never survive!"

I glance back at Conner, who is humming to himself and staring out the window, oblivious to us. "You're still alive."

We fall silent for a moment as we get closer to the airport. I can see the entrance just down the road.

"Have you thought about what I said a few days ago?" she asks quietly.

My heart fills with dread. I don't say anything for a long few moments.

"It's all I've been thinking about," I admit because, thanks to Callie's reaction, that's the truth. If it had been up to me, Ashleigh's request for reconciliation would have been nothing more than a passing thought, but Callie leaving me because of it made it impossible to forget.

"Any thoughts you want to share, good or bad?" she asks in a vulnerable voice that says she's terrified of what I'm thinking. "I can take it. I promise."

She pulls to the curb by the departures door. I glance out the passenger window and see my family is two cars in front pulling their luggage out of my parents' truck. I open my door and move to the back door, unhooking Conner from his car seat and carrying him to the sidewalk.

"Luc!" I call out and my brother turns. "Can you take Conner for a second?"

He nods and jogs over, taking him from me with a big smile. "Come and say bye to Rose, little man."

I slip back into the passenger seat and shut my door. Ashleigh is looking at me with an expectant stare and wide eyes. She has no idea what's coming but she knows it's big.

"I've been involved with someone," I tell her frankly.

She looks like she's been slapped but tries to recover. She swallows and nods. "Is it…I mean…I…who…how did you meet someone so quickly?"

"It's Callie," I admit without a shadow of guilt. "I've been seeing Callie."

Ashleigh's face drops; her glossed lips fall open. "Callie? As in *our* Callie? Caplan?"

I nod.

"Oh God," she says in a shocked whisper, but she's smiling. I'm completely confused.

"What are you thinking?" I can't help but ask.

She shrugs her shoulders a little bit. "Well, to be honest, I feel betrayed. By her, not you."

"Look, Ashleigh…"

"Let me finish, please, Devin," she insists and moves her hands off the wheel into her lap. "Callie was my friend too at one time. Or so I thought. So yes, it hurts. I feel betrayed. But…at the same time I'm almost relieved it's Callie."

"What?! Why?" I don't even try to hide my shock.

"Because at least it's not serious," Ashleigh explains with that little smile curving her mouth upward again. "I mean, we all know Callie is a good-time girl, not the settling-down type. If you were involved with someone else—someone who was actually in a relationship with you or wanted a future with you...well, then I would panic."

Ashleigh turns her body toward me and reaches out and places her hands on top of mine on my lap. I look down at her fingers as they curl around my palm and notice her wedding ring is still on—or back on, I'm not sure which. I wonder if she notices mine is gone.

"Devin, I have a different perspective now," Ashleigh insists, squeezing my hands. "I feel like I can learn to be happy. I can make this work."

"Can we talk about this when you get back to New York?" I ask, because I'm so overwhelmed with what I want to say, and what I need to say, and I know the curb in front of the departures gate is not the place for any of it. "Just enjoy the rest of your stay with your parents and let's talk when you get home."

"Let's have dinner at our place the night I get back, okay?" Ashleigh asks with a hopeful smile. "Conner would love that!"

"I've got to go," I say simply and see Luc walking toward the car with Conner. "Thanks for the ride."

She smiles brightly and nods. "Safe travels."

I nod back and get out of the car, helping Luc fit Conner back into his car seat. I kiss my son and promise to call him from New York.

As the car drives away and I wave good-bye, Luc stares at me.

"What the hell are you doing?" he wants to know.

"I have no fucking clue," I admit.

Chapter 53

Callie

Luc wanders out of his and Rose's bedroom looking disheveled and disoriented. He sniffs loudly and makes his way toward me at the dining room table just off the tiny kitchen. He looks down at my homemade blueberry French toast as he yawns and stretches. I point to the oven.

"There's more warming in the oven. Help yourself," I say quietly.

"Thanks, Callie," he says as he grabs a plate and opens the oven.

As he drops his giant frame into the chair across from me and reaches for the maple syrup, he gives me a soft smile. I take a small bite of my food. I cooked the breakfast mainly for Luc. I appreciate them letting me crash in their guest room, in the two-bedroom condo they're renting until Luc figures out more permanent housing, and I want to show my appreciation. Also, I miss cooking for people. I loved making meals for Devin and Conner.

"Why don't you hate me the way everyone else does?" I finally ask him. I've wanted to ask him for a while now. He doesn't glare at me or call me names like Jordan did. I think it might be just so he can keep from making waves in his own relationship with Rose, but I want to know for sure.

"Because I kinda get it." Luc shrugs and shovels a heaping forkful of syrupy toast into his mouth. When he finishes chewing and swallows it down, he continues. "I mean, growing up I watched my chosen brothers do and say the stupidest shit because of love. Seriously, Jordy lost his mind so many times over Jessie. And Devin wins a freaking Stanley Cup and he jumps right into a big serious thing with Ashleigh. And then Cole…"

Luc starts to laugh. "Cole was a total asshole when he and Leah broke up. He would mouth off to everyone. Tried to start fights in bars. Yelled at everyone about everything. Total nightmare."

I nod and try to envision that. During the six-month period when Leah and Cole broke up, Jordan and Jessie had already stopped talking, so I wasn't really around the Garrison family much at that point. I have a very hard time picturing Cole screaming at anyone, let alone his family or random guys in bars.

"I tried to avoid love myself," he tells me as I get up and go to the fridge to pour us both some orange juice. "I mean, I was in denial over how deep my feelings for Rose were. And when I realized how I felt about her, I panicked. Freaked out."

"But you never left her," I say.

"Nah." Luc smiles at something he's thinking. Something

intimate, I can tell. "Don't tell her this but…your sister owns me. I'm, like, totally her bitch."

I laugh out loud at that as I place a glass of OJ in front of him. It's the first time I have laughed since Christmas Eve. It's fleeting. My thoughts get dark again very quickly.

"But doesn't it terrify you?" I want to know. "The idea that someone could very easily hurt you?"

"No. For two reasons," he says simply and smiles this deep, sexy grin. "For one thing, I trust your sister would never do that to me. And for another, I'm not a control freak like you are."

"What?"

"Devin has been calling you Callie Control Freak since you were a kid," Luc reminds me as he finishes the last of his French toast. "And the thing about love is—you lose all control."

"I've always *had* to be in control," I argue back. "All three of us had to be in control of everything in our lives because no adult was there to do it for us."

He nods at that as he stands up and brings his plate to the sink to rinse the excess syrup off it before he puts it in the dishwasher. "You're completely right. But at the same time, Rosie and Jessie learned to let go of that closed-off, controlled mindset and let love do its thing."

He wiggles his eyebrows at that last comment and I roll my eyes.

Their bedroom door opens again and a freshly showered Rose comes sauntering out in a pair of well-worn jeans and a soft, clingy, crimson V-neck sweater. Luc's whole face lights up at the sight of her, his big brown eyes filled with love.

"Morning, *Fleur*," Luc says to her softly, calling her flower in French, a nickname that used to make me roll my eyes at the romantic cliché of it, but now I almost smile.

"Morning, babe." She smiles and winks at him.

My heart drops into my socks. They look so happy. I had started to feel happy with Devin. Because of Devin—but even though I was dealing with it, it still terrified me the entire time. It didn't seem to terrify either of them. I wonder if I would have ever gotten past that. Not that it matters now that Ashleigh wants him back.

Rose lets her eyes sweep over my appearance and then she sighs. "Callie, if you're intent on living your life without him, at some point you have to live your life without him. You've barely left the apartment since we got back from Silver Bay."

She was right. I had gone out only to jog or buy groceries. I spent most of my time locked in my bedroom—asleep or at least trying to sleep. The TV show was still on winter break so I didn't even have work to distract me.

"I have to go out, but when I get back we're doing something, okay? And sitting on the couch and moping is not an option," she says firmly.

I nod. There's nothing else I can do. I love my little sister but I don't want to hang out with her today. She's going to try to make me talk about it and the thought makes me want to vomit. So I shower quickly and leave the apartment before she comes back. Bundled up in a parka, a pair of giant winter boots, a scarf, mitts and a hat, I just start walking, wandering through Prospect Park and then down random streets. I find a movie theater and buy a ticket for the next movie and sit through some asinine comedy.

When I emerge from the theater, it's almost seven and everything is dark, just like my mood. I had turned off my phone and am not about to turn it back on because I know there will be a billion texts and voicemails from Rose—and maybe even Jessie, if Rose was worried enough to tell her I took off.

I start to walk aimlessly again until I see a neon sign and peek in a window to see a relatively full bar. The sign says Black Horse Pub and it looks like a bit of a dive bar, but hey—I suddenly feel like a drink…or ten.

When I get inside, it's definitely a bit of a dive but none of the patrons look all too scary. I sit down at the bar and the bartender looks up at me and smiles. He's cute with shaggy dark hair and a brightly colored tattoo sleeve on his left arm.

"A shot of Jack and a bottle of Sam Adams, please," I say and attempt to smile.

He nods and brings my order quickly. I down the shot and immediately order another. He raises an eyebrow but it's more like he's intrigued than concerned. His eyes are very blue and he's got a pretty little dimple in his left cheek.

Maybe Rose is right. Maybe I need to start living my life again. I wanted to be the old Callie again and old Callie would totally hit on this guy.

"Can I buy you a shot?" I ask him with a wink. "I don't like drinking alone."

Chapter 54

Devin

I'm sitting alone eating a box of takeout pad thai and flipping through the sports channels when my text message alert goes off. It's from my teammate Tommy Donahue, which is surprising.

Your girl Callie is at Black Horse Pub and she's wasted!

I read the sentence three times before it registers. Callie is drunk. Who cares? Not my concern. I text Tommy back.

Typical Callie. FYI, she's not my girl.

A few minutes later as I stare at what is left of my pad thai, with no urge to eat it suddenly, Donahue texts me again.

Dude, she's a little out of control. She needs rescuing.

I don't respond. I don't know what to say. My heart starts to beat a little faster as I think about all the things that statement could mean. All the very bad, dark things…But Callie isn't mine to rescue.

Then it occurs to me that Callie isn't the type who ever needs rescuing. Even Donahue should be able to see that. No matter the crazy situation she seems to get herself into, she's always in control. She's Little Callie Control Freak.

My text message goes off again and this time there are no words, just a picture. It's of Callie looking incredibly drunk sitting on the actual bar, her head tipped back with a hipster douche bag–looking bartender pouring vodka straight out of the bottle into her open mouth. His tatted-up arm is wrapped around her middle and his big fat hand is nearly groping her breasts. I feel nauseated and furious all at the same time. I can't dial Luc's number fast enough.

"Callie is at a bar called Black Horse Pub on Fifth and she's obliterated," I blurt out as soon as he says hello. "You need to go get her."

There's a slight pause as he takes in the information. "You go."

I want to reach through the phone and punch him. "Luc, stop being a fucking moron. Go get her! Something could happen to her!"

"Donahue already texted me, Dev. I told him to text you," Luc explains. "Tommy told me he tried to get her to leave and she won't listen to him. She isn't going to listen to me or Rose either, but she'll listen to you."

"Luc. No," is all I can get out.

"Devin. Yes," he responds and then hangs up on me.

"Fucking goddamn asshole," I swear under my breath as I storm into the front hall and shove my feet into my shoes.

Chapter 55

Callie

Callie! Callie, come on...please?" Tommy's voice is incessant in my ear.

Geoff, the bartender who is now finished with his shift and is completely focused on being my entertainment for the night, kisses my neck again where remnants of the salt he put on there to lick off before his tequila shot still remain.

"Callie!"

I sigh and turn my barstool to face Tommy and promptly fall off it. My ass hits the tile floor with a hard, painful smack. "Ow! Fuck!"

Geoff laughs and slaps the bar with his tattooed arm. Tommy bends and scoops me up under the arms, pulling me to my feet. I let my body drape over him. He tenses.

"Thanks, Tommy," I whisper in his ear and kiss his cheek, leaving my lips there long enough to get a flush. The kid so wants me. So does the bartender. This is what used to thrill Old Callie. I should be thrilled right now.

I try to turn and walk away but Tommy grabs me around the waist. For such a young pup, with a gimp knee, he's incredibly solid and strong. He turns me back to face him.

"Callie, you can't go home with that dude," he tells me in a tense whisper. "Devin and Luc will kill me if I let you."

Geoff stands up and stares at Tommy menacingly. "Dude, I was here first."

I giggle at that. "Wow. Suddenly I feel like a fire hydrant in between two Chihuahuas."

"Did you just call me a Chihuahua?" Geoff asks, unimpressed, but I ignore him and so does Tommy as he starts to pull me toward the table where he and his buddies are sitting. I don't fight him. When we get there, he drops me into a chair and I lay my head on the table to stop the room from spinning.

Tommy turns back to Geoff. "Dude, she's related to three of the biggest hockey players in the National Hockey League and they're coming to get her right now, so if you want to take that on, be my guest. But I wouldn't if I were you."

Geoff thinks about it and then shrugs and walks away.

"Wait!" I call out way too loudly, but he keeps walking anyway. I glare at Tommy. "I am *not* related to any NHL players! Those boys aren't my family."

Donahue smirks at that like I'm the most amusing thing in the world and sits down in the chair beside me, propping his leg with the knee brace up on the chair across from us.

"Callie, that dude was a sketchy loser. You can do better." He reaches out and pushes my hair off my cheek.

"Do you think I'm hot, Tommy?" I ask him bluntly in slurred speech.

He looks embarrassed by the question and his young cheeks flush again, but he answers just as bluntly. "Fuck, yeah."

"Well, I want to be kissed and no one has kissed me," I say and make a sexy little pouty face that, even drunk, I know turns men on.

Donahue shifts in his seat. "That bartender dude kissed you."

I shake my head. "Not really. I was holding his lemon for his shot in between my teeth so our lips touched, but that's not a kiss."

Tommy shifts again and blushes more deeply and smiles at me. "Callie, you're drunk."

"Of course I'm drunk," I reply and give him a smile as I lean forward and put my hand on his knee. "But even drunk girls deserve to be kissed."

I stand up, turn and drop myself down onto his lap. He winces and I shift to make sure I'm not putting pressure on his injured knee. I wrap my arms around his neck and stare at him. He bites his lower lip and takes a deep breath, holding it for a long minute as an internal debate rages within him.

But then Tommy stands suddenly and I'm thrown off his lap onto my own legs, which start to wobble. Tommy steadies me and calls out. "Devin! Over here!"

He's storming toward us, his light hair messy, his jaw set tightly and his eyes clouded with anger. *Please let this be a drunken hallucination*, I pray fruitlessly. He grabs my coat off the barstool a few feet away and then he's right in front of me—so close I can feel the heat radiating off his beautiful, perfect, sexy body. He doesn't look at me; he looks over my shoulder at his teammate.

"Thanks, Tommy," he says gruffly and grabs my arm. "You should be at home recovering from surgery, not out drinking."

Before Tommy can respond, Devin wraps his long fingers tightly around my wrist and pulls me out of the bar.

Outside, the air has gotten cold and the wind is blowing like a storm might be coming. Hard. Devin still hasn't let go of my wrist and he's dragging me toward a cab double-parked at the curb.

I want to scream at him to let me go or to go away but I don't say anything. I'm drunk. I'm weak. And the feel of his hand, even wrapped harshly around my wrist, is amazing. I missed his skin, his touch, his face, his…

"Get in the fucking car," he demands gruffly as he throws open the passenger door.

I do as I'm told and he slides in beside me and slams his door. As the driver pulls into traffic, Devin glares at me. "Did you kiss him?"

"Who?"

"Donahue. That douche pouring liquor down your throat. Anyone. Are you fucking someone else already, Callie?" Devin's voice is low and venomous.

"Are you back together with Ashleigh yet?"

"You were all over Donahue when I got there. My fucking

teammate!" Devin is yelling at me now. Loudly. Really loudly. My head hurts.

The driver's eyes flare in the rearview mirror, and he turns a corner too quickly and my stomach lurches.

"Were you really going to FUCK my teammate?"

"I feel sick."

"So do I," he snaps back and the driver turns another corner a little too quickly. My hand goes to my mouth and I try to focus on anything but the drunken nausea growing in my gut. "You don't want a relationship? Fine. But stay the fuck away from my teammates," Devin yells.

"Pull over," I tell the driver.

"Don't," Devin barks at him.

"PULL OVER!" I yell and he finally does.

I throw open the door and stumble out and manage to make it to a garbage can near a bus stop before my stomach lurches and I bring up the last four hours of alcohol. Oh my God, I wish I were dead. I think I may be at any moment now. At least I feel like I'm dying.

The wind is still blowing and freezing rain has started falling in thick, heavy drops. I'm getting very wet, very fast. My stomach starts lurching again and I feel Devin's hands on my neck pulling my hair away from my face and the mess I'm making. When my stomach finally stops once and for all, Devin is still there, crouched beside me, one hand holding my hair and his other rubbing my back.

It makes me feel better and worse all at the same time. He pulls me gently to my feet and I turn away from him, using the sleeve of my shirt to wipe my mouth. We're both drenched.

"Are you okay?" he asks tenderly, and my heart cracks again. *I'm not okay, Devin. I miss you. I feel like I'm dying inside.*

"I'm okay," I whisper back hoarsely.

"Let's get you back to Rosie and Luc's, okay?" he says, moving away from me and back to the cab.

As soon as Devin opens the door, the driver starts to complain that he doesn't want to drive us. He's scared I'll puke in the cab. Devin tells him there's a hundred-dollar tip in it if he'll just take us a few more blocks.

He nods and we slide into the backseat. The cabbie drives much more carefully now and my blurred drunken vision and my still unsettled stomach are grateful. There's not a lot of traffic this late at night on a Tuesday, so we get to Luc and Rose's rental apartment in Williamsburg pretty quickly.

A block away he stops at a red light and I jump out of the car. I try to race my way to their apartment but I'm still way too drunk and I'm weaving all over the sidewalk, which is slippery from the freezing rain. I feel a hand under my elbow and suddenly Devin's guiding me in a straight line.

"I'm not letting you fall on your damn face," he says almost begrudgingly.

Oh God, he must hate me. He must think I'm just a dirty little drunken bimbo who can't hold her liquor. Just some crazy girl he was stupid to ever get involved with. Who would want me? He deserves way better than me. Now he knows it.

"Stop." I glance up and his face swims into focus as he tugs me into the waiting elevator. He looks…broken. It takes my drunken brain a few seconds to realize I just said all of that out loud. "I don't think you're a crazy bimbo. I'm just...I'm upset. I'm hurt."

The elevator opens on the third floor, Luc's floor, and I wrench my arm free from Devin and mumble, "I have to go."

Then I promptly drop my keys. I bend to retrieve them and almost fall flat on my face. He saves me once again, scooping me and my keys up and leaning me against the wall. He's right in front of me now. Staring at me.

"You're not happy, Callie," he says flatly, his eyes hooded and sexy as all hell. "Look at you. *This* is not happy. Why are you insisting on being unhappy?"

"I wasn't happy with you either," I slur and sniff back tears. "I was scared. I knew you'd leave."

"I didn't leave. *You* left!" he argues, his voice rising.

"She came back."

He sighs and shakes his head in frustration. "You're drunk. You're not going to remember any of this in the morning anyway. Why am I even trying to talk to you?"

He guides me down the hall and leans me against the wall again as he opens the apartment door. I stumble straight to the guest bathroom and puke again. He holds my hair again as I pray to the porcelain gods. I have never been this drunk in my life.

Half an hour later I finally start to feel better. I'm still drunk, but the room isn't spinning and my stomach is done rejecting its contents, mostly because there are no contents left. I stand up and reach for my toothbrush.

He stays there in the bathroom while I brush my teeth, leaning on the marble countertop like I've just gone three rounds in a boxing ring—at least that's what it feels like. I brush my teeth twice and swirl a copious amount of mouthwash.

"You look like shit," he tells me flatly as he turns, pulls back the curtain and starts the shower behind him.

I glance in the mirror. My hair is matted and there's vomit in the ends. I'm pale, sweaty and my makeup is smeared. I probably smell too. I start to peel out of my clothes.

Devin watches me, his face neutral. I'm still too drunk to care if he leaves or not. Completely naked, I step out of the piles of my clothing at my feet and attempt to climb over the tub but start to lose my balance.

I am never drinking again.

Devin's there once again, holding me under the arms and helping me into the warm, soothing spray. I hold on to the tiled wall for balance and close my eyes.

A minute later, the shower curtain is pulled back, I feel a waft of cool air circle me and then his hands are on my waist. My eyes open. He reaches past me and grabs my purple shower pouf off the hook under the shower nozzle. I don't turn around. Not because I don't want to see his perfect naked body behind me but because I'm scared I'll lose my balance again.

I hear the body wash container lid flip open and seconds later he's washing my back in slow, easy circles. Foamy soap slides down my front as he pushes it over my shoulders.

"Face me," he whispers and I slowly turn. He steadies me with his hand on my shoulder.

He runs the soapy pouf over my breasts, my abdomen, my hips…

I let my eyes drop and run over the hard planes of his athletic body. His skin is glistening with water drops and it enhances the hard cut of his stomach muscles at his hip and the solid curve of his well-developed thighs. He's hard, his thick, long cock pointing skyward, but he isn't acting like he knows it. His free hand cups my cheek. I finally raise my eyes to his. We stare at each other. He leans forward and presses his thick, soft lips to my forehead.

He wraps his arms around me and we hold each other, the water bouncing off us. Thankfully, the spray on my face masks my tears as he finally pulls back and drops the pouf. Devin pulls back the curtain and steps out of the shower, carefully guiding me out after him.

Devin stands in the middle of the bathroom, soaking wet and gloriously naked. He turns off the water and wraps me in a towel. He wraps one around his own waist and then opens the bathroom door and holds my hand as we walk to the office and he lays me down on the futon, pulling the comforter up over my still damp body.

"I'm going to get you some water and an Advil," he says softly near my ear.

He starts to stand up and I reach for him. "Devin…stay with me."

I wrap a hand around the back of his head, my fingers slipping through his damp golden hair. My lips graze his and I feel him respond, pushing his lips into mine for just a second before he pulls away. I want to scream in protest.

"I could stay," he replies with a small sad smile. "I want to so fucking badly. But…you'll blow it off in the morning as a drunken mistake. And I'm not your mistake, Callie. I'm the best thing that ever happened to you. If you can't admit that, then it's over and it's staying over."

He tugs his hand out of my grip and turns and leaves the room.

That's the last thing I remember.

Chapter 56

Callie

I'm not sleeping. I'm just lying there in the fetal position in my pink sweats and my oatmeal-colored tank top with my head buried in the pillow. I did get up and shower earlier. Even washed my hair and styled it a little. It's the first time that has happened since Devin left my drunken ass forty-eight hours ago, so today is a victory in my opinion.

There's a knock at my door and Rose wanders in without waiting for a response from me. I stare at her through one open eye and she stares back with her dark eyes narrowed and her face full of judgment.

Still, I can't help but notice Rose looks fucking gorgeous. Her thick, straight, almost-black hair is shimmering down her back. She's wearing a crimson empire-waist minidress with a satiny white ribbon around her torso just under her breasts. Her long, lean legs still look miraculously tanned and her tiny size six feet are wrapped in a pair of amazing black patent leather stilettos, making her look taller and giving her calves a pretty curve. Her makeup is darker than normal, with smoky gray eyeliner and shimmery translucent shadow, and her lips are glossy and pink.

"You look like a fucking supermodel," I tell her in a croaky voice, probably because it's the first thing I have said to anyone all day—and it's after five in the evening.

"And you look like a reject from *Celebrity Rehab*," she counters with a wry smile. "You know we're having company in a couple of hours, right?"

"I know *you* and the French Disaster are," I confirm and sit up. "The only company I'm keeping is Ryan Seacrest on my TV."

Rose gives me a long, stern stare and then sighs dramatically. "Be right back."

I watch her disappear out my open door again and come back a few minutes later holding her laptop. "Move over," she demands and I slide over on the bed so she can sit beside me.

She plops her laptop half down on my leg and half on hers, and I look at the screen and see Jessie's face and the background of her bedroom in Seattle. Fucking Skype. I groan loudly.

"I love you, too, little sister," Jessie sarcastically says in response.

"I hate technology," I complain and cross my arms like an angry child. "I swear it was only invented so you two could tag team me."

"And porn," I hear in the background. "It was invented for porn."

"Is that Big Bir—I mean Jordan?" I say, not wanting to start a tirade because of the nickname. I always said it in jest but he hates me now and that means there are no more friendly barbs.

Jessie's pretty auburn head nods confirmation. I hear a door open and close.

"He's getting ready. We're going out with Chooch and Ainsley for New Year's," Jessie explains.

"I thought you hated Ainsley."

Jessie shakes her head and her perfectly tousled auburn hair cascades over her shoulders. "She hated me. But she's slowly gotten over it. She's even almost nice now. Besides, I love her boyfriend, Chooch."

"So…you and Jordy are okay?"

I see her eyes darken and she shrugs. "As long as your name doesn't come up. But if it does, well, one of us usually ends up slamming a door or sleeping on the couch."

I let out a gust of air at that. It's like someone has hit me in the chest with a sledgehammer made of pure guilt.

"Jessie, let him hate me," I urge quietly.

"No. You hate yourself enough for everyone," Jessie argues back with a frown on her perfectly glossed lips. "Besides, he hasn't gone through what we've gone through. Sure, he saw it, but he didn't live it, so he doesn't get to judge how you handle your life."

I don't say anything. I don't know what to say.

"But we get to judge it!" Rose adds almost happily. "And we think you're an idiot."

"Yeah. I get that," I tell her and roll my eyes. "You've made it perfectly clear. It's his *wife*. She loves him."

"And you don't?" Rose questions, eyebrows up.

"I'm not his wife."

"Look, Callie," Jessie starts, her voice flipping into a soothing tone. "Whether we think you are an idiot or not doesn't matter. This is your choice. It's your life. I can't make you fall in love any more than I can make you jump out of a plane or off a bridge. And I shouldn't be trying."

"She can jump off a bridge. I'll help her do that," I hear from somewhere off in the room.

"Jordan! Stop it," Jessie snaps and I see tears instantly fill her eyes.

"Okay, that's it." I sit up straighter on the bed and grab Rose's laptop in both hands. "Rose, give me a minute. Jessie, please put your fiancé in front of the computer and leave the room."

"What?" both my sisters question in shock and in stereo.

"Do it."

"I don't want to talk to you." I see Jordan's midsection float by behind Jessie as he walks by. She tilts her head upward and watches him go by.

"Well, do you want to marry my sister?" I call out loudly. "Because that's not going to happen unless you talk to me."

"Oh, so now you're not happy just ruining my brother's life? You've got to ruin mine too?"

"Jordan! I told you I'm not putting up with this anymore!" Jessie snaps and stands. Now our view through the screen is nothing but both their midsections until Jessie turns, and now it's just her ass we can see. It's perky and perfect in a pair of dark jeans.

"Jessie! Just go and let me talk to him!" I holler at the computer and nudge Rose until she almost falls off the bed. She stands up and huffs, but leaves the room.

Jessie turns and bends in front of the computer screen. "I'm sorry for anything and everything he will say to you. I love you."

I just nod and watch her storm out of the frame. Jordan moves into focus, sitting swiftly at the desk in front of the computer Jessie just vacated.

"Jordan, stop upsetting Jessie," I say sternly. "After everything you two went through, are you really willing to fuck it all up? *Again?*"

"She loves me."

"She loves me too, no matter how much you tell her not to," I counter flatly.

His normally good-looking face pinches up and he looks furious. He takes a deep breath.

"I know you like people to think you're a hard-ass bitch, and trust me, I used to believe it," he tells me and runs a hand through his short blond hair—a typical sign that Jordan is frustrated. "But you're fucking not. You're capable of loving someone. You love Jessie and Rose. You love my mom and dad. I think you might even love Luc and me."

I don't say anything; I just stare at him through the screen. He's right: I do love them. All of them.

"Do you love us?" he questions outright.

I sigh. I want to tell him to get bent. I hate sharing my feelings, especially with him. But I really want to make things right with him for Jessie's sake. "Yes, Big Bird. I love you, all of you. Immensely."

"And Devin?" he questions, his crystal blue eyes boring into me. "You love Devin?"

Fuck. I keep my face neutral and nod calmly.

He smirks at that, but it's not his usual cocky, sexy smirk. It's contemptuous and taunting. "Say it."

"Oh, come on. What the fuck are you trying to do here?" I ask hotly, quickly losing my patience. "Just stop upsetting my sister, for fuck's sake."

"Do you love Devin?" he demands angrily.

"Yes. Fine. I love all the Garrison brothers like they're my own," I snap, and I mean it but I wish I didn't. Jordan's such an annoying fuck.

"Bullshit." He almost laughs. Almost. "You love Devin the same way Jessie loves me, not like a brother."

"Nobody loves anybody the way Jessie loves you, which is why you are a dumbass for screwing it up," I respond instantly and I mean it.

He shakes his head, his smile confident. "You never said it. Say you love Devin."

"Are you high or just stupid?" I argue and I can feel the anger making my face flush. "I just said I love all the stupid Garrison brothers."

"Say, 'I love Cole.'"

"I love Cole." I roll my eyes. "And Leah."

He nods. "Now say 'I love Devin.'"

"No."

"Callie."

"What the fuck is your problem?" I yell. It's loud. It's venomous. It brings Rose rushing to the door of the room, a concerned look on her stunning face.

"Say it," Jordan says, leaning back in the leather chair he's sitting in and placing his hands behind his head. "It's not a big deal, right? I mean, you say you love your sisters all the time. I hear it. 'I love you, Jessie. I love you, Rosie.'"

"It's not a big deal, it's just ridiculous and I'm not a child like you, Big Bird," I argue back.

He chuckles. "You just said you weren't a child and called me Big Bird in the same sentence."

"Fuck off."

"Callie, if you say, 'I love Devin Garrison' out loud—right now—then I will back off. I won't bother you ever again. You can live your life alone, without my brother, and sleep with whomever you want. I'll set you up with all of my teammates. And most importantly, I will never say a derogatory thing about you that will upset Jessie ever again," he promises.

"That's a fucking lie," I retort and run my hands through my hair. I feel a wave of panic rise up in me and I don't know why.

He raises one of his giant hands like he's taking an oath. "If I am lying, may I never win another Stanley Cup again."

"Whoa," I hear from the doorway and look over to see Luc has joined Rosie and is also eavesdropping. "That's serious, Cal. He's serious."

I jerk my head in that direction and point, even though Jordan can't see them. "I said I love you all like brothers. Why the fuck isn't that enough? I don't hear you confessing your love to anyone but Jessie ever. Because it's stupid."

"Hey! Luc!" Jordan calls out.

"Yeah?"

"I love you, bro."

"Aw…" Luc bursts out laughing. "You're such a chick."

"I love you," Jordan calls out again loudly like he's almost singing it. I want to punch my fist through the screen.

Luc is still laughing. "Whatever. I love you too. You and your vagina."

I'm fuming. I'm so angry I'm almost delirious from it. "This is fucking stupid. You're a piece of shit."

"Callie," Rosie warns me. "What's the big deal?"

"Yeah, Callie, I mean like I said, you say I love you to Jessie and Rosie all the time and they're sisters. I just said I love my moronic immature best friend," Jordan states, and I see Luc flipping his middle finger at the laptop from the corner of my eye. "So if you love us like brothers, just say, 'I love you.' I promise I will stop hating you."

"I love you, Jordan, you stupid jerk-off."

"Great. Right back at ya, bitch," he replies with a sarcastic roll of his eyes. "Now say you love Devin."

"Oh my fucking God, you're a fucking idiot!" I scream.

No one says a word for a long moment. I take a deep breath and roll my eyes and try to swallow down all the emotions roaring inside me like freight trains headed right for each other.

"I love him."

"Who?"

"You fucking little…" My chest tightens. "I love Devin."

My breath catches in my throat. My eyes instantly fill with

tears. I feel like I might choke—like those emotions I swallowed down are actual solid objects. My heart starts to hammer. I might pass out. A sob breaks from my lips suddenly like an errant hiccup and I cover my mouth with a shaky hand. "I love Devin."

Jordan's smile turns from confident and annoying to satisfied and sympathetic.

"And there you go," he says, like he just solved a particularly hard sudoku or explained why the sky is blue or something.

I start to cry. I can't stop. And it's not a pretty cry. It's a full-on messy, meltdown cry. Rose rushes to my side and wraps her arms around me. Through my blurry vision I see Jessie pop into view next to Jordan on the laptop.

"I love Devin. I love him," I repeat in a stunned panic. "I love him so much."

"We know," Jordan says casually, not at all disturbed by my tears, which I want to find perplexing, but I am too much of a mess. "But he doesn't know."

"Why the fuck would you do this to me?" I sob as Rose pets my hair.

"Because I knew if you just said it out loud, you'd be forced to admit it to yourself," he says happily as he pulls Jessie down on his lap. "When we were kids and Jessie left me, I lost it. I ran from my feelings. I was too young to deal with it, but you're an adult, Callie. You've been an adult since you were a kid, thanks to your shitty parental problems. And adults face their fears and go for what they want in life. So fucking stop sobbing and go tell my brother you love him."

I take a deep, almost-calming breath and nod shakily.

"Go fast," Luc warns seriously. "He's supposed to spend tonight with Ashleigh."

My heart plummets.

"Not because he wants to but because *she* wants to—and because he thinks you're not going to love him," Luc adds hastily. "Callie, you need to get your ass over there."

I stare at nothing in particular and blink my eyes. He's with Ashleigh. I have actually driven him back to her. I thought I wanted that and I got it. I may have ruined my own life. Broken my own heart.

"He loves you too, Callie," Jordan assures me as Jessie beams lovingly at him and plays with his moppy blond locks. "And he deserves you as much as you deserve him."

"I am so going to have sex with you right now," Jessie announces giddily.

"Gotta go!" Jordan blurts out, grinning, and then Skype goes black as he logs out.

Rosie pulls me off the bed and to my feet. "Come on! Let's get you dressed and cleaned up ASAP."

I let her pull me to the bathroom.

"Are you sure?" I ask her when we're alone in the bathroom and she's pulling out my makeup case.

"Yes! Callie, he loves you. You love him!" she tells me urgently, her eyes wide. "I know why our childhood would make you believe unconditional love isn't something that happens to you. But it happened, Callie. You've got the chance to be loved by someone who loves you back and will love you back forever.

Go for it! You deserve to be happy, Cal. I swear to God you do!"

I take a deep breath and wipe my eyes. "I have to go."

Before Rose can put makeup on me, I charge out of the bathroom, out of my bedroom, grab my jacket off the coat rack and run out the door.

Chapter 57

Devin

I'm shifting from the ball of one foot to the other nervously as I stand in the living room window, waiting for the car service to drop Ash and Conner off from the airport. She told me to meet her at her place—our old place. I'd spent ten minutes trying to remember where I'd put the keys. It is weird being here without her. If I'm honest, it is just weird to be here in general. Ashleigh hasn't changed anything since I moved out—everything looks exactly the same but somehow it doesn't feel the same. This house is no longer my home.

When we bought this place, our first married year, Ash was so excited. She thought it was a palace. It had been gutted and redone with the best finishes like the marble counters and dark hardwood floors. To be honest, at first the space seemed a little cold to me, but I loved the fact that it made her so happy. The longer I lived in the brownstone, the more it felt like a perfect fit—especially after Conner was born. I loved to come home from a long road trip to a living room full of toys, and everything in what Ashleigh referred to as "chaos" because, after growing up in a tiny house with three other boys, that's what love looked like to me. It wasn't pristine or refined; it was sloppy, loud and real. Which is why I had such trouble in my rental before Callie came along. I hadn't realized it at the time, but just like Conner needed things to make him feel at home, I needed her. Callie was loud and messy and…Callie was love.

I sigh and stare at my winter jacket hanging on the banister in the hall. Tucked into the inside pocket are the terms of our divorce. My intention is to go over it with Ash tonight, and if all goes well, the paperwork will be filed by the end of the week.

I sigh. I still don't have Callie but that doesn't mean I should go back to Ashleigh. I try to push Callie from my mind just as a town car slows to a stop at the curb. I stride to the hall and pull open the front door, eager to see my son.

As the driver struggles to pull Ashleigh's three oversize, overstuffed suitcases out of his trunk, I march over to Ashleigh, who is climbing out of the backseat. Her head spins and I see a stern frown covering her whole face. Her eyes lock with mine and the disdain becomes mixed with relief.

"I've been trying your cell and you didn't answer. I thought maybe you forgot us," Ashleigh admits as I reach her.

"I have my phone on silent. We had a team meeting and I guess I forgot to turn it back on," I explain and dig it out of my back pocket. I see her missed call and shake my head, taking it off silent mode. "Sorry about that."

I lean into the back of the car. Conner sleepily opens his

eyes, says "Daddy" and reaches for me. I take him out of the car seat and lift him into my arms.

"A team meeting? On New Year's Eve?" she says, not hiding the annoyance in her voice.

"Yes. We're struggling to make the play-offs, Ash. Management thought we could use a bit of a pep talk," I tell her, trying not to be annoyed at her clear annoyance.

"Well, I'm just glad you're here now," she says and I can literally see her force her face into a serene smile.

She reaches up and gives me a hug, which is awkward with Conner in my arms. I gently hand him over to her and turn to pay the driver. She carries our son inside as the driver leaves and I haul her bags up the steps and into the house.

"How was the rest of your time in Silver Bay?" I ask casually as I carefully pile her bags in the corner of the hall next to the stairs.

She starts to chat about her parents, the snow, Conner's adventures on the outdoor ice rinks, my parents, and on and on and on. I'm not completely interested in what she's saying but I do appreciate having her to talk to. It's been so long since I have had simple, inane conversation, and I can't believe how comforting it is.

"So I thought I would fix us some dinner," Ashleigh says quietly. "Maybe watch a movie? I just have to head to the store."

I nod. "How about dinner and maybe we can talk after Con goes to bed?"

"Sure. Whatever you want."

Fifteen minutes later we're walking through the grocery

store aisles together. Conner, who is tired and cranky, is in my arms again, trying to sleep as he clings to my neck. Ashleigh happily pushes the shopping cart as she loads it with fresh veggies, milk, steaks and cheese.

We move into another aisle to grab some of Conner's favorite yogurt snacks and almost run cart-to-cart into Loops, his wife, Tara, and their son, Henry, who is cooing happily in his BabyBjörn strapped to the front of his dad.

"Devin!" my goalie says in a shocked voice.

"Hey," I say and feel instantly uncomfortable.

Tara smiles at me and gives Ashleigh a tight smile and a short nod. The two women have never been close, which has always bothered me. Loops is one of my best friends on the team and Tara is just a doll. She often coordinates events and charity work for the wives and I've never been able to figure out why the two don't get along. But I blame the tension as the reason Ashleigh rarely participates in the team's charity work.

"You two doing New Year's together?" Loops can't keep the disbelief out of his voice.

I nod firmly and smile as big as I can. "Yep. Just a lazy night in as a family. How about you guys?"

"Yeah, we're taking it easy." Loops nods and looks down at his perky, pretty wife who grins and blushes. "Tara is feeling a little nauseous."

Conner stirs in my arms and I pat his back to settle him down as I watch Tara put a hand on her stomach, and for the first time I notice a small bump on the usually fit woman.

"We're having another one," Loops says happily.

"Man, that's great!" I say excitedly and I mean it. I lean forward and give him a clumsy hug—as best we can with two kids in between us. Ashleigh plasters a smile across her face. "That's amazing, Tara. So great for you! Congrats!"

"Thank you, Ashleigh." Tara smiles appreciatively. "It's a little sooner than we'd planned, but we're just thrilled."

"We want three or four so might as well crank 'em out quickly!" Loops announces and laughs. Tara laughs with her husband, her face beaming.

I laugh too, but it's not nearly as merry. Ashleigh is just standing there with her overly bright smile.

"Well, happy New Year, guys!" I say, and they say it back, and we continue in different directions.

"Do you want spaghetti or penne?" Ashleigh asks as we approach the pasta aisle.

On the short walk home we keep our talk on anything but our encounter in the store with Loops and his pregnant wife. It's almost painfully obvious we're talking around it. When we get home, Ashleigh heads straight to the kitchen to cook up dinner and I deal with an overly tired, super cranky Conner.

He whines and cries the entire time no matter what I do. It's frustrating but at least it takes my mind off how weird I feel being back in this house. This house Ashleigh and I painstakingly picked as our dream house—the place where we would live, laugh and love together as we grew old. Once again I miss the rental brownstone I used to dread. I miss Callie in the townhouse with me bringing it to life—filling it with delectable aromas and wild laughter. Ashleigh just doesn't have the fire that Callie has. Ashleigh simply has a more restrained personality than Callie. I used to love how serene and mellow Ashleigh seemed, but now...well, I would sell my soul for a little Fleetwood Mac and errant cake batter all over the appliances.

"Ashleigh, do you have any snacks he can have?" I call from the family room, where Conner is whining and throwing his Duplo blocks at the wall. "I think he's hungry."

"Dinner is in a half hour! He has to wait."

"Come on, just some carrot sticks or something," I call back. "He's exhausted and probably won't even make it to dinner. Let's give him something and settle him into bed."

She turns to look at me from where she is stirring the pasta on the stove. "Fine. Fine. Give him a yogurt and some raw veggies. But now his sleep pattern will be messed up and you'll be the one who has to get up with him tomorrow morning. I need my beauty sleep."

She winks at me, grinning. I smile back and grab some baby carrots and a tiny yogurt cup out of the fridge. I try not to act shocked when I realize that her jovial comment means she expects me to be here in the morning.

Almost an hour later, I head back downstairs after putting Conner to sleep. Our dinner is warming in the oven and she frowns as she pulls it out.

"It's probably ruined now," she huffs as she brings it to the table. "Dammit!"

I start uncorking the wine and lean over and stare down at the steaks, Parmesan pasta and steamed broccoli. "It looks great. Don't worry about it. I'm so hungry I'd eat a horse."

She gives me a small smile but I can tell she's still bothered by it. "I think he might be coming down with a cold. He's been fussy for a few days."

"He'll be okay," I reply and the cork comes out of the bottle of Merlot with a loud pop.

She stares at me as I fill her wineglass and then she suddenly reaches up and presses her lips to mine. The kiss shocks me. My instincts kick in and all I want to do is shove her away—jump back like I've been assaulted, like her lips are causing me physical pain. But she's the mother of my only child, so I pull back and gently but firmly push her away.

"What was that for?" I can't help but ask as we both sit down at the table across from each other.

"For being you," she says simply. I reach for my wineglass and take a big sip.

"So Loops and Tara are having another one," I say as I cut into my steak, which is a little tough. "Henry is barely one year old."

Ashleigh shakes her head and frowns. "Tara is going to regret that. Conner was so much work once he was a toddler. I can't imagine having an infant to breastfeed, change and burp and deal with on top of that."

"I'm sure she'll do fine," I say confidently. "Lots of moms handle it."

"Lots of moms have dads to help them. Tara doesn't," Ashleigh reminds me in a low voice and it makes my muscles tense. "Mitchell is gone all the time."

She glances up at me and must see my disdain because her long face softens and she shrugs. "Maybe they'll hire a nanny. That would help."

"My mom raised all three of us and did just fine without a nanny," I counter quietly and chew on a piece of broccoli, barely tasting it as I swallow it down. "My dad was out working on the blueberry farm sixteen hours a day and she did fine."

Ashleigh says nothing. Her face is expressionless and the air in the kitchen is suddenly cool. But I'm not backing down. I know what I want from a relationship—from life—and I'm not ashamed of it. "Ashleigh, I want more kids."

She puts down her fork and raises her face to me. "Fine."

I blink. "Fine?"

She shrugs and nods. "Fine. Let's have another kid."

We stare at each other across the table. Her face is so stoic and resigned, like she's just agreed to live in Siberia for the next fourteen years.

"Ash…" I swallow and put down my fork and knife. "I wasn't asking you to have them."

Her mouth falls open but suddenly the doorbell jingles followed by a loud, hard thump of a fist on the door. We both jump.

"Are you expecting someone?" I ask skeptically.

"No."

We both stand and make our way through the house and into the front foyer. I swing the door open, tense and unsure of what will greet me. When I see Callie's tearstained face and giant, puffy parka over sweats with her giant brown Ugg boots, I almost smile. She's a hot mess and that's honestly how I love her best. But the fact that she is so disheveled and teary makes me worry something is terribly wrong with someone we love.

"Callie…what's wrong?" I ask cautiously. "Is everyone okay?"

It's a crazy moment where everyone I love flashes through my head. My mom, dad, Luc, Jordan, Cole, Rose, Jessie, Leah…Our lives—mine and Callie's—are so completely linked that if anything happened to any of our loved ones, we'd both be affected dearly.

"Everyone is fine," she says in a shaky voice and glances over my shoulder at Ashleigh. "But I'm not fine. I need to talk to you. Alone."

Ashleigh pushes me out of the doorframe and glares at Callie. "We're in the middle of dinner, Callie. Please leave."

Callie ignores her completely and looks at me. "Devin, please."

I open my mouth but nothing comes out. Ashleigh doesn't have that same problem. "He is *my* husband. Go find another man to be your bed buddy. We're working things out here, Callie."

"Really, Ashleigh?" Callie shoots back suddenly, letting anger slip into her vulnerable disposition. "How, exactly, are you doing that? Are you going to unfuck the accountant?"

"Callie…let's not go there," I say defensively.

"I'm sorry, Devin," she says, her big brown eyes wide and pleading again. "But she doesn't deserve you."

"And you do?" Ashleigh snorts in disgust. "You don't love him. You don't know what love is."

Callie straightens her shoulders and gives me a strong, intense stare I don't have time to even figure out the meaning of before she turns a hard, cold stare at Ashleigh.

"I know that he's the strongest, kindest, sexiest man I have ever met," Callie tells my wife with a hard edge to her voice. "I know he'd do anything he could to help me or save me from something. Even now after I fucked it all up, I know he'd be there for me. And I know that I would rather die than watch him suffer with a woman like you who has no idea how amazing he is and doesn't appreciate everything he does and gives to a relationship."

My heart is racing a mile a minute. I feel almost woozy, like I might pass out.

"I don't want to mess up your marriage, but I know this…" Callie smiles at me and her eyes fill with tears and then she turns back to Ashleigh. "I know I would never, ever have even thought of cheating on Devin. I know that I could spend a million nights alone while he was on the road if it meant having even one night with him when he got home. I know when I'm with him, I am everything I never thought growing up I would ever be—happy, content and loved."

I feel a lump start to form in my throat.

"Callie, you don't know anything," Ashleigh says, her voice high and grating like nails on a chalkboard. "You haven't lived it."

"I did live it," she argues back. "I lived it when you kicked him out. I lived with him and Conner. I fed them and I cleaned the damn house and I sat home alone worrying he might get injured in away games."

"And you made cupcakes," I croak out for some reason.

Callie turns her face to mine and she grins, a tear slipping down her cheek. "And I made fucking cupcakes."

"He chose me to live it with him. You were just there by default," Ashleigh says in an angry whisper. "And now I choose him too."

"I chose him all along." Callie turns her eyes from Ashleigh and focuses on me again. "I'm sorry I didn't make it seem that way. I was scared and stupid. But, Devin, I…I want to be with you."

I gently move Ashleigh out of the way and place my hand on the doorframe and lean toward Callie on the front stoop.

"Do you love me?" I whisper to her, my brain still reeling from the tornado of words and emotions swarming around me.

"Yes." She swallows hard and I see her hands shaking a little as she pushes them back into her pockets. "I love you."

"Devin, I love you!" Ashleigh says as she bursts into tears beside me.

I turn to Ashleigh and hug her. "Go inside. Go inside and wait for me."

"You'll make her leave and you'll come back, right?"

"Yes, Ashleigh. I'll come back. You and I have to talk," I tell her honestly and watch as she hesitantly wanders back toward the kitchen. I close the front door behind her and turn to Callie.

"Walk with me," I urge in a choked-up whisper. She looks wide-eyed and terrified but she follows me down the path to the driveway.

"Devin—"

"I don't want to make this any harder on Ashleigh than it has to be," I cut her off as we walk side by side, not touching, to the sidewalk. "But please know that if I didn't think she was watching out a window I would grab you and kiss you senseless right now."

"Really?" she says and her eyes fill with tears again.

She faces me and I turn and lean against the stone ledge that borders the sidewalk. I smile at her, my back to the house and Ashleigh's prying eyes.

"I was going to make sure Ashleigh knew we were over before you even showed up," I confess. "I have the divorce papers in my jacket inside."

"You should have said something; then I wouldn't have had to emotionally vomit everywhere," she jokes as tears stream down her face.

"Are you crazy?" I almost laugh and wipe her tears with the pads of my thumbs on her cheeks. "I needed to hear that more than anything in the world. I deserved to hear it."

She takes a shallow breath. "You did. I'm sorry I didn't say it sooner."

"You said it now and that's all that matters," I say and smile, my own eyes brimming with tears. "Now I need to make sure Ashleigh is clear that we have nothing left. Make sure she's okay, for Conner's sake, and then I'll come home to you."

"Tonight?" she asks meekly.

"Tonight and every night after that," I promise. "Let's get you in a cab."

She shakes her head. "I'll walk. I need the air."

"You better be in the house when I get home."

"I promise."

She steps away and the wind catches her long, crazy hair and swirls it around her pretty face. God, I wish I could kiss her right now. Kiss her and so much more.

"Callie," I say as she turns to walk away. "I love you too."

She smiles over her shoulder at me and takes a ragged breath. "You know what? I know."

I watch her walk away until she's completely out of sight and then turn back to face my soon-to-be ex-wife.

Chapter 58

Callie

It's the sound of the car in the driveway that startles me back into consciousness. My eyes fly to the digital alarm clock on the bedside table.

11:41 p.m.

I have been waiting for him for almost five hours. I had come straight to the rented brownstone, just as he'd asked, and used the key I still had to let myself in. I'd waited patiently for half an hour downstairs perched on the edge of the living room couch. Then I'd realized when I glanced at myself in the bathroom mirror that I was a bit of a disaster. So I went into the master bedroom and dug around for a hairbrush and washed my face and combed my hair.

Then I'd plopped down on the bed, which was unmade, and lay back in the rumpled sheets. I had turned my face to the pillow and inhaled the scent of him on it. God, I missed him. I missed this bed. I missed being in this bed with him. Naked.

I waited and waited and, as the hours passed, I tried not to let nerves and paranoia set in. He would come. He was going to leave Ashleigh. It was just taking longer than expected. He wanted me. He loved me. He would be here. I had fallen asleep repeating those thoughts over and over in my head.

I hear the key in the front door and sit up, my spine ramrod straight, my ears straining. I hear the door open and his keys drop onto the hall table.

"Callie?" he calls out.

I swing my legs off the side of the bed and walk out into the hall. As my bare feet reach the landing at the top of the stairs, I respond. "Up here."

His head flips up and his eyes lock with mine and then he starts up the stairs, taking them two at a time, and the next thing I know he's crashing into me, pushing me back against the wall behind us. His hands push into my hair and his body presses into me, and his lips cover mine.

I kiss him back with the same overwhelming intensity he's kissing me with. Our tongues push forcefully against each other but there's also an underlying tenderness in our actions, as he gingerly scrapes his fingers against my scalp and holds the sides of my head with his palms. I have my hands up under his shirt and my arms wrapped around his back holding him tightly to me.

I can feel his hardening cock against the front of his jeans, pushed up squarely against my thigh. He finally breaks the kiss, pulling his head back so he's half an inch from me, like moving farther away would be devastating. I know it would be for me.

"I'm sorry," he says and his breath tickles my cheeks and the bridge of my nose. "I wanted to be here way sooner but she…It was hard. And I wanted to make sure she understood everything."

"Is it okay?" I ask stupidly because no, it's not okay. It's the end of a marriage; it will never be okay. "I mean, is she okay to be left alone? Because if you have to go back…"

"It's not my job to help her through this," he responds and his big, warm caramel eyes are soft and slightly sad. "I told her to call Andrew and ask him to come over."

"You did?" I'm stunned.

"She still has feelings for him." He shrugs and I can tell it doesn't bother him at all anymore, which is amazing. "It was guilt and fear that had her trying to get me back, not love. I think she is starting to realize that."

His lips brush mine again and the pads of his thumbs slide over my cheeks, tracing the line of my cheekbones. He smiles. It's not his usual confident, almost snarky smirk. It's boyish and shy.

"I'm just glad you finally came to your senses," he whispers happily. "I mean, I wasn't going to get back together with Ash anyway but…it's nice to know my feelings aren't one-sided."

"You have Big Bird to thank for that," I explain and lightly scratch his back with my fingernails as I let my hands fall down to his hips. "He forced me to realize my feelings."

"Jordy?" He looks completely stunned.

"That giant doofus loves you more than you know. It's rather atrocious, actually. If I hadn't taken you back, he said he would make my life a living hell," I say, half joking, and give

Devin a small grin. "What he didn't realize was being without you was living hell."

Devin smiles and kisses me again. This time it's slow and methodical and he takes his time running his tongue over my bottom lip and slowly sliding it against mine as I open my mouth to his. He pushes his whole body against mine again, slowly and softly, and I let my hands slide down to his ass and cup it gently.

"I love you so much, Callie," he whispers hoarsely against my lips.

"Prove it," I counter hotly and move my hands to the front of his jeans, unbuckling his belt. "Please."

Chapter 59

Devin

She doesn't have to ask me again. I let her unbutton my jeans as I slip my hands under her tank top and push it up and off her body in one fluid motion. Her bra is a bright pink cotton racerback number with white polka dots. I run my hands over the fabric and lean down and kiss the swell of her breast that pushes up from the demi-cup.

Her hands push my jeans off my hips and they drop around my ankles. As I pull her off the wall, moving my hands behind her to undo her bra, she slips one of her delicate hands into the front of my Tommy Hilfiger boxer briefs and wraps it around the base of my cock.

"Fuck, Callie, I have missed you so much," I whisper as the clasp on her bra unhooks and I move my hands to her shoulders to pull down the straps. "Your fucking touch makes me insane."

I press my lips to the curve of her neck and suck on the flesh there. It earns me a tiny mew of pleasure from her. Her bra slides down her arms and she moves her hand from my cock long enough to let it drop to the ground. I reach up and cup her breasts, rolling her tiny pink nipples between my fingers and thumbs and tugging ever so slightly. She mews again. God, I fucking adore every sound she makes. I adore everything about her.

I kiss her passionately again. Her hands hook the waistband of my underwear and slide them over my ass and down my thighs. And then she starts to follow our discarded clothing, dropping to the floor on her knees.

Before I can speak she's got my entire length in her warm, wet mouth and her left hand is tugging gently on my balls. My eyes literally roll back in my head and I place my hands on the wall above her and let my head hang down.

"Holy fuck…" I grunt and resist the urge to push into her. I don't want to choke her, and besides, any more friction and I will explode. I don't want to lose it all like this. Not tonight. I have other plans. But, fuck, does she feel glorious. Her mouth starts moving quickly. Her lips tighten around me and her tongue swirls around and around the tip as she moves.

"Callie…I'm going to lose it…" I warn but she doesn't stop, so I use my hands to push off the wall and move my body out of her reach. My dick slips from her lips with a wet pop sound.

She looks up at me with a disappointed stare. "But I was having fun!"

I laugh and pull her to her feet. As I step out of my pants and underwear, I bend and push my shoulder into her abdomen, flipping her whole body up, and carry her to the master bedroom. She's giggling the whole way and smacking my ass in mock protest.

I flip her back onto the bed and she lands in the middle of it, her breasts bouncing and a giggle still escaping her lips. I glance at the clock. It's exactly midnight. Her eyes follow mine and she glances at the clock as well.

I yank my shirt up over my head and toss it on the floor as I drop down on top of her, pressing my entire naked body into her and pushing my hard-on into her leg. I kiss her wildly. She wraps her legs around my torso and pushes herself into me.

"Happy New Year, baby," she coos against my ear before nipping my earlobe.

"First of many," I promise and move my hands to her thighs, untangling her legs from my waist and then grabbing the waistband of her sweats and underwear and pushing them down her legs in a few short, erratic shoves. I get them as far as her knees before I give up and move my hand back up to her center. I skim my fingers over her opening—she's drenched. I groan in lust and she takes my hand and pushes it into her, two of my fingers pushing straight inside her. And now she groans.

"Everything about you makes me so fucking wet," she whispers, her eyes closed and her head tilted back. "I've dreamt about your fingers, your cock, your tongue...you make me fucking insatiable."

"I would lick you and suck you and finger you and fuck you all day, every day, if I could," I promise, sliding my fingers in and out of her, moving my thumb to her clit and my lips to her throat.

Her hips tilt up into my hand. I bite down lightly on her

collarbone. She grabs onto my bare ass with both hands, her longer fingers pressing hard into my flesh. She spreads her legs so they fall on either side of my hips and I glance down between us and watch my fingers slide in and out of her beautiful pussy, coated in her slick juice. My cock wants to be in there so bad it starts to ache.

She pulls on my ass and I have no choice but to move my hand away from her core to the bed beside her hip. I kiss her, slipping my tongue into her mouth and sliding it over hers as she tilts her pelvis and pushes on my ass, and my dick slips down through her folds. I feel her wet center perched perfectly at the tip of my dick. Her hands on my ass guide me into her.

She's so wet and so warm and so tight and I know we can't do this. We have to stop. She's not on the pill and I don't have a condom on, and holy fuck, she feels so fucking blindingly spectacular. I grit my teeth and fight like hell not to come immediately.

"Callie…I'm not wearing…" I grunt as I move my cock deeper and deeper into her pussy. "Fuck."

"I know. I just…wanted to feel it…" she pants back, struggling to keep her eyes open, her eyelids fluttering. "I just…it feels so good like this…"

I'm completely inside her now. My dick is twitching mercilessly, begging for the euphoric friction of a thrust or two or ten or a hundred. But I remain still.

"We can't…" I say grudgingly. "I want to. Fuck, I want to…but we can't."

"I know," she relents. "Not yet."

"You mean not until you're on the pill?" I ask, too scared to believe it means something else—what I want it to mean.

Her eyes open a little more and she gives me a look like I'm absurd and then it softens.

"No, I mean not until you're officially divorced," Callie whispers back and runs a hand over the side of my face gently. "Things are messy right now and I don't want to risk bringing a kid into our life until it's completely our life."

I blink. "But you would bring a kid into the world? You'd consider…"

"Not any kid, no," she explains softly, biting her lip like she's nervous. "But your kid, yes."

And then she tilts her hips and grinds herself downward. My erection responds to the friction and I give her a quick, hard thrust and then use all the willpower I have to pull completely out of her and reach for the condoms in the bedside table.

I'm sheathed in seconds, and just as urgently as before, she's taking me into her body. The sensation isn't as full but it's still fabulous. Everything about Callie is fabulous.

"Fuck me, Devin," she begs.

"This is more than that," I respond and take my first soft strokes inside her.

Epilogue

Devin

The NHL awards were long and although they had amusing moments I was itching for them to be over. Jordy was up for, and won, the Lady Byng Award. Our family is peppered throughout the auditorium—Luc and I are with Rosie and Callie and our team toward the middle of the auditorium. Jordan and Jessie are with the Winterhawks to the left; Cole and Leah are in the balcony with my parents. We all jump up and give Jordy a Garrison family ovation. He thanks his coach, his teammates, his family and "the love of his life and future wife, Jessie." I'm thrilled for Jordy but for a quick second I'm also a little jealous that he can make a public declaration to Jessie like that.

Later that night we all head to the club at the Palms, which they have reserved for players and families only. It's a catered event and we chat, laugh, and eat and drink. At nearly midnight I decide we should head home. My mom and dad had relieved Conner's babysitter hours before and said he could stay in their room tonight, so I was looking forward to alone time with Callie.

We hold hands as we make our way down the long, luxurious hallway at the Mirage to our suite. She's holding her shoes in her free hand and I've got the keycard in mine. I swing open the door and she kisses me softly as she slips inside. A few minutes later she calls to me from the bathroom. I walk in to find her lying in the enormous round tub brimming with bubbles.

"Get in." She smiles and winks at me.

I strip out of my boxers, the only piece of clothing I still have on, and slip into the tub facing her. The heat of the water stings a little as my cool skin adjusts but it feels delicious once I settle in. She turns and slides over to my end, leaning her back into me. I wrap my arms around her middle, placing my palms gently across her abdomen.

"Mmm…this trip is heaven," she says and shifts so her perfect little butt slides across my growing erection. We say nothing for a few long minutes. She runs her hands over my thighs in the warm water and I let my hand slide upward and caress her breasts.

"You naked in the bubbles is heaven," I murmur as I kiss the tattoo at the back of her neck.

As my hands move south, slipping between her spread legs, she grips the sides of the massive porcelain tub and slides herself away from me. She turns in the water so she's facing me now and then comes back toward me. I move so my back isn't against the tub anymore and she floats into my lap, wrapping her legs around my waist.

I run a wet hand over her hair and cup the side of her face as I guide her lips to mine. The kiss is scorching and needy. I could spend my whole life attached to her lips, with her tongue in my mouth, and it wouldn't be long enough. She presses herself against my cock and bobs up and down against it.

"Fuck…" I murmur into her neck as I suck the flesh there. "I want to be inside you."

"So be inside me," she whispers back and repositions her legs so she's kneeling on either side of my thighs. She tilts herself up, her bare breasts breaking free of the water, and I clear the bubbles clinging to her skin so I can wrap my lips around one of her perfect nipples. I feel her reach for my cock under the water and position it at her center before pushing down on it. Suddenly I'm surrounded by her hot, wet heat pressing in on me.

"You feel so fucking good," I moan and grip her hips. "But we have to stop."

She smiles shyly at me and rotates her hips. My dick twitches in pleasure at the friction.

"What's the worst that could happen?" she asks and kisses me softly, tugging on my bottom lip with her teeth.

"You get pregnant," I reply and slide my hands to cup her perfect ass.

She smiles more brightly this time. "We can handle that."

"We can," I agree and stare lovingly into her big brown eyes. "I want to handle that. But we have to break it to my mom that we're doing this out of wedlock. That should come before the pregnancy. Give her a chance to get used to it."

She looks thoughtful for a long moment as her eyes leave my face and stare out the window across from us. Then she looks back at me and smiles. It's shy, which is a new look for Callie Caplan. She bites her bottom lip as she slightly rises up and pushes back down on my cock. I fight the urge to buck up and meet her. We can't do this. But, fuck, I want to...

"Do you not want to get married again?" she asks softly, her eyes closed as she pumps me slowly one more time.

"I would marry you in a heartbeat if you wanted it," I reply quickly and honestly. "But I don't need it. I just need you."

She becomes perfectly still. I watch her chest move up and down and her eyelids flutter. "I want it."

Holy fuckballs, she did not just say that. I swallow hard as my heart starts to hammer excitedly in my chest. Her big brown eyes open and look up at me. "I mean...why not make it official?"

"I'd love to," I say in a whisper. "Are you serious, though? Are you sure? You hate weddings."

"I'm fairly certain I'll like mine." She smiles and lifts herself up and down on me one more time.

"You'll marry me?" I ask again in complete shock.

"Yes," she says as she leans forward and kisses me.

I kiss her back with everything in me and feel tears prick the corners of my eyes. When I pull back, her eyes are swimming too, but she's giving me a look of mock disdain.

"Relax, Garrison, this isn't going to be some romantic sappy affair," she warns me, blinking back her tears.

"I don't care what it is, as long as it happens. And soon," I reply and kiss her again.

"Well, I was thinking we do it tomorrow," Callie says with a grin. "But tonight you have to fuck me. Now."

I pull her close and push up into her and she moans.

Epilogue

Callie

I swear to God, if you two do not stop blubbering, I am going to slaughter you both," I warn them sharply as I stare at their teary faces through the mirror I am currently fixing my hair in.

"Oh, shut up," Rosie tells me bluntly, wiping at her eyes to ensure her makeup doesn't run. "This is a sign of the apocalypse. I'm allowed to cry."

"Thanks a lot," I snark and can't help but grin. I turn my focus back to my reflection. I have to admit, I get why they might be tearing up. I look fucking awesome.

The dress they'd helped me pick out was strapless, slightly off-white, with delicate flowers cascading down the front and around the train in chiffon and sparkly beads. There was a sash tied around the middle and I could have had it in any color—I'd picked apple, which is similar to the Barons red and gives the Vera Wang dress a modern pop that is so me.

We'd announced the whole getting married thing over breakfast. Devin had simply said, "Guys, don't make plans for tonight. Callie and I are getting married by the pool and we'd like you to be there."

Luc had dropped his orange juice on the floor. Jessie and Rosie screamed so loudly security came over to our table to make sure they weren't being murdered. Jordan choked on his eggs. Cole and Leah clapped. Donna started to cry, which made Conner cry because he thought she was sad. I even saw tears well up in Wyatt's eyes and he excused himself from the table, which made me want to cry like an idiot.

When Wyatt came back, he hugged me so hard he lifted me off my feet. And then he almost lifted Devin off his feet. After that the day had been overtaken by my sisters, Donna and Leah, who had traipsed me all over Vegas finding my dress, flowers and a ring for Devin.

I hadn't even thought about a ring until they mentioned we had to have them. So I'd picked out a simple, thick platinum band for him and spontaneously engraved numbers on the inside—the geographical coordinates for the barn at his parents' place. Where this all began so many years ago.

There is a knock at the door of the room we're hunkered down in just off the pool area. When Rosie opens it, Donna and Wyatt come rushing in.

"You're so beautiful," Donna gushes. "Oh, Callie."

She hugs me tightly. I hug her back. Wyatt clears his throat. "Don't blubber too much, Donna. You have to do this again in a month."

Jessie laughs. Donna lets me go and Wyatt steps forward and hugs me. He pulls back and looks in my eyes. "I always worried about you the most, but I don't have to anymore."

"Oh, Wyatt…" I hug him tightly.

"It's Dad to you now, kiddo," he warns and I start to cry. Full-on waterworks.

"Makeup!" Jessie yells. "You'll ruin your makeup."

I laugh. "Okay. Okay. I'll stop…I hope."

"We'll give you girls a minute," Donna says with a smile. "Devin and Conner are outside when you're ready."

My future in-laws disappear back out the door and I turn and stare at my sisters for a long time. We're all smiling from ear to ear.

"I knew when Grandma Lily died that these hometown hockey boys would infest both your lives again," I say, looking from Jessie to Rose and back again. "But somehow I'm the one marrying one of them first? How the hell does that happen?"

Jessie kisses my cheek. "You're just lucky, I guess."

I laugh, hug them both and then follow them out the door. Devin and Conner are in the hall in matching black suits with red ties that match my sash. They both look amazing. Devin's hazel-colored eyes fill with tears as he sees me. I jump into his arms.

"If you cry, I cry and then Con cries and it's a total mess," I whisper in his ear, cupping the back of his neck gently. "So suck it up, Garrison."

He nods and takes a deep breath. "You're the most beautiful thing in the world," he announces in a throaty whisper.

Conner beams up at me. "You're really pretty, Callie."

"Thank you, little man!" I ruffle his hair. "You look very handsome."

"Ready?" Devin asks and his voice is tentative, like he thinks I might have cold feet. Hell, no.

"Totally," I say confidently.

We decided to walk down the aisle together, with Conner. It just seemed right. We were doing this together—to become a family. I would never be Con's mother—and I would always respect Ashleigh's place—but he was becoming my stepson. I wanted him to know he was a part of this.

The ceremony starts off on the perfect note as the pianist plays my musical choice, an instrumental version of "Don't Stop Believin'" by Journey. Everyone laughs. An arch of white hydrangeas is set up in front of the waterfall and we follow the white carpet, sprinkled with red rose petals, past the rows of white chairs containing our relatives. Conner skips ahead waving to everyone excitedly. We go with the traditional vows. Everything else I want to say to him has been said or could be said in private.

Jessie hands me Devin's ring and Jordan hands Devin mine. My eyes grow wide at the sight of it. I had told him I only wanted a simple band. He got a band but it's platinum and covered in sparkling princess-cut diamonds all the way around.

"Sorry." He shrugs with a smirk, which says he's not sorry at all. I let him slip it onto my finger and can't help but gape in awe at how incredibly gorgeous it is. I slip his on his finger and he grins like an idiot.

"Kiss now, Daddy?" Conner asks loudly.

Everyone laughs and the minister looks at him and grins. "Yes. Kiss now!"

Devin kisses me and everyone erupts with cheers.

We had reserved a private room at Le Cirque for a late dinner. We drink way too much Champagne and eat way too much seafood and steak. Conner falls asleep in my lap as Devin pays the bill.

We say good-bye to everyone as we get off the elevator on our floor and Devin carries a sleeping Conner into our suite. I follow them into Conner's bedroom and help Devin change him from his suit into pj's. He whines and fusses a little bit because he's overtired. We finally settle him down and tuck him in, and before we're both done giving him a kiss on his forehead, Conner is passed out again.

We make our way back through the living room and into our own bedroom. Devin literally attacks me as soon as the door is closed, pulling off his tie and grabbing my face, pressing his mouth to mine in a hot, searing kiss.

"This was the most perfect night of my life," I confess softly and pull at the buttons on his shirt, forcing them open.

"Mine too, Mrs. Garrison."

"Caplan-Garrison," I correct him and he smirks.

"Of course you're hyphenating." He laughs and nips playfully at my neck and he unzips my dress. "Mrs. Caplan-Garrison."

"The baby can just be Garrison," I assure him as my wedding dress slips from my body and pools at my feet on the carpet.

"The baby…" he repeats and his face lights up. "We should get right on that."

"We totally should." I smile back and let him toss me back onto the bed.

I kiss him wildly as we remove layer after layer of clothing—bra, thong, his shirt, pants, socks and underwear. When we're finally naked and he pushes into me, I tip my head back and sigh. He kisses my earlobe and whispers, "I love you so much, Callie. I'll always love you."

He means it. And more important, I believe him.

"I love you too, Devin," I assure him with a grin, because I'm not scared anymore.

Want more? Start at the beginning of Victoria Denault's Hometown Players series with

One More Shot!

Prologue

Jordan

Five years earlier

Y*ou're drunk. Again. I told you I'm not talking to you when you're drunk. Not about this."*

She doesn't even look at me. She keeps her eyes on the tabletop she's wiping down with much more vigor than necessary. I sigh and run a hand through my hair. "Callie, I've had a few beers. I'm not drunk."

"Five. You've had five beers. I know because I served them."

"Not drunk," I repeat even though... Yeah, I may be a little drunk.

She looks up, but not at me. She looks at the group I walked into O'Malley's with—Luc, my ex-girlfriend Hannah, one of her friends and two girls Luc and I met at the lake today. "Really? If you're not drunk, then you're just plain stupid to come in here with your girlfriend and ask me for my sister's phone number."

"Okay, now you're the one who must be drunk," I bark back. "Hannah and I haven't been together since last year."

"Then why are you always with her?"

"She's dating one of the guys on the Royales now so she's decided we should be friends." I roll my eyes and then lean forward and put my hand over hers so she stops the incessant table scrubbing. "Callie, please. Just give me her new number."

She pulls her hand away and straightens up, pushing her shoulders back and stepping around the table to stand toe to toe with me. She's maybe half an inch taller than Jessie, with the same petite build, but Callie has this way of carrying herself when she's pissed off that makes her seem more intimidating than an MMA wrestler.

"No."

She turns on her heel and storms off. I follow her because I can't let this go. I haven't been able to let it go since I got back to Silver Bay last month. And Callie's right—when I'm sober I can convince myself I'm okay with the way things are. I use the anger in my heart to justify the choices I've made. It worked without a hiccup while I was living in Quebec, playing in my first NHL season. But since I've been back in Silver Bay for the summer, it's been harder. I don't know if it's because there are so many memories here or because I see her sisters around town or what. But lately, after a few drinks…the anger starts to feel like longing. Longing for her.

Callie walks over to the server's station in the corner and starts to tap an order into the screen. I walk over and cover it with my hand. She swats it away and swears under her breath.

"Do it again and I will punch you." I know that's not an idle threat.

"If you don't give me her number, I'll tell the police to raid this place and you'll get caught working here underage. Poor old Billy will get fined and you might even go to jail."

She looks up and levels me with an icy stare. *"You're here underage too, jackass. And the NHL would just love for you to get busted for underage drinking."*

Fuck. She's right. So much for that plan. I go back to my original idea—begging.

"Please. I just want to know how she's doing," When once again my pleas are met with a cold, impassive stare, I grab a pen off the servers' station and grab Callie's hand. She tries to pull away but my grip is firm. I flip her hand over and scrawl my number neatly on the skin of her wrist. *"If you won't give me her number, then please just give her mine. Because maybe she wants to know how I'm doing too."*

"She knows exactly how you're doing." Callie tugs her wrist out of my hand. *"She's got the Internet in Arizona, you know."*

"What the fuck does that mean?"

"There are hockey websites that report more than just stats," she explains bitterly.

I feel defensive suddenly—and embarrassed. *"She left me, Callie. What was I supposed to do?"*

"Not fuck half of Canada," she snaps.

"You? You're going to judge my sexual history? Really?"

A flicker of pain ripples over her face, replacing the anger for just a moment and I feel like a sack of shit. Did I really just imply Callie's a slut? What the fuck is wrong with me?

"Callie. I'm sorry. I didn't mean it that way. I just—"

"She's seeing someone else."

"She's what?" The music is pretty loud in here. And there's a ton of people chattering all around us. I must have misunderstood what Callie just said because it sounded like she said…

"Jessie is seeing someone," Callie repeats slowly and clearly.

Callie turns and marches back to the tables she's serving. I stand there for what feels like forever, just staring after her. My chest starts to feel tight, like my rib cage has shrunk, and my limbs feel cold, like my blood has stopped circulating. Jessie is seeing someone. Not casually dating again, not hooking up, not thinking about me. She's seeing someone else. She doesn't give a fuck if I'm thinking about her or missing her or regretting anything. She's gone. It's over.

"Hey!" Luc wanders over, one arm over each of the girls from the lake. "Emily and Lisa want to show us the hot tub at their place."

I walk over numbly and join them. "I don't have my suit."

"Then I guess you'll have to go without one." The sultry brunette smiles at me and winks. "Don't worry. I won't wear one either so you'll feel more comfortable."

Her hand loops around my back. "I like the way you think, Lori."

"It's Lisa," she corrects, like it matters.

"Sorry, honey. I'll make it up to you," I reply suggestively as we all head toward the exit. I catch Callie staring at me as I go and I turn away. Fuck her and fuck her sister. I'm done with giving a shit.

Chapter 1

Jordan

Despite my better judgment, my eyes flutter open. I'm not at home. I think I knew that before I opened my eyes, but I'm not sure exactly where I am. I'm...on a bed. A big bed. Probably a king. But not *my* king. I would have nicer sheets.

I squint against the light, not that there is much of it, but it's still more than I would like to have hit my pupils after what feels like only fifteen minutes' sleep. There's a desk in the corner and a flat screen on the wall and dark blue and white striped curtains. There is also a naked woman lying facedown beside me.

I shift onto my side, ignoring the mild throbbing in my foot, and as the sheets turn and twist around me, I realize that I'm naked too. I look down at her. All I can see is pale skin—like never-been-on-a-beach pale—and dyed blond hair. I'm thinking it's enough to take care of my morning wood.

I run a hand down her bare back, over her ass and down

the back of her thigh. She stretches and makes a little moaning sound as my hand makes it to the back of her knee.

"Round three?" she giggles into the pillow.

Three? I guess I was a busy boy last night. A drunk, busy boy. She rolls toward me.

"Such big blue eyes…" She leans closer and kisses me, her hands wandering under the sheets. "Such big everything."

The night is slowly coming back to me. We won a home game. I sat and watched from the team box high above the ice, ridiculously frustrated. Afterward, I joined my teammates at a bar to celebrate. I wanted to drink away my frustration at not being able to play thanks to my stupid ankle.

Hours later, my teammate Alexandre invited a bunch of people back to his place. That's when I had decided to screw my frustration away with one of the girls who tagged along because obviously drinking alone wasn't going to improve my mood. It never does but I've yet to stop trying. Fucking random girls has never helped my problems either, but I keep doing it. I've never been one to learn from my mistakes, at least not quickly.

Her name was…Jenny? Julie? Jackie? It began with a fucking J, I know that because I avoid girls whose names begin with J. Normally that's a deal breaker for me, especially when I'm drunk. But desperate times called for desperate measures, and I was so over being injured and unable to play hockey—the only thing I've ever done for a living—that I was desperate for a distraction. This J girl was it.

"You're a freaking animal," she coos, her hand moving from

my ass to my hard-on. "I had no idea hockey players had so much stamina."

I just grunt, gently turn her toward the mattress and move myself over her back. I nudge her legs open, kneel between them and then pull her backward by her hips so she's on all fours.

I grab a condom off the bedside table where there is a pile of them in a bowl. I realize I'm still at Alexandre's apartment because he's the only one ballsy enough to leave condoms around his house in candy dishes.

I tear the condom wrapper with my teeth and start to put it on when my cell phone starts ringing. My head begins to pound in rhythm with the shrill ring. Great. I stop what I'm doing and extract it from the back pocket of my jeans, which for some unknown reason are draped over the lamp beside the bed.

I see my parents' number on the call display and roll my eyes as my dick deflates.

"I have to take this," I tell Julie-Jenny-Jackie.

She groans in dismay and I ignore her.

"Hi, Mom. It's a little early to call," I say into the phone as I yawn.

"Jordan, it's one in the afternoon," she lets me know tersely.

I blink. Shit. "Sorry, it was a late night."

"Should you be having late nights when you're still injured?" she asks pointedly.

I try not to be annoyed and remind myself she's just doing her job. Moms are supposed to ride their son's asses.

"We won and went out to celebrate," I defend myself. "It's

fine. I'm fine. The ankle is getting better every day."

"Okay, then…" I can still hear the judgment in her voice, but we both ignore it.

"When do you leave for New York?" I ask, changing the subject. My parents were supposed to be going to Brooklyn this weekend to visit my older brother, Devin, his wife, Ashleigh, and their two-year-old son, Conner.

The girl beside me gets out of bed and gathers her clothes. "I have to go. Work," she whispers, and disappears into the bathroom.

"Well, we were supposed to go tomorrow but we had to push back our flight to Monday. Honey…" She pauses and there's something in her tone that makes my stomach clench uncomfortably. "Lily Caplan died."

I feel a wave of relief to hear that my parents aren't sick, but as the news settles in, it instantly feels like a bomb has exploded in my chest. My heart skips a beat and my mouth goes dry. "Mrs. Caplan?"

The name conjures up images in my head of three beautiful, spirited but sad teenage girls, not the silver-haired shrew of a woman it belongs to.

"Yes. I guess it happened a couple days ago. I just found out this morning," she says, and her tone is soothing. I know she knows this news makes me feel off-balance—like a hormonal, impetuous teenager, because that's what I was the last time the Caplans were in my life. She also knows that because of my turbulent past with one Caplan in particular, this news hits me harder than the rest of my family. "It was sudden but not completely unexpected. She had those heart problems."

"I know..." I swallow and ignore the dyed blonde with the J name as she leans in and kisses my cheek before heading for the bedroom door.

"Call me," she whispers a little too loudly. I nod quickly at the blonde and she frowns as she leaves the room.

"Are they back?" I bark out the question gruffly because I don't want to be asking it. I don't want to care. I don't want to know...only I do want to know. Badly.

"Rose arrived last night. Callie got here this morning," my mother volunteers easily. "Jessie is supposed to be arriving this afternoon."

She's back. She said she would never go home again. Everyone swore she was gone forever. But Jessie is back. The vault in the recesses of my brain, the one where I crammed all the memories of her, suddenly bursts open, and my breath catches in my throat and I cough.

"The funeral is Saturday. We're going, of course, but I thought it would be nice if you could come as well," my mom goes on. "You boys were all so close to them, and Devin and Luc can't make it because they're playing. But since you're not playing right now..."

"Isn't Cole going to go?" I ask quickly, almost nervously. I fucking hate that I feel this out of sorts all of a sudden.

"Yes, but Cole wasn't best friends with Jessie," she says simply. My mom has never been one to get too involved in our romantic lives. She doesn't want to be that kind of overbearing woman. But clearly she feels strongly about this. "You should be here, Jordan."

"I'll see what I can do," I mutter. "Thanks for telling me, Mom."

"Do you want me to say anything to...them? From you specifically?" she asks quietly in a voice full of unspoken words.

"No." My mother sighs her discontent so I clear my throat, roll my eyes and add, "Fine. Tell them I'm thinking of them and everything."

"I will. I love you, Jordy," she says in a voice that clearly says she approves of my message.

"Love you too," I say, and hang up.

As I throw on my underwear, slide my injured foot into my aircast and dig around the room for the rest of my clothes, Alexandre appears in the doorway. He's in nothing but Seattle Winterhawks track pants and he's holding two coffee mugs. His dark blue eyes are twinkling and his dark brown hair is askew.

"You sure know how to make a girl scream," he says with his heavy French Canadian accent and a wry smile. He hands me one of the mugs. "I'm surprised you didn't set off car alarms last night."

I smile, but it's short-lived, and take a sip of the coffee before putting it down to pull my shirt over my head. "I have to go to the rink. I need to talk to Coach."

"Why? Did she rebreak your ankle or break some new part of your body?" He laughs.

I make a face at his crappy joke and shake my head. "A friend of the family died."

"Je suis désolé, mon ami," he says, offering condolences in his native French.

"Yeah," I reply because I don't have time to explain to Alex that after the way Lily Caplan treated her grandkids, she wasn't exactly my favorite person.

I grab the mug again and take a few more sips as I walk out into Alex's main living area, which has floor-to-ceiling, south-facing windows and reclaimed barn board floors. A sultry-looking brunette in nothing but Alex's plaid dress shirt from last night stands behind the kitchen island cooking eggs on the stovetop.

"Hey." I give her an awkward wave.

"Jackie says to tell you to stop by Hooters any time and she'll get you free wings," the brunette tells me.

"Tell Jackie thanks," I say, and try not to roll my eyes. Even after all these years as an NHL player, I'm still always shocked when the same girls who throw themselves at you the first night they meet you just because you're a professional athlete expect a shot at girlfriend status. Of course, in their defense, I'm not turning them down.

"Why do you need to talk to Coach?" Alex wants to know.

"I need to go back home," I explain, and try to tame my wild bedhead with my hands. "For the funeral. Just a couple of days."

Alex shrugs and then gives me a hug. "Okay. Take care, eh?"

I nod and smile. "Thanks for the guest room."

"Sure." Alex smirks. "But next time remind me to buy earplugs for my neighbors."

Outside I'm greeted with a crisp, sunny fall afternoon. It's not raining, which in Seattle is always a plus. When I was traded to the Seattle Winterhawks last season, I wasn't all that thrilled about living so far from home. At least when I played in Quebec City, it was only an eight-hour drive from my hometown in Maine. But Seattle is fun, my team has been great and the fans here are a small but passionate bunch. I'm happy now professionally. At least I was until I broke my left ankle. Hockey is the only thing I've ever wanted to do with my life. It's the only thing I've ever been *great* at and the one thing I have never screwed up. This is the first injury in my professional career. It's a big one, and I couldn't be handling it worse if I tried.

As I drive to the rink I call my older brother, Devin.

"Hey, Jordan," he says easily, answering on the second ring. "What's up?"

"Lily Caplan died."

"I know." Devin sounds stunned for a minute. "Mom told Ashleigh."

"She wants me to go home for the funeral," I respond as I pull my SUV off the I-5 and down the familiar downtown Seattle streets to the hockey arena.

"Makes sense," he says.

"How does it make sense?" I demand. I was calling him for support—so he could help me brainstorm excuses for not showing up. "Mrs. Caplan hated me. She hated all of us. She thought we were—and I quote—derelict hockey punks."

"She's dead," Devin reminds me snarkily as I slow at a stop sign and lean my head against the leather headrest. "This isn't about her. It's about supporting your best friend."

"Ex–best friend," I retort. "We haven't talked in years."

"And whose fault is that?" Devin mutters almost under his breath—almost inaudibly—but I hear it and it pisses me off.

"She left town, remember? Why does everyone blame that on me?"

I wave my players' pass at the security guard at the gate to player parking. He's obviously a little surprised to see me on a day off, but he raises the gate without question. "I should be concentrating on getting my leg healed. My family should be supporting that."

"Oh, I'm sorry," Devin counters, and the sarcasm rings loud and clear through the Bluetooth. "Is your leg going to stop healing just because it's in Maine instead of Seattle?"

"Go fuck yourself."

"Love you too, bro." He laughs, enjoying this way too much if you ask me. But when the laughter dies, he grows serious. "Look, Jordy. I would be there if I could and so would Luc. The Caplan girls are family. We've all given you and Jessie enough time to figure out how to be grown-ups yet you can't seem to do it. So I'm telling you be a grown-up and go and support her."

"Fine. I'll go if the coach lets me."

"He'll let you."

"Shut up."

"Shutting up," Devin promises, and then the line goes dead. I sigh loudly, get out of the car and slam the door. Hopefully Devin is wrong and Coach Sweetzer has some reason he needs me here. Because as painful and frustrating as it was to be here dealing with my injury and not being able to play hockey, seeing Jessie Caplan again would be worse—*much* worse.

About the Author

Victoria Denault loves long walks on the beach, cinnamon dolce lattes and writing angst-filled romance. She lives in L.A. but grew up in Montreal, which is why she is fluent in English, French and hockey.

Learn more at:
VictoriaDenault.com
Facebook.com/AuthorVictoriaDenault
Twitter: @BooksbyVictoria